I0671693

THE SHERIFF 6

A POST-APOCALYPTIC SCI-FI WESTERN

M.R. FORBES

Published by Quirky Algorithms
Seattle, Washington

This novel is a work of fiction and a product of the author's imagination. Any resemblance to actual persons or events is purely coincidental.

Cover illustration by Tom Edwards
Edited by Merrylee Lanehart

CHAPTER 1

Sheriff Hayden Duke snapped awake with a start, covered in sweat, heart hammering in his chest like an out-of-control freight train. Nightmares weren't new to him. He'd lost count of how many visions of Natalia—usually with a knife in her back, sometimes a bullet, occasionally his fist wrapped around her throat, choking her—that he'd woken up from in the last four months. Ever since they'd found Grimmel.

Ever since he was forced to end her life.

After every nightmare, he'd had to remind himself that the Natalia he'd killed wasn't his Natalia. She was a clone. An imperfect copy, controlled by the Relyeh Ancient, Iagorth, who sought to gain control of Earth through his moieties, through Natalia and Grimmel.

But the moieties and Natalia were gone, and Grimmel was now under New Eden's control. In the hands of Nathan and Chandra, trusted allies in his fight to bring Earth back from the brink. Time wasn't on their side. The enemies of humankind, Relyeh and Axon, wouldn't leave the planet alone forever, and there was no way they could win in the state they were in right now. Scattered, divided, cynical, and fighting one another when they should be working together.

They had directed Grimmel to work on a new solution, but it was a problem even the advanced artificial intelligence struggled to solve.

Maybe it was stubborn on his part, but Hayden truly believed the only way to bring civilization back was to rebuild the bridges the trife had burned, one settlement at a time.

Blinking the sleep from his eyes, he registered the gray predawn light filtering into his austere bedroom in the Greens. He just stared at the ceiling for a moment, breathing hard.

His nightmare had seemed so real. But then again, they were always like that. He figured it was on account of Shub'Nigu pressing at his mind, always searching for a way through the walls he had built against the eldest of the Relyeh. Lately, it seemed the so-called World-god had become more desperate to reach him. To punish him for defeating Iagorth's plot or to praise him for blocking a rival? It was hard to know which with the Relyeh, and he didn't much care either way. The last thing he needed was to let old Shubbie back into his head.

Shaking off the sense of dread, Hayden glanced at the freshly laundered clothes piled on a table beside the door to his room. No matter how many times he told Alina she didn't need to do his laundry, it was always the same story. Her gratitude for him trying to help her find her son was unwavering even though it had been too late.

He rolled out of bed, dressed only in his long johns, and crossed the small room to the table. There was no sense trying to go back to sleep now. But even as he went through his morning routine, he couldn't shake the feeling that something was wrong. Very wrong. He'd learned long ago not to ignore this tightness in his gut. Whether instinct or paranoia, experience had taught him to stay alert, and this was a sort of doom he hadn't sensed in some time. He decided to check in on Kady and the others to ease his mind.

After donning a black linen shirt that was beginning to fray at the cuff, homespun tan pants that were getting a little thin in the seat, and his oldest pair of western boots, Hayden tightened his gun belt around his waist and tied the two holsters down to his thighs. After shrugging into his vest and buttoning it, he draped his bandoliers over it before leaving his room and going downstairs. The silence in the small home suggested Alina and Kady had already gone out.

Exiting the home, Hayden followed the street a couple of blocks to the Greens' bustling downtown. What had started as a relatively small settlement had grown exponentially in the last couple of years, the population swelling from a few hundred to over a thousand. Farmers tended to plentiful crops, market stalls had popped up selling salvaged goods, and kids chased one another up and down the thoroughfare, laughter echoing long after they had vanished from sight. It was all proof that life could thrive again after unspeakable horror. That humankind could rebuild and prosper if only given the chance.

His boots crunched along the path to the big communal barn the residents had converted into a schoolhouse. Being unseasonably warm today, both sets of double doors, one in front and one in back, were open to let a breeze through. Walking through the front doors, he spotted Alina Prior helping the younger children with their prior day's assignments. The sight brought a thin smile to his weathered face.

"Sheriff Duke!" called the first of the children to notice him. The other kids turned their attention away from Alina. "Morning, Sheriff!" they cried in unison.

"Good morning, kiddos," Hayden replied. "Hard at work, I see?"

"Algebra stinks," one of them said.

He laughed. "I remember when I was your age and I had

to do algebra. I thought it stunk, too. Now that I'm older, I realize how important a good education is."

"Maybe," the child replied, pausing to consider. "But it still stinks."

"What can we do for you this morning, Sheriff?" Alina asked, her expression curious. "You're up and about early today. Eager to get back on the trail?"

Hayden shook his head. "Not just yet. I wanted to see how things were holding up here first." He glanced around. "Have you seen Kady this morning?"

Alina looked around the room. "She was here a minute ago. If I had to guess, she probably skedaddled up to the loft. She likes to go up there to be alone sometimes."

"Everything okay with her?"

"She seems fine, and she says she's okay. But you know how girls her age can be, Sheriff."

A wave of sadness washed over Hayden, and he bowed his head. "Pozz. I'll go check on her."

She waved him on, turning back to her students. Hayden climbed the ladder to the loft two rungs at a time. The loft held a recreation space for the kids. An old couch, a pinball machine Oz had fixed up and somehow managed to get up there, something called a foosball table, and lots of books. Kady had probably read all of them at least twice.

What he didn't see was Kady.

"Kady?" Hayden called softly, edging over the ladder into the loft. "Where are you?"

"Is that you, Sheriff?" a small voice drifted from above. "I'm up here." Craning his neck, he spotted her sitting up in the rafters, in the shadows, hugging her knees to her chest. He could just make out tear tracks glistening on her cheeks.

"How'd you get up there?" he asked, worry permeating his tone.

"Climbed," she replied simply. "I...I had a bad dream, and I can't stop thinking about it. I needed to be by myself for a bit."

Ice water trickled down Hayden's spine. "A dream? What about?"

"A city filled with monsters. You were there, too. Looking for me." Her eyes were haunted, brimming with confusion and fear. "It seemed so real..."

He opened his mouth, searching for some words of reassurance, when a burst of gunshots, along with wailing and shouting from outside, interrupted his thoughts. Screams of surprise and pain and mortal terror all blended into a hellish chorus that sent every instinct in his body slamming to red alert.

"Stay up here!" he barked at Kady, pounding back down the ladder. He burst out of the barn to find utter chaos erupting around him.

Marauders had descended on the Greens, tearing through the streets on modified hovercycles. The bikes were decked out in spikes and armored cages so heavy they could barely float, their repulser pads kicking up whirlwinds of dust.

The bandits were unfamiliar. Strips of leather armor peeked out from under white robes, their feet clad in crude sandals. Opaque breathing masks completely covered their faces, giving them an inhuman insectile appearance. They clutched pistols and sawed-off shotguns, firing indiscriminately as they cut a bloody swath through town.

Panic swept through the Greens as people fled in all directions, desperately trying to get away from the slaughter. A few brave souls grabbed weapons to defend themselves, but they were hopelessly outmatched.

"Oz!" Hayden shouted, spotting the burly ex-War Dog unloading his gun at the nearest marauder. "What the hell is going on? Who are these bastards?"

"No idea!" the big man yelled back, dropping a raider with

a shot to the face, his breathing apparatus shattering. "They came out of nowhere! Never seen gear like this before!"

Alina had emerged from the barn, the children huddled behind her in the doorway, all waiting to be told which way to run. Where to hide.

Alina had a pistol in her hand. Even as Hayden watched, she turned it on one of the hoverbikes, planting a few rounds into the rider's side. He lost control, his bike swerving until it crashed into a tree. The impact lifted him off the seat and slammed him into the side of a cage, bending his limbs at odd angles before his body disappeared in the billowing dust beneath the bike.

"Oz, help me with Alina and the kids! We need to get them to safety!"

Hayden and Oz moved to flank Alina, the three of them forming a protective cordon around her and her young charges.

"Look, there!" Oz cried suddenly, pointing with his gun. "APC!"

Hayden already had his eyes on the hulking armored personnel carrier entering the main thoroughfare, surrounded by another force of marauders on foot. Curiously, these raiders wore military combat armor, the chest plates painted red beneath their white robes, and they carried plasma rifles that he knew had originated on Proxima.

The hoverbikes swept past Hayden and the others to circle behind the barn, riders turning their heads to glare at him as they passed, none of them showing signs that they recognized or feared him. Alina pivoted to track one of them with her pistol, getting a bead, but Hayden laid his hand on her shoulder. "Save the rest of your bullets," he said. "They've made themselves known. Now let's see what they want." Alina lowered her weapon without question.

The APC ground to a halt near the center of town. The marauders quickly set up a perimeter, surrounding the frightened civilians still alive and in the street. The back ramp of the personnel carrier opened, and a single raider descended. He wore fully painted red armor beneath his robes, his breather stamped to resemble a pair of bloody jaws. "Stand down, you have been chosen!" he yelled, his mask rendering his voice flat and mechanical. "I know you're providing shelter to property that once belonged to Grimmel. Surrender his children and the rest of you will be spared!"

Hayden glared at the man. Who was he, and how did he know about Grimmel and the children?

"What do we do, Sheriff?" Alina whispered. "Turning over the children isn't an option."

"Same thing we always do," Oz growled. "Protect them with everything we got, right Sheriff?" He glanced at Hayden.

"Pozz," Hayden replied.

"I'll draw their fire, buy you some time to get in close. Make each shot count, yeah?"

Hayden nodded grimly, tightening his grip on the twin revolvers slung low on his hips. "Alina, take the children through the barn and out to the barge. Don't wait for me to catch up before casting off. Whatever happens, don't let them take the kids."

Tears glimmered in the schoolteacher's eyes, but her jaw was set with determination. "I'll die before I let them be hurt again. That's a promise." She turned and disappeared into the gloom of the barn's interior.

Hayden finally lifted his guns from their holsters, eying the hoverbikes on either side of them in his peripheral vision.

"Oz, on my signal," he said.

"What's your sig—?"

Hayden cut him off when he snapped both arms up in opposite directions, single rounds punching through the heads of the bikers on either side of them. Oz darted left, firing wildly at the group around the APC, drawing their attention while Hayden cut to the right, knocking down two more bikers before they knew what hit them.

The marauder leader whirled to face him. "Kill him!" he shouted, pointing to Hayden. The armored raiders in front of the APC raised their plasma rifles, and bolts flew. One grazed Hayden's right bicep. Another cut a swath through the flesh of his left thigh before he went down on one knee, emptying his revolvers into them.

Oz did his best to draw their fire from Hayden, but the raiders remained focused, suggesting something more than basic training. They weren't War Dogs, though. They were something else. Possibly Centurion deserters.

Not a single one of Hayden's rounds failed to hit them center mass or in the head, but all failed to penetrate the marurader's armor, forcing Hayden to run for cover. He dove behind a wooden barrel sitting beside the storefront adjacent to the barn. The plasma bolts followed him, burning into the wood and mortar over his head, and several more sank into the barrel.

An angry roar turned Hayden's attention to Oz. Realizing he couldn't get the raiders' attention, he had moved into the open, charging them like a bull. Finally, they swung away from Hayden, just in time for Oz to barrel into one of them, slamming the raider to the dirt.

Hayden dropped each of his revolvers to the ground in turn, rapidly reloading one and then the other with practiced speed and ease, but as fast as he was, he wasn't fast enough to help Oz. One of the raiders had grabbed him, and with the enhanced strength provided by his armor, had thrown him to the ground. Together, the raiders peppered him with plasma that tore into his unprotected chest and gut.

Oz looked past them to Hayden just as he looked up from reloading his guns. It wasn't fear the Sheriff saw in his eyes but acceptance of his fate and the pride he took in dying trying to save the kids he had come to love.

Hayden didn't intend to let his friend's death be in vain. He burst from cover as the APC circled the remaining raiders and Oz's body. They were headed behind the barn, worrying Hayden they would cut Alina and the children off and surround them before they could reach the barge.

Hayden put his teeth to his bottom lip, releasing a shrill whistle as he holstered one of his revolvers and charged into the midst of the armored marauders. They weren't the only ones with enhanced strength. His right hook into the helmet of the first raider he reached sent the man's head snapping to the side with enough force to break his neck. Stunned, the one beside him watched his fellow raider drop to the ground dead. Hayden took the opportunity to shove his gun between the man's helmet and collar. He squeezed the trigger, and his round burst through the man's jaw and sinus into his skull, killing him instantly.

From his periphery, Hayden caught sight of another raider rushing up on him. He whirled, kicking the man's plasma rifle aside before he could fire. He grabbed the man by the back of the neck and pulled him close to repeat the killing headshot, dropping him, too.

Searing heat burned into Hayden's back, and he spun again, drawing his second gun and emptying both into the faceplate of the shooter, doing enough damage to shatter the transparency and then the face behind it. Holstering one revolver, he reloaded the other just before a hand landed on his shoulder, twisting him around. The raider held another Centurion weapon in his free hand and pressed the muzzle against Hayden's temple.

"Who do you think you are?" the raider muttered through his breathing mask. Hayden smelled the stench of some kind of drug through it. No wonder they hadn't recognized him. They probably had no idea who they were, never mind who he was.

Shod hooves suddenly pounded the ground behind him,

and Hayden smiled, his levity surprising the man long enough to delay his trigger pull. A hind hoof slammed into the side of the raider's head, dropping him to the ground as Zorro blew by.

"Perfect timing." Hayden patted Zorro's neck when he returned to him. He grabbed hold of the stallion's mane and swung onto the stallion's bare back. Hayden turned the horse around, and Zorro took off, instinctively knowing exactly where Hayden wanted to go.

Hoverbikes closed on him from both sides, riders steering with one hand and shooting with the other. Hayden leaned low over Zorro's neck, firing on the enemy as plasma bolts zipped past his head. Others sizzled into the dirt near Zorro's churning hooves.

One hoverbike rider went down, caught right between the eyes by one of Hayden's bullets. Another collapsed a moment later. Hayden squeezed his thighs tight against Zorro's barrel and grabbed another quick loader from his bandoliers, refilling his revolver.

Screams from inside the barn fired his anger and determination. Zorro's as well, the big black picking up the pace, galloping through the barn's front doors. They raced between desks, heading for Alina, the children, and the raiders surrounding them. The APC sat just inside the barn's open back doors. The raiders were dispersed behind their leader, between him and the APC, all trying to get a bead on Hayden.

"Sheriff!" Alina shouted. "There's a—"

She gasped, swallowing her words as the raider leader backhanded her and then caught her from behind as she fell, drawing her in front of him as a shield. In his fury, Hayden didn't halt Zorro's charge. Nearing Alina's desk, the horse gathered itself and leaped, clearing the desk and landing without issue.

And that's where Hayden's luck ran out.

Before he could pull Zorro up, a rope shot up out of the dirt and snapped taut. High enough for Zorro to duck his head beneath it, it was just at the right height to catch Hayden full in the chest. The impact lifted him out off Zorro's back. His ribs broke, muscles strained, and the rope's impact knocked the air from his lungs. He landed on the ground in agony. Riderless, Zorro shied away and came to a stop at the back of the barn, snorting in anger and pawing the dirt.

Every rifle in the barn pointed at him, Hayden sat there, hand clutched to his chest, struggling to breathe. He could already feel his body beginning to knit itself back together, and given a couple of minutes he would be ready to fight again.

Of course, there was no way the raiders would give him a couple of minutes.

"Sheriff!"

Kady's cry drew his immediate attention as she ran out of the back of the APC, a raider right behind her. He reached for her, but couldn't grab her before she turned and let out a siren scream. An invisible wave of psionic energy blasted the raider up and back with such force that his back hit the top of the APC. He fell to the ramp and tumbled awkwardly down it to the ground, landing like a twisted rag doll.

As Kady ran toward Hayden, the raider leader threw Alina to the dirt and grabbed her, wrapping one arm around the girl's chest and both arms. "Sheriff, help!" she cried, struggling to break free.

"Not so fast, little one," he said, covering her mouth with his other hand to prevent her from releasing another psionic scream.

"Let her go," Hayden growled.

The raider leader chuckled. "She has a great purpose to fulfill. Greater than you know."

"You have no idea what you're dealing with," Hayden warned him, keeping his voice low and even despite the rage pulsing through him. "No idea of who you're messing with. Let the children go and I'll let you walk away."

Mechanical laughter filtered through the raider's mask. "Look at you. Your threats are useless. Our path is the path of righteousness. The Rebirth cannot be denied. So it is prophesied. So it shall be done." He smiled down at Hayden, no hint of malice in his eyes. "Kill him," he ordered.

Three raiders stepped forward, leveling their plasma rifles at Hayden. He gritted his teeth, pain arcing through his body as he pushed up to his knees.

Kady whined behind the leader's hand, tears streaming down her face. "Don't worry, child," he told her. "I won't expose you to such violence."

The raiders kept their guns on Hayden as the leader boarded the APC with Kady. The rear doors of the carrier slammed shut with a resounding clang.

"I'll hunt every one of you down," Hayden said, eyeing the marauders. "I'll find you. And when I do, there's going to be hell to—"

He was cut off as a barrage of plasma bolts slammed into him at such close range they burned right through him, quickly filling him with cauterized holes. Hayden gasped for air, looking down at his riddled body, then back up at his killers. His anger refused to abate, even as his vision faded.

This wasn't the end of this fight.

It was only the beginning…

CHAPTER 2

Hayden jerked awake with a gasp, his body drenched in sweat, heart pounding like a jackhammer. For a long moment he just laid there on his bedroll spread out on the rough wooden floor, staring up at the ceiling of the derelict farmhouse that had become his home over the last few months. The dream—no, nightmare—still gripped him, images of marauders slaughtering the people of the Greens, of Oz dying to protect the children, of Kady's tear-stained face as she was dragged away by the mysterious raiders.

It had all seemed so real. Too real. With a shuddering breath, Hayden pushed himself up to a sitting position, raking his fingers through his shaggy hair. He was still wearing the same clothes he'd had on yesterday—dark pants and a sweat-stained homespun cotton shirt, a pair of Centurion-issued military combat boots on his feet. His ever-present gun belt and bandoliers rested on the floor beside him, within easy reach. Sleeping in his clothes had become a habit, a precaution born of necessity.

The floorboards creaked as he rose to his feet, joints popping. He picked up the bandoliers and slung them over his body before cinching the gun belt around his waist, the familiar heft of his twin revolvers one thing that made him feel most like himself. Careful to step around the rotted floorboards as he left the room, he crossed to the staircase.

Descending to the main floor, he checked the makeshift traps and noisemakers he'd rigged around the staircase along the way. Tin cans strung on wires. A bell attached to the banister. A tripwire that would send a cascade of empty shell casings clattering across the steps if triggered. It all remained in place and undisturbed, and he threaded his way past them to ensure they remained that way.

Early morning sunlight slanted through gaps in the boarded-up windows, illuminating motes of dust drifting lazily through the air. Hayden made his way through the kitchen to the back door, breathing in deeply as he stepped outside. The cool, crisp air refreshed him, helping him shake off the remnants of panic he had felt upon waking. He hadn't felt such alarm since Natalia's clone had suddenly appeared.

Calming, he still had a sense that there was a deeper meaning to the nightmare. That it wasn't just another of Shub'Nigu's efforts to throw him off his game. What would be the point, especially right now? After Natalia, he needed a break. Time to recover, reflect, and grieve all over again. Time he couldn't afford to spare but also couldn't afford not to take. How could he help anyone with his mind in such chaos?

Exhaling, Hayden collected a couple of eggs from the small coop he'd built for the wild hens he'd found wandering the property. He filled a dented pot with water from the old well and returned to the farmhouse to turn on the scavenged generator he'd repaired a while back. Eggs were cooking on an old portable electric hot plate he'd come across right there at the farmhouse, and he couldn't stop his mind from wandering back to the dream.

No, not a dream. He knew that deep in his bones, even if his waking mind didn't want to believe it. It was more like a vision, a glimpse of events happening elsewhere, without his presence or influence. The dread that had seized him upon waking still lingered, an icy fist clenched around his heart.

He ate his meager breakfast without tasting it, his appetite dulled by the gnawing worry. When finished, he rinsed his plate and fork in the bucket that served as his sink and then headed out to the oversized stable adjacent to the farmhouse. Once upon a time, the stable might have belonged to a thoroughbred breeder or at least a true lover and collector of horses. Now, three-quarters of it had collapsed, and he'd had to patch the roof over the last quarter to keep it relatively dry.

Zorro nickered in greeting as Hayden slid open the half-rotted stable door, the familiar scent of hay and horse filling his nostrils. He allowed himself a faint smile as he stepped up to his best friend, scratching him between the ears.

"Morning, old friend. I hope you slept better than I did."

As if sensing his troubled mood, Zorro butted his head against Hayden's chest. Hayden sighed, running his hand along the horse's neck before fetching a bucket of apples.

"I had a hell of a dream last night," he said as he picked an apple out of the bucket small enough to feed Zorro without cutting it up. "More of a nightmare, really. I saw the Greens under attack. Oz, gunned down trying to protect the little ones. And Kady..." His throat tightened, and he swallowed hard. "They took her. I don't know who they were, but I watched them drag her away, and there wasn't a damn thing I could do to stop it."

Zorro snorted softly as if in sympathy, as he munched down his apple. Hayden leaned his forehead against the horse's neck, drawing strength from the animal's steady presence.

"We both know Kady had some kind of psychic abilities as a result of the experiments Grimmel put her through. I can't shake the feeling that it wasn't just a dream, and not Shubbie, either. I'm worried what I saw really happened. Something like it, I mean. I'm worried about Kady and the children foremost. Alina and Oz, too." He straightened, jaw tight with resolve. "I don't know that I'm ready to get back in the saddle, partner. But it doesn't look like fate's giving me any choice."

He picked up another larger apple and held it while Zorro bit off half of it. He waited for the horse to chew and swallow it before feeding him the other half. "I won't be able to live with myself if I don't head to the Greens to check on them," he said, fetching the horse his morning bucket of sweetened oats and two flakes of hay. "So what do you say? Up for another adventure?" he asked, leaning his elbows on the stall gate to watch Zorro dig into his oats. The stallion threw his head up and down several times, ending his response with a snort before diving back into the bucket. Hayden found himself laughing. "Pozz." He patted the horse's neck and stepped back. "We'll head out right after you finish breakfast."

Hayden returned to the farmhouse to collect his gear and went to the cellar. He pushed an old bookcase out of the way, revealing a hole in the foundation hidden in darkness. He reached in to collect his packed saddlebags and plasma rifle, hefting the bags over his shoulder and climbing back up the steps. He would've liked to have headed to the river to wash, but he didn't want to take the time. What he had seen had either already happened, and he needed to get there before the trail went cold, or it had yet to happen, and he needed to get there to stop it.

Either way, he needed to get there. Fast.

When he returned to the stable, he quickly saddled Zorro and packed some oats for him into his saddlebags. His gaze drifted afterward to the wall of the stable, where his long coat hung on a peg. The duster still bore the scars and stains of past battles. Retrieving it, he shook off the dust of non-use and shrugged into the heavy garment, the weight familiar and oddly comforting.

"I need to go to the Greens," he said, more to himself than the horse. "I have to make sure Kady's alright. If something's happened to her..." He didn't finish the thought.

Mind made up, he led Zorro out into the pale morning light. The sun was just cresting the horizon, painting the sky in shades of pink and gold. Under different circumstances, Hayden might have taken a moment to appreciate the raw beauty of it. But now, all he could focus on was the sense of urgency spurring him back to the Greens. And hopefully, a happy reunion.

He swung up into the saddle, Zorro eagerly tossing his head. "Let's ride," Hayden murmured, and with the tap of his heels against Zorro's barrel, the stallion surged forward. His powerful muscles bunching and flexing, they galloped away from the lonely farmhouse, a cloud of dust billowing in their wake as they raced toward the rising sun and whatever destiny awaited them.

CHAPTER 3

Hayden rode hard for the Greens, Zorro's hooves eating up the miles beneath them. He barely stopped to rest, catching a few hours of sleep here and there, always with one eye open and his guns within reach while Zorro grazed on grass. The nightmare that had driven him from his self-imposed exile refused to fade, the image of Kady's tear-streaked face as she was dragged away by the raiders was seared into his mind.

Two weeks of hard riding found him on the outskirts of the Arches, the large monument coming into view over the city's ruins. It was where the Natalia clone had found him and where he'd destroyed Idhra before it could escape.

It happened six months ago, but for Hayden, it was still so raw in his memory that it felt like it had happened yesterday. He could see how much it had changed when he drew near enough to the settlement. Where before there had been only a few hundred people eking out a meager existence amongst the rubble, now there appeared to be thousands of survivors who called the Arches home.

There were also enough people that guards were stationed along the main roads in and out of the city. He also noticed sentries positioned at high points in the damaged buildings.

They had undoubtedly seen him coming from at least a mile or two away.

The guards blocked his path, but they were hardly threatening. Two older women with sun-bleached white hair and plenty of wrinkles carried hunting rifles and smiled up at him as he approached.

"This here's the Arches," one of them said. "Biggest metropolis in the world outside of New Eden. What's your business here?"

"I'm here looking for passage downriver," Hayden replied. "Preferably on a boat."

"Not on a log, then?" The other woman asked, cackling at her own joke.

"Never you mind, Beatrice," the first said, returning her attention to Hayden. "She's got a few screws loose."

"Please," Beatrice crowed. "Only one here missing pieces and parts is you, Milady. You old windbag."

"Who are you calling an old windbag? You're older than me."

"If you don't mind," Hayden said, getting their attention. "Is there a fee to enter?"

"A fee?" Beatrice laughed. "Well, why didn't I ever think of that."

"Sure is, Mister," Milady replied. "Ten notes."

"Plus ten for your horse," Beatrice added.

Hayden nodded to them, opening a saddlebag to take out a wad of notes that made the two women gasp.

"Best not make that roll of notes too public, Mister," Milady said. "You don't want to attract the wrong crowd."

"Are you blind?" Beatrice said. "Look at him. He could give the Sheriff hisself a run for his money."

Hayden counted out the notes, handing each of them ten. "Are we square?" he asked as they pocketed the so-called fee.

"Fair and square," Milady said, moving out of his path. "In you go."

Zorro eased forward, stopping next to Beatrice when Hayden pulled gently back on the reins. "One question," he said. "Do you happen to know a woman named Tabitha? Or a man named Jack Colton?"

"Sure do," Beatrice said. "They're like celebrities around here. They're the ones helped make the Arches what it is today."

Hayden smiled, happy to hear that the pair had returned to the Arches as they'd said they would. "Do you know where I can find them?"

"Yup," Milady said. She turned and thrust her finger down the street. "Two blocks, turn left on Main, go another two blocks. You can't miss the sign to their place."

Hayden tipped his hat to them. "Thank you kindly. Have a nice day."

"You, too, stranger," Beatrice said.

As Hayden continued down the street, he could hear them bickering.

"I think he really was the Sheriff."

"You are so full of it, Milady."

"He was so the Sheriff," Milady insisted. "Did you see his chiseled jaw? And those guns he's totin'?"

"If he's the Sheriff, where are his metal arms?" Beatrice countered. "Everyone knows the Sheriff has metal arms except you, dummy."

Chuckling, Hayden turned left where Milady had said, riding down a bustling city street before the trife and a ruin before Idhra. Cleared of debris, clay planters lined the ancient, battered asphalt while dozens of people worked on restoring levels of the buildings flanking the street one at a time. People stopped to stare as he passed, some with suspicion, others with open curiosity. He kept his head down, the brim of his hat pulled low over his eyes.

It didn't prevent him from spotting the sign Milady had mentioned. It would have been nearly impossible to miss.

Hanging from the sixth-floor window of one of the buildings were what appeared to be several white bed sheets sewn together, with Hotel Colton printed vertically on them in giant red letters.

"Hotel Colton?" Hayden said softly, surprised at the swanky name. He smirked as he guided Zorro the rest of the way to the building. An attendant waited there. He recognized her as one of the former prostitutes from Girls in Walville.

"Well, as I live and breathe," she said excitedly as he hopped off Zorro. "If it isn't Sheriff Duke in the flesh." She smiled widely. "I owe you more than I can ever repay, Sheriff."

"You don't owe me anything except your name," Hayden replied.

"Gerta," the woman said, reaching out. "I assume you're here to see the owners? I can take care of Zorro for you, Sheriff. He looks like he's been movin' hard lately."

"For the last two weeks," Hayden agreed.

"Well, I'll make sure he gets a nice bath, a massage, and plenty of good food. I can do the same for you, if you want." She eyed him suggestively.

"Like I said, Gerta. You don't owe me anything except your name, and you've already given me that."

"I don't mind, Sheriff."

"I appreciate that, but my mind, body, and soul are already spoken for."

"In that case, go on inside. Tabby and Jack should be in the back. Him behind the bar, her cooking up a storm in the kitchen."

"Thank you kindly," Hayden said, passing her Zorro's reins. He turned to his stallion. "Now, you behave yourself." He tapped the horse lightly on the nose.

Zorro snorted, lowering his head to Gerta for some attention. She laughed and stroked his mane.

"Come on, Zorro. I've got a couple apples with your name on them. See you around, Sheriff."

"Bye, Gerta," Hayden replied.

He walked up to the door, removing his hat as he pushed through it, a bell above his head jangling merrily. The lobby was empty, but he heard voices from the back room.

He followed the sounds to a dining area decked out with freshly constructed tables and chairs, simple in form but perfectly functional. A half-dozen people sat scattered around the room, digging into some kind of stew. It took a few seconds for the smell to reach his nose, but when it did, he breathed deeper, drawing in the aromas.

"Hon, we need another bottle of Jack's Finest out front," a familiar voice called from the bar. Hayden turned his attention that way, laying eyes on Jack. He looked the same as the last time Hayden had seen him, with the addition of a thick mustache.

"Coming," a voice sing-songed from beyond an archway behind the bar. Hayden remained fixed in place as he watched Tabitha emerge.

She had definitely changed, having trimmed down some in the last few months. Everywhere except her belly, bulging slightly beneath her apron

She was handing Jack a bottle of moonshine when she noticed him standing in the doorway, grinning at them. In her excitement to see him, the bottle fell from her hands. Jack barely caught the bottle as she rushed to the end of the bar and threw the partition out of the way.

"Sheriff!" she cried, rushing across the room toward Hayden in a dozen quick strides. Throwing her arms around him, she hugged him tightly. Hayden stiffened for a moment before slowly returning the embrace.

"It's damn good to see you," Tabby said, her voice muffled against his chest. She pulled back, holding him at arm's length, her gaze roaming over his face. "You look like hell, though. And smell even worse. When's the last time you had a proper meal? And a bath?"

Hayden chuckled, running a hand through his hair. "It's been a while," he admitted. "I've been...away."

"Natalia?" Tabby asked, her brow deeply furrowed.

He nodded.

"I can tell by your reaction and the fact you're here alone that it didn't end well. I'm so sorry, Hayden. Truly I am."

He nodded, swallowing past the lump in his throat. "Thank you," he managed. "It's been...." He trailed off.

"Of course," Tabby said, squeezing his arm. "Losing someone you love like that...I can't even imagine."

"Sheriff? I can't believe it!"

Hayden looked up as Jack approached, a broad grin splitting his face.

"Jack," Hayden greeted, clasping the man's hand firmly. "Good to see you."

"Likewise," Jack said, clapping him on the shoulder. "Though I have to say, you're looking a little rough around the edges. Not that you don't always look a little worn, but more than usual. And..." He paused as if remembering their last meeting for the first time. A glance at Tabby confirmed it. "Oh. Sheriff, I'm sorry. I take it you found Natalia."

"I did," he replied. "She uh...she's gone." He forced himself to spit it out. "Again. For good, this time."

"I wish I knew what to say, Sheriff," Jack said. "If there's anything you need, you know Tabby and I are here for you."

"I don't need much," Hayden replied. "I knew you said you planned to come back to the Arches, and I'm passing through, so I thought I would stop by and catch up with you."

"Well, we're glad you did," Tabby said. "I've got dinner cooking in the back. We'd be happy to have you join us."

Hayden considered before nodding. "Pozz. Two weeks on the road has helped give me more of an appetite, at least."

"It's settled then. Jack, why don't you go check the stew while I get our guest settled?" She turned to Hayden. "Nothing but the best for you, Sheriff. Our most expensive room happens to be vacant at the moment. It's yours for as long as you need it."

"I appreciate that, but no need to fuss over me."

"Don't be ridiculous. You saved my life. It's the least we can do."

"I'm sure we can let you pay if you want, Sheriff," Jack said. "Since I know you have the means." He raised a suggestive eyebrow, aware that Hayden could print notes as needed.

"It's not about that," Tabby reminded him. "It's a gesture of goodwill and thanks, and I won't take no for an answer."

"In that case, show me to the room."

"This way, Sheriff."

CHAPTER 4

Jack went off to check the meal while Tabby led Hayden to the stairwell. Initially intended for emergencies, she'd painted the gray walls in bright colors and added rugs to the cold concrete steps, giving them as homey a look as possible.

"Tabby," Hayden said as they went up the stairs. "Are you...?"

She followed his gaze, one hand coming to rest on her stomach. "Pregnant?" she finished for him. "Sure am. About four months along now."

"And Jack is the father?"

"Sure is," Tabby confirmed with a nod. "I know what you're thinking, Sheriff. Jack and me were just friends last time we were all in the same place. And that's how I intended it to continue, but..." She shrugged, a wry smile tugging at her lips. "Things change. Jack, he...he really stepped up, you know? After everything that happened with Grimmel and the moieties, he was there for me. For everyone, really. He's a good man, Hayden. Better than he gives himself credit for."

"I'm happy for you both," Hayden said sincerely.

"Thank you," Tabby said, her eyes shining. "That means a lot, coming from you." She clapped her hands together briskly. "Now, enough of that. Let's get you settled in a room, and then we can catch up over dinner. I want to hear all about what you've been up to."

Hayden followed her up the stairs. She led him to a small but clean corner room at the end of the hall, with a simple bed, a washstand, a tub, and a freshly upholstered winged chair by the window.

"I know it doesn't look like much," Tabby said apologetically. "We're still saving up for better furniture. Jack knows a guy who makes some really fine quality frames and mattresses. Trouble is, most folks come to the Arches to stay, not to pass through, so business is just good enough to stay above water." She turned to him, putting up a hand. "Don't think I'm telling you that because we want your help. What you have at your disposal suits what you do, but Jack and I want to make our own way."

"I never thought otherwise," Hayden replied. "And you're doing well for yourselves. I'm happy to see it."

"The bed's comfortable, and there's hot water for washing up. I can have Gerta fetch you bath water while we eat, if you'd like. You just holler if you need anything else. Dinner will be ready soon."

"It's perfect," Hayden assured her. "Thank you, Tabby."

She smiled, patting his cheek affectionately. "You're family, Hayden. You don't ever have to thank me." With that, she left him to get settled, closing the door softly behind her.

Hayden set his saddlebags on the bed, suddenly feeling the weight of his exhaustion pressing down on him. He splashed water on his face from the washstand, scrubbing at the road dust and grime until his skin was pink and raw. Catching a glimpse of himself in the mirror, he grimaced. Tabby was right; he looked like hell. His face had grown gaunt and hollow-cheeked, his eyes shadowed by dark circles. His hair had grown too long, and he had two weeks of scrub growing on his chin and jaws.

He then realized that he'd spent too long feeling sorry for himself. Nat had been gone for years. The clone...as much as it had looked like her, it had never been her.

Sighing, he changed into a clean shirt from his saddlebags and returned downstairs, promising himself he would shave before he departed. The smells of cooking food wafted up to greet him, making his stomach growl.

Jack and Tabby were already seated at the table closest to the kitchen when he entered the hotel dining room, their heads bent close together as they spoke in low voices. They looked up as he approached, identical welcoming smiles on their faces.

"There he is," Jack said, pulling a chair out for him. "Come on, sit down before the food gets cold."

Hayden took the offered seat, his mouth watering at the spread before him. There was a steaming pot of stew, thick with vegetables and tender-looking chunks of meat, and a loaf of what smelled like freshly baked bread. There was even a jug of what smelled like real ale.

"I think you've outdone yourselves," he said honestly. "I can't remember the last time I had a meal like this."

Tabby beamed at the praise, ladling a generous portion of stew into his bowl. "Well, you just dig in and enjoy," she said. "And if you want more, there's plenty where that came from."

For a few minutes, there was no sound but the clink of spoons against bowls and the occasional appreciative murmur as they ate. The food was every bit as delicious as it looked, and Hayden found himself going back for seconds and then thirds.

Finally, when the last morsel had been scraped from their bowls, Jack leaned back in his chair with a contented sigh. "That was a fine meal," he said, patting his belly. "My compliments to the chef."

Tabby grinned, her cheeks flushed with pleasure. "You're just saying that because you have to," she teased.

Jack held up his hands in mock surrender. "Guilty as charged," he said with a wink. "But it's still the truth." He turned his attention to Hayden, his expression growing serious. "So, not that it's not great to see you, but what brings you back to our neck of the woods? Nothing bad, I hope."

"I'm not sure if it's bad yet or not," Hayden replied. Noticing their confused expressions, he took a deep breath, steeling himself. "I had a dream," he explained. "More like a vision, really. I helped a woman a while back, name of Alina Prior. She was looking for her boy. Sadly, he was killed. But we uncovered a research facility run by Grimmel while we were looking for him, and rescued a bunch of kids from the facility. We brought them back to this settlement called the Greens to live."

"I've heard of the Greens," Tabby said.

"You have?" Hayden replied, surprised.

"Yep. Some folks have come to the Arches and decided the environment isn't right for them. We still have lots of ruins, and we're growing too quickly for some. They hear the Greens is smaller, and under the protection of the Sheriff. Which I suppose is right."

"Sure is," Hayden replied. "As best as I can protect anywhere on my own."

"So what about this dream?" Jack asked.

"I saw the Greens under attack by these marauders, dressed in white robes and wearing masks to breathe in some kind of hallucinogenic vapors. They were after Kady and the other children from Grimmel's facility. I tried to stop them, but they overpowered me. I watched as they dragged Kady away."

Tabby gasped, her hand flying to her mouth. "Oh, Hayden," she breathed. "That's awful."

Jack frowned, leaning forward. "What makes you think it was more than a dream? I mean, a bunch of raiders overpowering you doesn't sound too likely to me."

"That's the thing. They had more advanced tech, and some gear from Proxima. Stuff normal raiders don't have. And there were a lot of them."

"No offense, Sheriff, but that doesn't make it real. Tabs and I hear a lot of stories from the guests, and I don't think either one of us has heard a peep about white-robed nomads in masks."

"Nope," Tabby confirmed. "Though I have to admit, we don't get much traffic coming north. Most folks are going the opposite way."

"I'm just trying to be helpful is all, Sheriff," Jack said. "You've been through a lot. Maybe…"

He trailed off as Hayden shook his head. "Neg. It's not me looking for something to get my mind off Natalia. Kady is different. Special. The experiments she underwent at Grimmel's facility gave her psychic abilities. And the dream felt too real. I think she might have been reaching out to me, somehow. Calling for help. I could be wrong, but there's no harm in me making sure."

"Is there any way we can help you?" Tabby asked immediately.

"I need to get to the Greens as fast as possible. I intend to take a boat down the Ole Miss to Memphis, if there's one available."

Jack rubbed his chin thoughtfully. "I might know a guy," he said after a moment. "Let me ask around, see what I can do."

"I can—" Hayden started to argue.

"Don't be ridiculous. Jack Colton is a master of connections. If you need a boat, I'll get you a boat." He pushed back from the table, dropping a kiss on top of Tabby's head as he stood. "Sit tight. I'll be back as soon as I can."

Tabby laughed as Jack hurried out the door. "See what I mean, Sheriff? The old Jack would have made sure he got something out of helping you. Which, in a way, I suppose he has." She rubbed her belly before standing to clear the table.

"Let me help you with that," Hayden said, hopping to his feet.

"Oh, it's no trouble," Tabby replied. "You're a guest. You just relax."

Hayden started collecting bowls. "What would make this guest happy is helping you clear the table."

Tabby laughed. "Suit yourself, Sheriff."

They set about clearing the table and washing dishes, chatting about this and that before returning to the dining room. Hayden sat again while Tabby helped their serving girl check on the few other guests in the room.

Jack came bursting back in, a triumphant grin on his face. "I found you a boat," he announced. "Friend of mine, name of Hank. He's carrying four other passengers down that way. Says he can take you to the Greens, no problem."

"That's great news," he said, standing. "When does he leave?"

"First thing in the morning," Jack said. "Hank wants to get an early start and make the most of the daylight. Though with you on board, he might stay on the river at night, too. Not that I told him who my traveling guest is. I know you don't like to advertise. By the way..." He reached into his pocket, pulled out a rolled-up pamphlet and passed it to Hayden. "...your latest escapade just hit the presses."

Hayden unrolled the pamphlet, looking down at a stylized version of himself with two metal arms and a cybernetic eye. He was facing off against a Goliath, its hulking form only a silhouette in the background.

Sheriff Duke vs. the Goliath, by M. Friend

"The author's selling so well, he's not making the books by hand anymore," Jack said. "Blaze's store got in a delivery of fifty of these a couple days ago. Sold out in a few hours. I nabbed this copy from Hank for twice the going rate."

Hayden shook his head, struggling to believe the popularity of the tall tales. And the author's name...he had a feeling he knew who was behind the stories.

"You have nine hours, Sheriff," Jack continued. "Why don't you head on up and get some rest? You look like you could use it."

"Pozz," he agreed. "But just for a few hours. I want to be ready to go as soon as Hank is."

Jack clapped him on the shoulder. "I'll make sure of it," he promised. "Now go on, get some shut-eye. We'll see you in the morning."

Hayden climbed the stairs to his room, finding a nice hot bath waiting for him when he arrived. Grateful to Tabby and Gerta, he stripped naked and climbed in, the water quickly browning from the road dust. Slipping deeper in the water, he leaned his head back until his neck rested against the rim. Closing his eyes, he exhaled a long breath, releasing some of his built-up tension.

"Sheriff Duke!"

Hayden's eyes snapped open, head turning to look for Kady. The voice sounded like it had come from inside the room.

"Sheriff Duke!" she repeated, frightened voice echoing in his ears. "Help me!"

CHAPTER 5

Hayden had just finished his morning bath and was toweling off when a loud knock sounded at the door, startling him. He quickly pulled on his pants and cracked the door, revealing Jack's grinning face.

"Rise and shine, Sheriff!" Jack chirped. "Hank's ready to cast off. Time to hit the road. Or river, as it were."

Hayden rubbed a hand over his face, feeling the stubble rasp against his palm. He hadn't slept at all. He hadn't been able to sleep after hearing Kady's voice. Waiting for the morning had become almost too much to bear. He was more certain now than ever that she was in real trouble, and he was anxious to be on his way.

"I'll be right there," he said, returning to the door to grab his shirt and vest. He quickly finished dressing and strapped on his gun belt and bandoliers before gathering his few belongings and stowing them in his saddlebags. When he stepped out into the hall, Jack was waiting for him, bouncing on the balls of his feet with barely contained energy.

They made their way downstairs, where Tabby was wiping down the bar. She looked up as they approached, a warm smile spreading across her face.

"Leaving so soon?" she asked, coming around the bar to give Hayden a hug.

"Afraid so," he said, returning the embrace. "Duty calls."

Tabby pulled back, searching his face. "You be careful out there, you hear me? Those kids need you. And so do we."

Hayden nodded solemnly. "I will. And Tabby..." He glanced down at her stomach. "Congratulations again. You and Jack are going to make great parents."

Tabby's eyes misted over, and she hugged him again. "Thank you, Hayden. Now go on with you, before I start bawling like a baby."

With a smile and a final squeeze of her hand, Hayden followed Jack out into the early morning light. The streets were just starting to come alive as they made their way down to the docks, the first rays of sun glinting off the water."Now, don't you worry a bit about Zorro," Jack said as they walked. "You know I'll take great care of him while you're gone."

"I know you will," Hayden agreed.

"And you know the best part about me and Tabby watching him for you, Sheriff?"

"What's that?"

"We get to see you again when you come back to get him. It's been great having you here. The world always feels a little bit safer when you're around."

"It was good to see you and Tabitha too, Jack," Hayden replied. "With any luck, this business won't have me gone too long."

"I sense a but in there, Sheriff."

"Kady called out to me last night, telepathically. Begging me for help."

Jack raised an eyebrow. "That's a thing that can really happen?"

"It is if Grimmel altered your DNA with Relyeh code."

"I don't know what that means, but it sounds bad."

"Not on its own. But yes, it is possible. Just like I can heal faster than a normal man. Anyway, I know she's in trouble. Now I'm just going to find out how bad it really is."

"I hope things turn out okay for little Kady. I'd go along with you for sure if it weren't for the baby."

"I appreciate that, Jack. But there isn't much you can do for me out there. Stay here and enjoy your growing family and the peace you have here in the Arches. I'll do my best to keep the peace for you."

"Deal," Jack said, stopping at the gangplank leading up to where an old shrimp boat was docked at the end of the pier. "Well, there she is…" Jack shoved his hands deep into his pockets. "…the Salty Dog."

Hayden took in the vessel before him. It was faded and worn, its hull composed of multicolored wood planks that looked like they could start taking on water at any moment. Not the most stable vessel from what he saw, but beggars couldn't be choosers, and he was just grateful to have a ride.

The other passengers were already on deck, their meager belongings piled at their feet. There were two men, one older with a grizzled white beard, the other younger and clean-shaven. A woman with long dark hair pulled back in a braid and a girl of about ten clutching a raggedy doll, her blonde hair in pigtails.

Hayden and Jack crossed the gangplank, the passengers turning to stare just as Hank walked out of the wheelhouse to greet them. He was a tall, wiry man with sun-weathered skin and a shock of white hair. He wore faded denim overalls and a corncob pipe dangled from the right side of his thick lips. His eyes suddenly widened when he saw Hayden, the pipe nearly falling from his mouth.

"Well, I'll be damned," he drawled, looking Hayden up and down. "Jack, you son of a gun. Why didn't you tell me I'd be ferrying an honest to gods legend?"

Jack held up his hands, a mischievous twinkle in his eye.

"Hey now, I said I had a friend who needed passage. I didn't think it mattered who it was."

"Are you kidding me?" Hank replied, sticking out a gnarled hand to Hayden. "Pleasure to meet you, Sheriff. Welcome aboard the Salty Dog."

Hayden heard several of the passengers gasp as he shook Hank's hand. "Thank you for taking me with you on such short notice," he said. "I appreciate it. How did you know who I am?"

"I saw you in Memphis some time back," Hank replied. "You probably didn't notice me. Anyways, any friend of Jack's is a friend of mine. Besides, having you on board will make me feel a sight safer, especially at night. Never know what you might run into on the river these days."

Hayden nodded, his thoughts turning once again to Kady and the Greens.

The older man among the passengers stepped up to them. "Did I just hear Hank right?" He looked from Hayden to Hank. "Did you just call him Sheriff?" he asked, but before Hank could answer, the old man's head swiveled back to Hayden "Are you?" He looked back at Hank. "Is he?"

Hank looked at Hayden. Shrugging, he waited for permission. Hayden would have rather kept a low profile, but it would be hard to spend the next day or two in close quarters with these folks. He gave Hank a resigned look and nodded.

"Yep," Hank confirmed. "This here's Sheriff Duke. In the flesh."

"Well, I'll be," the old man said, grabbing Hayden's hand and vigorously shaking it.

"But you have two regular hands," the little girl said.

"Molly, you can't believe everything you read," her mother said.

"Sheriff Duke, as I live and breathe," the older man said. "Ain't this a stroke of luck?"

The others murmured their agreement, eagerly crowding around Hayden.

"Is it true you fought a whole army of trife single-handed?" the younger man asked.

"I heard you killed a queen with your bare hands," the woman chimed in.

Hayden held up a hand, feeling a bit overwhelmed by the attention. "Now, now, let's not get carried away. Most of those stories are just tall tales."

The little girl tugged on his coat, looking up at him with wide, solemn eyes. "But you are the real Sheriff Duke, aren't you? The one who protects people?"

Hayden crouched down to her level, giving her a gentle smile. "I am. And I promise, as long as I'm on this boat, no harm will come to you or anyone else. Okay?"

With a timid smile, the girl nodded, hugging her doll tighter. Hayden straightened up, looking around at the other passengers.

"I don't suppose any of you have heard rumors about men in white robes and breathing masks?" he asked, not expecting an affirmative answer but having to ask anyway.

They all shook their heads, looking puzzled. "Can't say as I have," the older man said. "What's this about, Sheriff?"

Hayden hesitated, not wanting to alarm them unnecessarily. "Just something I'm looking into. Probably nothing to worry about."

He could tell they weren't entirely convinced, but thankfully, Hank chose that moment to bellow from the wheelhouse.

"All right, folks, time to cast off! Next stop, Memphis!"

"I'll get the lines for you, Hank," Jack said, giving Hayden a two-fingered salute before running back over the gangplank to the pier.

Behind him, Hayden pulled in the gangplank and stowed it alongside the rail where he found fastenings for it while

Jack released the stern line first and tossed it into the boat. He ran back to the boat's bow, taking care of that line before shoving the boat's bow away from the dock. He remained to wave from the pier as Hank guided the Salty Dog away from the Arches and out into midriver.

Hayden moved up to the bow and he stared downriver. It was too bad he didn't have the means to reach Nathan on short notice. A Centurion starhopper could get him from the Arches to the Greens in fifteen minutes, but at least he was on his way.

The sun crept higher in the sky as they chugged south at a snail's pace. The boat's old diesel engines shot plenty of dark smoke into the sky as the muddy waters of the Mississippi flowed beneath them. Hayden continued to stand at the bow like a figurehead, but his nerves and the boat's slow progress finally got the best of him. He began to pace the deck, eyes constantly scanning the riverbanks, his right hand resting on the butt of his pistol.

The passengers kept their distance, sensing his agitation. Occasionally, the little girl would wander over and tug on his sleeve, offering a shy smile as if to comfort him before scampering back to her mother. Hayden smiled back, but her childish attempts to ease his anxiety only reminded him of Kady when they first met, leaving him ever more eager to reach his destination.

As the day wore on, they passed the occasional settlement, usually clusters of ramshackle buildings clinging to the water's edge. People came out to wave as the boat went by, excited to see signs of life on the river. Hayden barely noticed them, his thoughts consumed by his mission.

The sun was just setting when Hank throttled back the engines, guiding the Salty Dog towards a sheltered cove."We'll anchor here for the night," he called down from the wheelhouse. "Too dangerous to navigate the river in the dark."

Hayden wanted to protest, to insist they keep going, but he knew Hank was right. With its shifting sandbars and hidden snags, the Mississippi was treacherous enough in daylight. And at night, the river wasn't the only thing to worry about.

The trife used to mostly come out at night. Mostly. Now, the raiders, bandits and brigands stalked the dark, looking for easy prey. They wouldn't find it on the Salty Dog, but they wouldn't know it until and if they showed up. Hayden preferred not to waste bullets on them, but he would if he had to.

Hayden threw out the anchor, and the passengers set up camp in the two cabins below deck, spreading out bedrolls and starting small fires in metal buckets to ward off the evening chill. Molly helped her mother heat up some canned soup provided by Hank, proudly carrying bowls to each of the men.

Hayden stayed topside, accepting his bowl with a nod of thanks. Molly blushed and rushed back to her mother, pleased the Sheriff had spoken to her. He ate quickly and quietly.

As the others settled in for the night, talking quietly amongst themselves, Hayden remained on watch, his eyes never leaving the darkening shoreline. The moon rose, painting the river in shades of silver and shadows, and still he kept his vigil.

It was deep into the night when he heard it, a soft splash of something entering the water. He was on his feet instantly, gun drawn, scanning the riverbank. There, just visible in the moonlight, was a small boat, little more than a canoe. And in it, two figures obscured in shadows.

As the boat drew closer, Hayden made out a pair of rough-looking men, their faces obscured by bandanas. A rifle lay across the lap of one man. The other had a revolver on one hip and a large hunting knife on the other. There was only one reason they might be paddling silently toward the Salty Dog under the covers of darkness, their faces masked.

"Hold it right there!" Hayden called out, his voice ringing across the water as he drew one of his guns and pointed it at them. "Turn around now or meet your maker. Your choice!"

The men froze, caught off guard by Hayden's challenge. They hadn't expected to be spotted so soon.

"W-we don't want no trouble, mister," one of them stammered, holding up his hands. "We was just lookin' for a place to rest for the night, that's all. We thought your boat was derelict."

"Right. I ought to put a bullet in both of you, so you stop preying on the innocents trying to make their way downriver."

"Preying?" the man replied. "N…no sir. We're just travelers ourselves."

"Well, rest somewhere else," Hayden said coldly. "And hope our paths don't cross again. I won't be so forgiving next time."

"Y…yes, sir," the man said.

They grabbed their paddles and started backing their canoe away, muttering curses as they paddled. Hayden trained his gun on them until they pulled the canoe up on the bank and moved well out of range, disappearing into the darkness.

Behind him, he heard the creak of the wheelhouse door and turned to see Hank emerging, shotgun in hand.

"What's going on, Sheriff?" he asked, hurrying over. "I heard shouting."

Hayden gestured out at the river. "Couple of masked robbers trying to sneak aboard. I sent them packing."

Hank whistled low, shaking his head. "Varmints. Who knows what kind of mischief they would've caused if they'd made it on board. We're lucky you were on watch, Sheriff. Mighty lucky indeed."

Hayden just nodded, holstering his gun. "Just doing my job."

Hank clapped him on the shoulder, his weathered face splitting into a grin. "Well, I for one am glad you're here. Makes me feel a sight safer, knowing we've got Sheriff Duke watching our backs. Tell you what, Sheriff. Why don't you let me take over watch for a spell? You look like you could use some shut-eye."

Hayden shook his head. "I appreciate the offer, but I don't need to sleep. I'll keep watch until morning."

Hank shrugged, shouldering his shotgun. "Suit yourself. We'll be on our way at first light. With any luck, we'll reach the Greens by midday tomorrow."

He headed back to the wheelhouse, again leaving Hayden alone on deck. The Sheriff turned back to the river, continuing his lonely vigil, a silent sentinel standing guard over the sleeping passengers, scanning the banks for any more signs of trouble. After a while, he watched the stars wheel overhead, the moon sinking slowly toward the horizon.

As the night wore on, quiet except for the night calls of wild animals and the gentle lapping of water against the hull, he could only hope that wherever Kady was, she was safe and that he would find her before it was too late.

CHAPTER 6

As dawn broke over the Ole Miss, the Salty Dog chugged steadily downriver, the muddy waters churning beneath its hull. Once again, Hayden stood at the bow of the shrimp boat, his eyes fixed on the horizon. Behind him, the other passengers began to stir, emerging from the cabin to stretch and greet the morning. Hayden paid them no mind, his gaze fixed on the river ahead.

It was nearly midday when Hayden first noticed a thin plume of smoke on the horizon, drifting lazily into the sky. Hayden's heart clenched, a cold knot of dread forming in his gut. He knew the smoke of smoldering wood all too well—the smoke of burned homes and ruined lives.

"Sheriff?" Hank called from the wheelhouse, his voice tinged with concern. "You seeing what I'm seeing?"

Hayden nodded. "How far are we from the Greens?"

"About as far as we are from the smoke, I reckon. You don't think…" He trailed off, realizing that was exactly what Hayden thought.

"Can you get us there any faster?" Hayden asked. "The threat may have passed, but what those folks need most right now is hope."

The old shrimper didn't need to be told twice. He pushed the throttle forward, the engines roaring as the Salty Dog surged ahead. The smoke grew thicker as they approached until they rounded a bend in the river and the Greens came into view.

Or what was left of it.

The once-thriving settlement was a smoldering ruin. The air remained thick with the stench of death and destruction.

Hank cut the engines, letting the boat drift toward a barge tethered to the Greens' dock, his face pale and drawn. As they drew closer, a group of armed residents rushed toward them, hunting rifles in some hands, pitchforks and other sharp implements in others. The Greens had grown so much that Hayden didn't recognize them.

"Stay back!" one of them shouted, his voice trembling with fear and anger. "We don't want any more trouble!"

Hayden stepped up to the bow, holding his hands out placatingly. "Easy now," he called out. "I'm here to help."

The man squinted, his eyes widening as he recognized the figure before him. "Sheriff Duke?" he said in disbelief. "Is that really you?"

A murmur went through the gathered residents, their weapons lowering as they realized who had come to their aid.

"Pozz," he said. "I came as quick as I could."

The residents lowered their weapons. A few crossed the barge to grab the boat as it coasted up to them, grabbing onto the railings and holding the boat in place so Hayden could get off.

"I can't believe you're here, Sheriff," one of them said. "The children…" He trailed off, eyes welling.

"I know," Hayden replied. "Don't you worry. I'll find the children." The man nodded before swiping away the moisture from his eyes.

Hayden disembarked from the boat and turned back toward it. "Hank, much obliged for the ride."

"My pleasure, Sheriff. You saved me from a reckoning with those thugs last night. I'm much obliged to you."

"Molly, Caspar, David, Laney," he said to the other passengers. "Thank you for being such fine company. I wish you safe travels down to Memphis. It's a nice settlement. I think you'll like it there."

"Thank you, Sheriff," David, the older man said. "Good luck to you. I hope you find those kids."

"That makes two of us," Hayden replied. He watched as the townsfolk pushed the Salty Dog away from the barge. Hank restarted the engines, guiding the boat back out into the river. He gave Hayden one final wave before opening the throttle and continuing south.

Hayden turned back to the gathered residents, about to ask them for more details on the attack, when a familiar voice called out, grabbing his attention.

"Hayden!" Alina cried, running toward him. "Oh, thank goodness you're here!"

She threw her arms around him, burying her face in his chest as she sobbed. Hayden held her, his own throat tight.

"I came as soon as I could," he said softly.

Alina pulled back, eyes wide. "How…how did you know we needed you?"

"Kady. She's been calling out to me. First in a dream, and then while I was awake."

"She has? Then you know…"

Hayden nodded. "I saw it all. The raiders in white, the masks, the children being taken." He related the entirety of his dream to her and how, at first, he thought it had come from Shub'Nigu before worrying the Greens were in trouble. "It happened just like I dreamed it, didn't it?"

Alina nodded, fresh tears spilling down her cheeks at the recounting. "Almost exactly. Except…" She swallowed hard. "You weren't there. In your dream, you tried to stop them. But in reality…"

"In the dream, I failed," Hayden said. "In reality, I wasn't even here. Oz. Is he…?"

Alina's face crumpled. "He's gone, Hayden. Him and Sam both. They died trying to protect the children."

Hayden's chest clenched, remembering the boy who had wanted so much to be like him. He had given Sam his Sheriff's star and put him in charge of protecting the Greens. It seemed the boy had taken the job seriously and had paid the ultimate price. And Oz had been a good man and loyal friend. Grief and rage flowed through him, not only for them but for everyone in the Greens.

"Alina," he said, his voice low and intense. "Do you have any idea who these raiders are? What they wanted with the children?"

She shook her head, wiping at her tears. "Their leader called the kids the 'Children of Grimmel.' Said they had some great purpose to fulfill. But beyond that, I don't know. What I do know is that they came out of nowhere, and when they left, after burning down half the settlement and taking the children, they headed north."

Hayden frowned, his mind racing. North wasn't much to go on. They could have scattered in any direction from there. With the hoverbikes and APC, it would be no trouble for them to cross the river. He would have seen them if they had kept following the Ole Miss. They must have headed overland.

"A group that size can't travel unnoticed for long," he said, almost to himself. "Wherever they went, I'll find them. I promise you that, Alina."

She looked up at him, hope and despair in her eyes. "I know you will, Hayden. If anyone can bring the children home, it's you."

"What about transportation?" Hayden asked, glancing around at the ruined settlement. "I had to leave Zorro in the Arches. I'll need a ride if I'm going to catch up to them."

Alina's face brightened slightly. "I think we have something you can use. Follow me."

She led him across the settlement to the large schoolhouse barn, the same one he had ridden through in his dream in a futile attempt to save the kids. One of the raider's hoverbikes sat inside, past the overturned desks and scattered books.

"Oz managed to take out the rider before..." Alina trailed off, swallowing hard. "Anyway, there's no reason it shouldn't still work."

Hayden circled the bike, inspecting it with a critical eye. Outfitted with a spiked cage to help protect the rider from trife, it was in relatively good shape considering its age. Even better, when he tapped on the display between the handlebars, he discovered the battery was still well over half charged. It would do nicely, at least for a couple hundred kilometers. The raiders would need to power back up, too. If he found out where they had, he would have a better idea which direction they went.

"The rider," he said, looking up at Alina. "I need to see the body."

She bit her lip, looking uncomfortable. "I'm sorry, Hayden. We didn't know you were coming, and we couldn't just leave them lying around. We burned the bodies."

Hayden nodded. He had hoped to find some clues about the raiders themselves, some hint of their origins or allegiances. But their ashes would tell him nothing.

"What about personal effects?" he asked. "Clothing, weapons, anything like that?"

Alina's face brightened. "Actually, yes. We gathered up what we could use. Just a moment."

She hurried out of the barn, returning a few minutes later with a battered metal box. Inside were the raider's robes, still reeking of acrid smoke, his breathing mask, cracked and stained with blood and still attached to the canister, and an assortment of smaller items — a few coins, a tarnished locket, a set of car keys.

And a pair of dog tags.

Hayden picked them up, his eyes narrowing as he read the stamped lettering. They were United States Marines tags, the kind the War Dogs liked to wear. But these were no War Dogs, he was sure of that much. But then, how had these raiders gotten their hands on such high-quality gear?

He turned the tags over in his hand, his mind whirling with possibilities. Could the raiders have attacked a War Dog platoon and won? It seemed impossible. The Dogs were the best-trained operatives born on Earth. But what if…

He dropped the dog tags into a pocket and picked up the mask, smelling the inside. It still had a strong odor, even though the canister had released its contents days ago.

"Alina, do you have any idea what was in the canister?" he asked. "Some kind of drug, I'm sure. But it's nothing I've encountered before."

"No idea, Hayden," she replied. "It's the first I've seen of anything like it."

Hayden turned the mask over, looking for an inscription or something that might give him an idea of where it came from. He was doing the same with the canister when he was interrupted by approaching footsteps. He looked up to see a group of residents gathered at the barn door, their faces lined with grief and exhaustion.

"Sheriff Duke," one of them said, an older man with a grizzled beard. "We just wanted to say thank you for coming. I know it doesn't change what happened, but knowing you're here means a lot to us."

Hayden nodded, touched by their gratitude. "I'm just sorry I couldn't get here sooner," he said. "But I promise you, I won't rest until I find those children and bring them home."

"Will you stay?" a woman asked, hopeful. "Just for a little while? I'm sure a hot meal wouldn't go amiss."

Hayden smiled sadly, shaking his head. "I appreciate the offer, ma'am. Truly. But every minute I spend here is another minute those raiders have on me. I need to get moving."

The woman's face fell, but she nodded in understanding. "Of course. We wouldn't want to keep you from helping the children."

Alina stepped forward. "I'm coming with you," she said. "Kady and the others are my responsibility too. You saw in the dream, Oz taught me to shoot."

But Hayden was already shaking his head. "I'm sorry, Alina. I know how badly you want to help." He held up a hand to forestall her protest. "The fact is, those raiders have a few days on me, and I can travel faster alone. You know I don't need much sleep, and I can push harder than most."

Alina looked like she wanted to argue, but she couldn't deny the truth of his words. Finally, she nodded, her shoulders slumping in defeat.

"Just bring them back to us, Hayden," she said, her voice thick with emotion. "Bring the children home. Bring Kady home."

"I will," Hayden vowed. "I swear it."

With that, he swung a leg over the hoverbike, settled into the saddle and flipped a switch. The machine thrummed to life beneath him, its repulsors glowing a soft blue. He gave the gathered residents one last nod of farewell before twisting the throttle and rocketing out of the back of the barn.

CHAPTER 7

Hayden sped north on the hoverbike, the ruined settlement of the Greens quickly disappearing behind him. He kept to the back roads and trails, avoiding the main thoroughfares where he might be spotted. The last thing he needed was to tip off the raiders that he was coming.

As he rode, his mind raced, trying to piece together the scattered clues. The War Dog tags, the white robes, the strange breathing masks. He had crossed the continent west to east and north to south and had never heard of a group like this before. Somehow, they had slipped his notice or only come together in the last few months. Both seemed unlikely, but one of them had to be true.

The raiders had intentionally targeted the kids from Grimmel's facility. How had they known about them? What did they want with them? They were a target because they had been experimented on. But of the ones who had survived, only Kady ever manifested supernatural abilities. How long might it take for the white robes to figure that out? And what would they do with the other children when they did?

It was a chilling thought.

He pushed the bike harder, angling away from the river,

the landscape blurring past in a smear of green and brown. There was no way the white robes had followed the riverbank and evaded his attention. They had to cut further overland. But there was no way to know if they had kept north or gone east. Not until he found a trace of them. He lamented that Kady had only called him for help and hadn't given him any actionable information. Then again, the leader had thrown her in the back of the APC. She couldn't see where they were going. Had any of the white robes let that information slip in her presence? He wished he could reach out to her the way she reached out to him and tell her to give him more details.

The sun was just setting, painting the sky in shades of orange and gold, when Hayden spotted a row of houses in the distance. Slowing when he approached, he noticed one of the homes didn't match the others. Instead of being rotted and decrepit, there were signs of recent repairs. Fresh boards nailed over broken windows. A door that looked like it had been recently rehung. A patchwork of reinforcement to keep the place upright. It wasn't all that common to find homes like this anymore. Nearly five years on from the trife, most folks were looking to join communities, not eke out an existence alone. But it wasn't wholly unexpected either.

He turned off the bike and dismounted, drawing one of his revolvers as he approached the house. Better safe than sorry, he climbed creaking porch steps and rapped on the door with the butt of his gun.

"Hello?" he called out. "Anyone home?"

Silence. Hayden was about to turn away when he heard a faint thumping sound, like someone pounding on a door. It seemed to be coming from inside.

Frowning, Hayden opened the unlocked door, leading with his gun, sweeping it across a simple living room. Immediately, he noticed blood on an already aged and worn sofa. It looked relatively fresh. Breathing in, he noticed a lingering smell that reminded him of the dead raider's canister.

"Hello?" he called out again. "Anyone here?"

The thumping intensified and came with a muffled voice. "Hello? Help me, please!"

Hayden crossed the living room to the source of the noise, a door leading to the basement, the deadbolt locked. He unlocked the door, stepping back as he pulled it open, aiming his gun into the darkness. "All right," he said, his voice low. "Come on out of there. Nice and slow."

For a moment, nothing happened. Then a figure emerged from the gloom, hands held high. An older woman, her face weathered by age and hardship. She squinted at Hayden, her eyes adjusting to the light.

"Don't shoot," she said, her voice trembling slightly. "I'm unarmed, and no threat to you."

Hayden lowered his gun but kept it ready at his side. "Who locked you down there?" he asked.

The woman lowered her hands, her shoulders sagging with relief. "Men in white robes. Ugly men. Evil men."

Hayden's heart skipped a beat. "White robes?" he repeated, taking a step closer. "They hit a settlement just south of here. The Greens. I'm trying to catch up to them, to give them what they deserve."

The woman cackled at that. "I hope you do. I've heard of the Greens. Nice place, if the rumors are true."

"It was," Hayden replied. "Then the white robes came."

"Same thing happened to me."

"What's your name?"

"Lonnie. What's yours?"

"Hayden." He tipped his hat. "Pleased to meet you, Lonnie. Tell me what happened."

"I was just minding my own business," Lonnie said, brushing dirt from her faded dress. "Tending to my chickens, working in the garden. Then this army comes roaring up on their fancy bikes, demanding I give them all my food." She shook her head. "They took everything. Every last scrap of food, every chicken in the coop. Then they locked me in the basement and left. I've lived here twenty years, well before the trife up and vanished. I never had a single one of those demons bother me. Never a single robber or raider. I knew how to make myself scarce. Then, I finally start to relax a little, and this happens." She spat on the floor. "Bastards."

"You're lucky they didn't kill you," Hayden said.

Lonnie laughed bitterly. "Lucky?" she said. "I'm not sure how lucky I am. They left me with nothing. No food, no way to get more. I'll starve out here on my own."

Hayden holstered his gun, his mind racing. "I can help you with that," he said. "But I need you to help me first."

She eyed him warily. "Help you how?"

"I need information about the men in the white robes."

"What kind of information?"

"Did you hear them say anything?" he pressed. "Anything at all about where they might be headed?"

Lonnie frowned, thinking. "They were talking to each other a lot," she said. "I could hear 'em through the door. Sounded like they were arguing about something. Supplies, maybe? Anyway, I heard one of 'em mention a place called the Fort. Don't know where that is, but it seemed important to 'em."

Hayden's pulse quickened. The Fort. It wasn't much, but it was something. A destination, wherever it might be.

"Anything else?" he asked. "Even the smallest detail could be important."

Lonnie hesitated, looking uncertain. "You know, there's something else I heard besides them talking. But it's going to sound crazy to you, I'm sure."

Hayden leaned forward. "I wouldn't be too sure. Tell me."

"I heard a voice," she said, her voice dropping to a whisper. "In my head. A young girl's voice, clear as day. At first I thought I was imagining things, but..."

"What did she say?" Hayden asked. It had to have been Kady reaching out.

Lonnie swallowed hard. "She said... 'Tell the Sheriff. We're going north.' That's all." She looked up at Hayden, realization dawning in her eyes. "You're not... Are you the Sheriff? *The* Sheriff?"

Hayden nodded. "I am."

Lonnie looked him up and down, a hint of disappointment in her eyes. "Huh. Always thought you'd be bigger."

Despite himself, Hayden felt a smile tug at his lips. "I get that a lot," he said. "Now, is there anything else you can tell me? Anything at all? Think back. Remember, no detail is too small."

Lonnie thought for a moment, then snapped her fingers. "Well, come to think of it, I did overhear one of 'em complaining about his 'Clear' running out. Don't know what that means, but he seemed pretty upset about it."

Hayden frowned. *Clear.* He'd never heard of any drug by that name before. Could it be the same substance as in the raiders' canisters?

"That's good," he said, straightening up. "Anything else?"

Lonnie pursed her lips, trying hard to remember. Finally, she shook her head. "I'm sorry, Sheriff. I'm not as sharp as I used to be. I just can't recall anything."

"That's okay, ma'am. What you've given me so far is helpful. One last question. Where's the nearest settlement?"

Lonnie pointed east. "About a half day's walk that way," she said. "Never had a problem walking it while the sun's up. Even without the trife, I'd never try to cross at night. That's how idiots get themselves robbed or worse."

Hayden nodded, reaching into his pocket and pulling out a wad of notes. He pressed them into the woman's hand, ignoring her gasp of surprise.

"That should be enough to help you recover," he said. "Head over to the settlement in the morning. Buy some food, maybe a gun for protection. And if anyone asks, you never saw me."

Lonnie clutched the money to her chest, tears welling in her eyes. "Thank you," she whispered. "Thank you so much." She paused, suddenly remembering. Oh, wait! There is one more thing."

Hayden paused halfway to his bike. "What is it?"

"The men, the ones in the robes...at least one of them was injured. I could hear him groaning, cursing. He was in the house, so he probably bled all over my couch." She scowled at the thought. "One of the others said he spotted an old factory on their way down, and he thought it was the kind of place they could scavenge for medical supplies. Asked for permission to check it out. The leader, I think, gave the go-ahead."

"An old factory? Do you know where it is?"

"Nope. Never been further north than this house. Not in sixty-three years."

"Have you been here alone this whole time?"

"I had a dog once, but that was a long time ago. With the trife, I was always better off solo and silent, if you know what I mean."

"Pozz," Hayden replied. An old factory. If the raiders were looking for supplies there, it might be a chance to catch them off guard and get the drop on them before they knew what hit them. "Thank you kindly. You may have just given me the break I needed."

Lonnie smiled. "I'm glad I could help, Sheriff."

Hayden tipped his hat to her, left the house, and returned to the hoverbike. As he swung his leg over the saddle, the woman called out to him from the doorway.

"Hey, isn't that one of the raiders' bikes?" she asked, eyeing the spiked chassis warily.

Hayden nodded. "It is. I took it off a raider at the Greens. He won't be needing it anymore."

Lonnie's face hardened. "Good," she said vehemently. "Bastard got what he deserved."

With that, Hayden gunned the engine and shot away, the farmhouse quickly receding behind him. He angled east toward the settlement Lonnie had mentioned. With any luck, someone there would have more information on the factory— and maybe even a lead on the raiders themselves.

CHAPTER 8

The settlement was small, a dozen recently constructed cabins clustered around a central square. Most of them looked abandoned, their windows dark and shuttered. Still, Hayden suspected people were inside, eager not to draw attention. A few showed obvious signs of life in the form of thin plumes of smoke rising from their chimneys.

Hayden stopped the bike at the edge of the square and dismounted, keeping his hands clear of his guns. The last thing he wanted was to spook these people, and judging by the strained silence that shrouded the area, they'd probably been through enough already.

Sauntering toward the center of the square, he trained his eyes downward, noticing ruts in the dirt that might have come from the raider's APC. Looking beyond the houses, he noticed pens and other simple shelters for chickens. But no clucking or any other sounds of animal life. The only animal life that seemed to be present was the dog.

To his left, a door suddenly creaked open, and a man stepped out, a battered shotgun cradled in his arms. He was large and barrel-chested from hard labor, with a scraggly beard. "That's far enough, stranger," he called out, his voice tense, a wary look in his eye. "State your business."

Hayden held up his hands, keeping his voice calm and even. "Easy, friend," he said. "I mean you no harm. My name is Hayden. I just came from Lonnie's house. A group of raiders in white robes locked her in her basement. I'm trying to track them down."

"What for?" the man asked. "That sounds like a quick way to get yourself killed."

"They attacked a settlement down south, took some children. They came through here before they got to Lonnie's, didn't they?"

The man's grip on his shotgun tightened. "Raiders? We ain't seen no raiders. And even if we had, we wouldn't tell you nothin'. We don't want no trouble."

"I understand. It isn't easy surviving out here, especially with such a small population. I don't want to bring any trouble down on you. The raiders had a military APC." He squatted down and pointed out a rut in the dirt. "It looks like it left these ruts in your streets. And I reckon they made off with most or all of your livestock."

The man took a step forward, shoving the shotgun closer. Hayden noticed his hands shaking slightly. He'd already been traumatized by the raiders, and he feared a lone man who had come searching for them.

"I didn't come here looking for a fight, except with them, " Hayden said gently. "All I need is information. The raiders, Lonnie told me they were looking for medical supplies. I heard they might try to scavenge from an old factory nearby. Do you know anything about that?"

The man didn't respond, keeping the shotgun trained on Hayden.

"Look, I know you're scared," Hayden said, trying to calm him down. "I bet those raiders slaughtered your livestock and butchered them while they held you and made you watch.

Probably took all of your grain, too. Everything but the secret caches you have stashed under the floorboards of your cabins. Maybe they were unkind to your wives."

The man's eyes welled in response to the last comment. "You should go."

"Sending me away isn't going to help you get vengeance for what they did," Hayden answered. "I know what happened here because I've seen it happen before, in places like yours all across the wilds. I don't like raiders much. What about you?"

The man hesitated, glancing back at the dark buildings behind him. He wanted to protect his people.

"Those raiders aren't coming back," Hayden said. "They already took what they wanted from you and moved on. I guarantee I'll be done with them before they could ever consider heading back this way."

For a moment, Hayden thought the man might simply turn and walk away. But then he sighed, lowering his shotgun a fraction.

"Might be I know some things," he said grudgingly. "There's an old chemical plant about four miles northeast of here. Trife lived there for a long time, till they all up and died. Been picked clean by scavvies since then, but my grandpappy used to tell stories of a hidden factory under the plant. Said his grandpappy worked up top. Long time ago. He swore it existed."

Hayden eyed the man, the sequence of events falling into place in his mind. The raiders had come to this settlement before moving on to Lonnie's. They probably never even planned to stop at the woman's home, but it could be their injured man needed a break. Might he have been their leader, and Lonnie was wrong about who was in charge? She couldn't see them, so it was possible.

Either way, they had done some awful things in this settlement. At least threatened the man's wife or daughter, even if they hadn't followed through with abusing them. They were looking for help for their wounded man, and to get them to leave, the man standing in front of him had told them about the factory.

"And this hidden factory, it made medical supplies?"

"That's what my grandpappy said. I have no reason not to believe him."

"Is there anything else you can tell me about the raiders?" Hayden asked. "Did any of them mention something called Clear?"

"Clear?" The man wrinkled his nose in thought before shaking his head. "Nah, can't say they did. What is that?"

"I think it's some kind of drug they were inhaling through their breathing masks," Hayden said. "Do you know anything about that?"

"I've heard from travelers of folks getting addicted to some kind of drink on the other side of the Ole Miss. I dunno if it's related." He shrugged. "Folks get addicted to drink all the time."

Hayden nodded. It probably wasn't related, but he would look into that, too, if it turned out the raiders had crossed the Ole Miss after all.

"Thank you, kindly, sir," he said, tipping his hat. "I appreciate your cooperation." With the shotgun still pointed at him, he turned and started back toward the hoverbike.

"Hey, mister, hold on a second," the man said.

Hayden stopped and turned around.

"Are you really going to find the devils who hurt my Sally?"

"Sure am," Hayden replied.

"When you give 'em hell, tell 'em it's for Sally and all the other folks they hurt."

Hayden nodded. "I will."

The man finally lowered his weapon and smiled. "A regular sheriff, you are. I wish you the best of luck, sir."

With that, he turned and disappeared into the building, the door slamming shut behind him. Hayden stood there momentarily, alone in the empty square, before returning to his bike.

An abandoned factory. It wasn't much, but it was something. Still a few days behind the raiders, he doubted he would find them still there, but if they had wounded, it wasn't out of the question.

He mounted the hoverbike and switched it on. He had enough charge left for another thirty miles or so before he'd need to switch rides or recharge. That would get him to the factory, at least.

He sat there a moment, hesitant, before dismounting and approaching the man's door. It opened before he could knock. The man didn't have the shotgun in hand this time.

"Is something wrong?" he asked.

"I'm sorry to bother you again," Hayden replied, eyes slipping past the man. A young woman with a black eye crouched on a bed in the corner under a blanket, obviously afraid. His heart broke for her immediately, fury lighting a new bonfire in his gut. "I was just wondering if you know of another settlement further north, past the factory?"

"There's a bigger town up north called Union," the man replied. "A little less than a day's ride from here, northeast from here. Most of the others here are from Union originally." He motioned to the shuttered houses.

"Why'd they leave?" Hayden asked.

"The whole place is run by a former War Dog, goes by the name of Tempest. He takes what he wants, if you know what I mean. Some folks, they accept that kind of leadership as the cost of safety. Others don't abide."

"I understand. Thank you again for your help." He tipped his hat again and turned away, the door closing behind him.

Swinging his leg astride the bike, he was sure the man meant a day's ride by horseback, not hovercycle. Four miles to the chemical plant and then something less than twenty-five miles to the town. If luck was on his side, he would have just enough range to reach it. Thankfully, it sounded like he could pick up new transportation there.

Activating the repulsors, the bike lifted a few inches off the ground. Hayden twisted the throttle and sped off toward his next destination.

And maybe confrontation with the raiders.

CHAPTER 9

The hoverbike ride from the settlement to the chemical planet only took a few minutes. Within no time, its rusted hulk loomed against the darkening sky, an ugly monument to a forgotten era. Massive cylindrical tanks and twisting pipelines sprawled across the complex, their once-gleaming metal now rusted and stained. The main building rose at the center, a behemoth of concrete and steel with rows of shattered upper-level windows gaping like empty eye sockets.

As Hayden drew closer, he noticed signs of recent activity. Fresh tracks cut through the overgrown lot, matching the tracks from the settlement. The APC had circled back this way, circumventing the small settlement on its return.

He had irrefutable proof as he glided around the storage tanks toward the main building's entrance. Three raider hoverbikes were parked outside.

Powering down his bike, Hayden dismounted silently and drew one of his revolvers. He crept towards the building, every sense on high alert. The massive steel door hung ajar, creaking softly as he slowly opened it enough to turn sideways and slip through.

The interior was a dark and dingy maze of shadows and

decay. Hulking machinery loomed on all sides, their purposes long forgotten. Pipes of all sizes crisscrossed the ceiling and walls, some broken and still dripping unknown fluids. The air was thick with the musty smell of abandonment and a sickly sweet odor he knew all too well. Immediately, he drew his second revolver, eyes narrowing in focus and confusion.

It couldn't be.

As his eyes adjusted to the gloom, he confirmed the source of the smell, though it wasn't as bad as he'd initially feared. He would never forget the smell of trife. He was relieved to see only their remains.

The desiccated corpses of the demons lay strewn about the facility by the dozens. While their innards had long since turned to dust, leaving them deflated, their razor-sharp claws and elongated skulls were still intact, along with their leathery skin. Hayden suppressed a shudder, remembering all too well the horrors the Relyeh creatures had caused.

He moved deeper into the plant, his footsteps echoing despite his best efforts at stealth. Ahead, he heard voices, low and muffled but definitely human. He was getting close.

A flash of movement caught his eye. Before he could react, a plasma bolt sizzled past his head, leaving a scorch mark on the wall behind him. Hayden dove for cover behind a drum tumbler as more shots followed.

"Damn. Missed him!" a gruff voice shouted. "Spread out and find him!"

Hayden remained in place as a few more bolts flashed overhead. Setting himself, he popped up from cover, firing back at his attacker. The raider ducked behind a massive storage tank just in time. Sparks flew off the pipe behind where his head had just been as the bullets missed their target. Hayden's eyes narrowed, surprised by the man's quick reflexes. Emptying his revolvers in the direction of the shooter, he used the distraction to reload as he sprinted down a narrow corridor lined with control panels.

The sound of heavy footsteps echoed behind him as the raider gave chase. Hayden zigzagged through the labyrinth of machinery and tanks, trying to lose his pursuer or at least find a way to circle back and get the drop on him.

He rounded a corner and found himself facing a dead end. Trapped.

As he spun around to try a different direction, the raider's triumphant laugh reached him before he came around the corner. "Nowhere to run now, scavvie," the man growled, leveling his plasma rifle at Hayden's chest.

"Who says I was running?" Hayden replied. He dropped his guns and lunged at the man, ducking beneath the raider's plasma bolt and slamming into him. They hit the concrete hard, Hayden throwing a punishing fist at the raider's face. Moving with unnatural speed, the raider caught Hayden's fist before it connected. His other fist slammed into Hayden's jaw, sending him tumbling.

Hayden rolled to his feet, fists raised as the raider scrambled up. They circled each other warily, looking for an opening. The raider threw another punch, but this time, Hayden was ready. He dodged, grabbed the man's arm, and using his momentum, swung him face-first into a storage tank.

The raider's mask cracked against the metal with a sickening crunch. He stumbled back, dazed, and Hayden pressed his advantage. A swift uppercut sent the man reeling, followed by a devastating right hook that dropped him to the ground.

Hayden stood over his fallen opponent, chest heaving as he caught his breath. He reached down to grab the raider's collar, ready to demand answers, but just as he opened his mouth, approaching footsteps had him scooping up his revolvers to retreat. He'd barely gotten them in hand before two more raiders rounded the corner, the first already getting back up.

"Drop the gun," one of the newcomers ordered, his voice distorted by his breathing mask.

Hayden hesitated, fingers tightening on his revolvers. He could take one of them down, maybe even two. But three? Those weren't odds he liked.

"I said drop it!" the raider barked, taking an aggressive step forward.

At that moment, Hayden made his decision. With lightning speed, he raised his guns and fired. The first raider cried out and went down, clutching his shoulder. They were on him before Hayden could line up shots to take the other two down.

Like the one he'd wounded, they moved with inhuman speed and strength. Hayden could only attribute it to whatever drug they were inhaling through their masks. Managing to land a solid punch on one it was like hitting a brick wall. The raider barely flinched.

A massive fist slammed into Hayden's gut, driving the air from his lungs. As he doubled over, gasping, the other raider wrenched the guns from his hands. A boot to the back of his knee sent Hayden crashing to the ground.

"Not bad for a scavvie," one of the raiders chuckled, pinning Hayden's arms behind his back. Stronger than an ordinary man himself, he still couldn't escape the man's grip. "But you're out of your league."

"Bastard! You broke my mask," the first raider said, more furious about the mask than Hayden shooting him. Clutching his injured shoulder, he picked up his rifle and pointed it at Hayden. "I'm going to burn a hole in your skull."

"Wait," one of the other raiders said, pushing the rifle muzzle aside. "Carver may have a use for him."

"I have a use for him," the raider argued. "Target practice."

The other raiders laughed. "We'll bring him to Carver. If

he gives the say so, you can burn holes in him until you're out of cell charge."

They marched Hayden deeper into the facility. He tried to memorize the route, looking for potential escape routes, but the plant was a maze of twisting corridors and massive machinery.

Finally, they emerged into what must have once been the central control room. Banks of computers and monitors lined the walls, their screens long dark. In the center of the room, a makeshift bed had been set up. On it lay a man, his face pale and drawn with pain.

"Carver, you still alive?" one of the raiders asked.

The injured man opened his eyes and turned his head their way. "What's this?" he demanded as they shoved Hayden forward. "Who the hell are *you*?"

Hayden straightened up, meeting the man's gaze steadily. "Just a scavenger," he said, keeping his voice neutral. "Wrong place, wrong time."

Carver's eyes narrowed suspiciously. "Search him," he ordered. "And check outside. Make sure he didn't bring any friends."

One of the raiders nodded and headed for the exit. Hayden's stomach tightened. It wouldn't take long for them to find the hoverbike and his saddlebags. When they did, his cover would be blown.

"So tell me, scavenger," Carver said, his voice dripping with skepticism. "What brings you to this lovely establishment? Hoping to score some pre-war tech?"

Hayden shrugged, buying time. "You never know what you might find in places like this. Sometimes the competition misses things."

Carver laughed, then winced as the movement jostled his injury. "Oh, I'm sure they do. But I think you and I both know you're not here by chance." His eyes hardened. "You must have seen the bikes outside, but you came in here anyway. Gutsy. Who are you really?"

Hayden's mind raced, searching for a way out of this. He needed to keep them talking. Distract them long enough to find an opening.

"I could ask you the same thing," he said. "Not every day you run into a bunch of guys in white robes and gas masks, and one of them is gut-shot." He glanced at the man he had just shot. "You're going to need another bed soon for this one, the way he's bleeding out."

The raider who had taken his guns punched him hard in the gut, doubling him over. "You think that's funny?"

Hayden spit blood on the floor. "I think it's the truth. Be glad I didn't have enough time to aim." He straightened, recovering quickly enough from the blow that the injured man seemed impressed. "I'm just a man looking for buried treasure. I don't care where it's buried, only that I find it. What's your story?"

Carver's lips curled into a smirk. "We are disciples," he said, his voice taking on an almost reverent tone. "And we are here to prepare the way."

"Prepare the way for what?" Hayden pressed.

"The Rise," the raider replied. "The rebirth of this broken world."

Hayden frowned, genuinely confused. "What does that mean?"

Carver leaned forward on his bed, eyes bright. "It means you need to open your eyes, scavenger. Look around you. Do you believe the world is as it should be?"

"No," Hayden admitted.

"Very good. And do you believe the destruction of civilization was humankind's rightful fate?"

"No."

The raider shook his head in disappointment. "Then that is where you and I differ. That is why you are destined to die without purpose. Without glory. The balance has been upset. Our future denied. But we will right the wrong."

Before Hayden could ask for clarification, the raider who had gone to search outside stormed back in, clutching Hayden's saddlebags in his fist. "He's not just some random scavvie," the man snarled. He's got one of our bikes out there!"

The atmosphere in the room instantly shifted. The injured man's face darkened with anger while the other raiders tensed, hands moving to their weapons.

"Is that so?" Carver said, his voice dangerously calm. "Are you from the Greens, by any chance? I don't recall seeing you there."

Before Hayden could answer, the raider who had found the bike stepped forward. "We should kill him," he growled. "He's obviously from that crappy little town we ransacked. We should put him in the dirt like we did the others who tried to stop us."

"Yeah," the first raider agreed. "He isn't one of us. And he just admitted he doesn't understand."

Carver held up a hand, silencing his companions. "Now, now. Let's not be hasty." A cold smile spread across his face. "I think our friend here might still be of use to us."

"As target practice," the first raider said again.

"Not entirely off the mark," Carver replied. "I want you to show him the door."

"You want us to let him go?" the third raider asked.

"Not that door, you imbecile," Carver snapped. "*The* door." He looked at Hayden. "We found the entrance to the underground facility, but we haven't been able to get inside. The door is stuck, and even if it wasn't, knowing pre-war facilities the whole place is probably rigged with traps." His gaze locked onto Hayden. "But now we have someone expendable to send in first. What do you say, 'scavenger'? Ready to make yourself useful?"

"What makes you think I can open the door when you couldn't?" Hayden asked. "You're all stronger than me."

"If you open the door or not is only a minor concern," Carver answered. "If you can't get it open, Zed there shoots you dead, and we keep trying same as before. If you can get it open, well maybe there's a chance you survive. A small chance, mind you, but it's better than nothing."

Hayden nodded slowly. The underground facility might offer a chance to escape, or it might be a death trap. Either way, he was out of alternatives. "All right. I'll do it."

Carver grinned, a predatory gleam in his eye. "Excellent choice, not that you really had one." He nodded to his companions. "Breaker, Justice, show him the door. And be careful that he doesn't try to do anything stupid."

CHAPTER 10

The two uninjured raiders grabbed Hayden's arms, their rough, vice-like grips a testament to their enhanced strength. They marched him out of the control room before shoving him forward, keeping their plasma rifles trained on his back as they made their way through the chemical plant, stomping over the decaying trife as they went.

Finally, they reached a nondescript storage closet from the entrance on the other side of the building, near where they had first spotted him. One of the raiders pressed the muzzle of his rifle against the back of Hayden's neck while the other heaved aside a heavy metal shelving unit. It slid along a hidden track with surprising ease, revealing a massive steel door in the concrete wall behind it.

Hayden's eyes widened as he recognized the insignia etched into the door's face—an eagle clutching a star in its talons, the unmistakable emblem of the United States Space Force. He eyed it curiously. What secrets lay hidden behind this long-forgotten portal?

"How did you find this?" he asked.

"Wasn't easy," Breaker, the larger of the two raiders,

replied. "But Carver's smart. He says to try to knock over anything and everything, and see what moves."

"And it moved," Justice agreed. He pressed his rifle harder into Hayden's neck. "Now, get to work. Open it."

Hayden approached the door, running his fingers along the cool metal surface. A control panel set into the wall beside it still glowed with a faint blue light, indicating it still had power even after all these years.

He reached out to tap the panel's screen, but Breaker barked out a harsh laugh. "Don't bother. We already tried every code we could think of. Damn thing's locked out now."

Hayden nodded, noticing the gouges and scrapes around the door's edges where they had attempted to pry it open. His hand unconsciously drifted toward his pocket, where his Relyeh microspear remained hidden. But he didn't want to reveal it until he was ready to use it, and he didn't intend to waste that surprise on a door.

"How exactly am I supposed to open this with my bare hands?" he asked, facing his captors.

Breaker shrugged. "That's your problem, scavvie. Like Carver says, figure it out, or die trying."

Hayden turned back to the door, making a show of trying to wedge his fingers into the seam where it met the wall. The raiders stood behind him, laughing and mocking his futile efforts.

"Look at him, brother," Justice jeered. "Like a rat in a trap."

Hayden ignored their taunts, sidling over to stand directly in front of the control panel. He began pounding on the door with his right fist, each impact timed precisely with subtle movements of his left hand across the panel's keypad. As he entered the master code that could unlock anything running USSF software, he continued his noisy assault on the unyielding metal.

"Are you serious, scavvie?" Justice called out. "That

metal's gotta be at least six inches thick. Nothing short of a missile's punching through that thing."

Hayden entered the final digit just as the raider finished speaking. There was a moment of tense silence, then a series of metallic clicks and whirs emanated from within the door. Slowly, ponderously, it began to slide open.

He turned back to the stunned raiders, unable to keep a hint of smugness from his voice. "You were saying?"

Breaker recovered quickly, shoving Hayden towards the now-open doorway. "Good for you, getting it open. Now get going."

Hayden stumbled forward into a long, dimly lit corridor. At the far end, he could make out what appeared to be an elevator shaft. He'd been in similar USSF facilities before, so he knew what to expect.

Possibly another factory hidden below, churning out military gear or parts for one of the generation ships. Or it could be a research facility, or perhaps a cache of advanced weaponry or medical supplies, like the frightened man he had spoken to had thought.

He stared down the passageway, hesitant to move forward. Using the master code should have disabled any traps set as part of the facility's security, but not taking extra precautions could prove a painful mistake.

Before taking another step, he knelt and scooped up a handful of gritty dirt that had accumulated on the floor over the years. He blew it gently into the air, revealing an invisible beam stretching across the corridor.

"Well, would you look at that," Justice muttered, sounding impressed despite himself. "How'd you know to check for that?"

"This isn't my first rodeo. I've been in places like this before." He carefully stepped over the laser, then repeated the process, revealing another beam a few feet further. After clearing the second trap, he tested the corridor again and found the rest of the passageway clear. Advancing without worry, he reached the elevator and pressed the call button. Ancient machinery groaned to life, straining cables echoing up the shaft as the car began its ascent.

The raiders had followed closely behind him, their earlier mockery replaced by wary respect. "I can't believe this place still has power after all this time," Breaker said.

"There's probably a generator hidden somewhere nearby," Hayden explained. "Probably uses runoff from the hills to keep the batteries charged. The USSF designed these facilities to be self-sustaining for decades, maybe even centuries. They always planned to return, even if that meant coming all the way back from the stars."

Justice's eyes narrowed suspiciously. "How do you know all this?"

Hayden shrugged. "I've been around. You pick things up in this line of work."

The elevator clanged to a stop, its doors creaking open. Hayden and the two raiders crowded into the small car, an oppressive silence falling over them as they descended.

Hayden's gaze shifted between the two raiders. In such close proximity, he could use the microspear to eliminate them both in seconds. But he still had questions that needed answers.

"So," he said, breaking the silence. "Tell me more about your group. I get that you consider yourselves disciples. Whose teachings are you following? Or what kind of movement do you belong to?"

"What do you mean?" Breaker asked.

"That's what being a disciple means," Hayden replied. "Or did you just pick the title because you thought it sounded important?"

Justice turned on him, putting his rifle under his chin. "Are you making fun of us?"

"Not at all. I'm just trying to understand your group. Carver wasn't very straightforward."

"We're disciples of the Rebirth," Breaker said. "That's the movement."

Justice spoke up, his voice taking on a fervent tone. "The Sheriff ruined everything. The new world order that was meant to rise from the ashes of the old. We're going to restore it and set things right."

"And how exactly do you plan to do that?" Hayden pressed.

"Through the Rebirth," the raider replied cryptically.

"Right. So what is the Rebirth? Are you trying to bring back Grimmel? Iagorth? Idhra?"

The two raiders stared at him like he was speaking another language. Neither seemed to know any of the names he had mentioned, including Grimmel, which surprised him.

Breaker laughed darkly. "You'd know the Rebirth when it happens. But don't worry your pretty little head about it. You'll be long dead before then."

The elevator shuddered to a halt, its doors sliding open to reveal a stark concrete hallway stretching into darkness. Hayden took a tentative step forward, every nerve on high alert, and for good reason.

A massive shape came lumbering out of the shadows, metallic feet clanging against the floor. Hayden's blood ran cold as he recognized the hulking form of a Butcher, apparently left behind to protect the forgotten facility.

With lumbering speed, the Butcher charged forward, axe-like appendages raised to strike the unwanted visitors.

Hayden dove to the side, narrowly avoiding the first brutal swing. He rolled to his feet, searching desperately for a weapon, anything he could use against the machine.

"A little help?" he called out, sparing a glance at the raiders. They stood in the back of the elevator cab, making no move to help as they watched the unfolding battle with cruel amusement.

The Butcher advanced, its axes whistling through the air toward Hayden. He ducked and weaved, his enhanced reflexes keeping him alive. But he knew he couldn't keep this up forever.

As the robot reared back for another strike, Hayden saw his opening. He lunged forward, grappling with the machine with all his considerable strength. His fingers found purchase on its head, straining to tear the vital components free.

He wasn't quite fast enough. One of the Butcher's axes fell, biting into Hayden's shoulder nearly to the bone. He cried out, the pain almost blinding, but he refused to let go. With a final, superhuman effort, he wrenched the butcher's head from its body. Sparks flew as vital connections were severed, and the massive form crashed to the ground, inert.

Hayden stumbled back, clutching his wounded shoulder. Blood seeped between his fingers as nausea swirled through his gut. The raiders' laughter echoed down the hallway.

"Not bad," Breaker called out. "Maybe you're not completely useless after all."

"Damn," Justice added. "That looks like it hurts. You should be more careful, scavvie."

Swallowing back the nausea, his teeth gritted against the pain, Hayden ignored them and pushed onward. The facility quickly turned into a maze of corridors and sealed rooms. He navigated carefully, wary of more traps. Twice more he narrowly avoided triggering deadly security measures, much to the amusement of his captors. Thankfully, he didn't encounter any additional Butchers along the way.

After some time, they reached what appeared to be the main security control room. Banks of monitors lined the walls, most dark and lifeless, but a few still flickered with ghostly images of long-abandoned corridors.

Hayden quickly scanned the control panels, piecing together the facility's general layout. He checked the primary control terminal next, tapping on the keyboard and staring at the output on the screen.

"You know how to work those things, too?" Breaker said, a hint of awe in his voice.

"It comes in handy," Hayden replied, checking the system logs. It seemed the security systems had been set only to be disabled from this very room. Whoever had done so must have never left, sealing themselves in with the facility's secrets. Of course, the raiders wouldn't know that. Their lack of interest in the screen's output suggested they didn't know how to read. Rather than disable the traps and recall three other Butchers guarding the place, he memorized their locations.

"There's nothing useful here," he announced, switching off the terminal display before heading for the door.

It wasn't long before Hayden's suspicions about someone remaining behind were confirmed. In a small office just off the main corridor, they found the remains of a woman slumped over a desk. Her withered fingers still clutched a datapad, its screen long since gone dark.

"Why didn't she leave?" Justice wondered aloud behind Hayden.

"She made sure to keep the security systems online," he replied. "Whatever is down here, she didn't want just anyone to find it."

"You mean filthy scavvies like you, don't you?" Justice asked.

"You're here to raid whatever supplies we find," Hayden answered. "That makes you a scavvie, too."

"No," Justice refused. "We have a great purpose, and finding something that can save Carver is part of that purpose."

"What's so special about him that he needs to survive?"

"He's a disciple, like us. What other reason do we need?"

Hayden raised an eyebrow, surprised by the answer. "That's not how things typically work out here."

"That's because the world is broken. But the Rebirth will fix it. The Rebirth will set everything right."

They continued deeper into the facility, emerging onto a vast factory floor. Hulking machinery and conveyor belts stretched as far as Hayden could see, the product it had been assembling spread across the belts in various states of completion. All of it was coated in a thick layer of dust.

Hayden stepped up to the closest conveyor belt, reaching out to wipe the grime from one of the produced squares. Unmarked and wrapped in dirty foil, Hayden could hardly believe his eyes.

"Well I'll be…" he commented.

"What is it?" Breaker asked.

"I'm not sure just yet," Hayden replied. He followed the assembly line to the end, where dozens of identical packets had been dropped into a box when the entire operation shut down for reasons Hayden doubted he would ever know.

Just the contents of the single box drove Hayden's imagination wild, thinking of how much good he could do with the stash. But it was what lay at the far end of the room that made his breath truly catch in his throat.

Stacked on pallets and rising nearly to the ceiling were hundreds of boxes just like the one in front of him. Each one, Hayden knew, contained hundreds of medical patches. He had always thought the patches were invented on Proxima, but this proved him wrong.

Staring at the boxes, a plan hatched in his mind.

"I can't believe it," he breathed. "Do you have any idea what we've found here?"

The raiders exchanged confused glances. "What are you talking about?"

Hayden gestured towards the towering stacks of boxes. "Those patches can heal even the biggest wounds within days. Think about that. They're worth more than you can imagine. With a haul like this, you don't need to be followers. You could buy yourself an army of your own."

He turned to face the raiders, his voice taking on an urgent, persuasive tone. "Forget about this Rebirth nonsense. Join me instead. We could split this find, make ourselves richer than you've ever dreamed. What do you say?"

For a moment, Hayden thought he saw a flicker of temptation in their eyes. But it was quickly replaced by the familiar fanatical gleam.

"I can't blame you for trying to save your skin, scavvie," Breaker laughed. "But we're loyal to the cause. The Rebirth is more valuable and more important than all the treasure in the world."

Justice nodded in agreement, then smiled coldly. "Besides, even if we did want all this for ourselves, now that we know what's down here, we don't really need you anymore, do we?"

Before Hayden could react, the raider raised his plasma rifle and fired. The bolt caught Hayden square in the chest, the searing energy burning through flesh and bone. He stumbled backward, his legs giving out beneath him.

He hit the ground with his eyes closed and didn't move.

"What an idiot," Breaker said, standing over him.

"Yeah, he should have seen that coming," Justice agreed.

"Come on, let's bring one of these boxes back to Carver. It sounds like one patch will fix him right up. Zed, too."

Hayden remained still as the two raiders collected the box at the end of the assembly line. He listened to their footsteps as they left the factory floor.

His shoulder and chest hurt like hell, but already his body worked to repair the damage. Either wound might have killed any other man, but not him.

Of course, the raiders didn't know that either.

He rose from the dead, a ghost ready to haunt them until he sent them to Hell.

CHAPTER 11

Hayden rolled to his side as the raiders' voices receded, their footsteps growing fainter. Slowly, he pushed himself up. Pain shot through his chest, burning through his lungs like fire with every breath he took, and the throbbing in his shoulder from the butcher's earlier attack didn't help matters. Even though his body worked to mend itself, it was a slow and agonizing process.

He questioned whether the pain was worth the extra information he'd extracted from the two raiders and if he should have stabbed them both in the elevator after all. Probably, he decided.

Nothing ventured, nothing gained.

He staggered to his feet, steadying himself against the conveyor belt's machinery. The darkness around him seemed to pulse and waver. He forced himself to focus, the pain a constant reminder that he was still alive.

And he intended to stay that way.

"One step at a time," he muttered to himself, heading for the office where they had found the woman's remains. There was something he hoped to find there, and if he did, the successful discovery would make all this pain much easier to bear.

The corridor seemed longer in reverse, but he knew that was just the pain talking. The raiders' voices had faded completely, and he guessed they'd reached the elevator by now. He figured he had five to ten minutes to get up there before they would finish patching up Carver and Zed and maybe make their way back down here for another box or two of the patches.

He approached the office, ears straining for any hint of danger. The skeletal remains of the woman remained slumped over the desk, the datapad clutched in her bony fingers. Hayden moved quickly, rifling through the desk drawers and the woman's pockets.

"Come on now," he grunted. "You've got to be here some-where." He gently pulled the corpse upright in her chair, her shrunken leathery skin the only thing keeping her bones from falling apart. Pressing his hand to her chest, an identifiable shape formed against his palm. He should have checked there in the first place. It surprised him the woman had made it so easy for anyone finding her corpse to find her transceiver.

He tore open her rotted shirt, looping a finger around the chain she wore, lifting it up over her head. The small, black transceiver attached to it bore an insignia—a tiny, detailed image of an eagle clutching a star—that matched the one on the door.

Exactly what he needed.

He pocketed the transceiver and went back out into the corridor. Knowing he needed to move faster if he would beat the raiders to the punch, he picked up his pace despite the surge in pain it caused.

Heading from the elevator, he rounded a corner and froze when a pair of red eyes activated at the far end. Immediately, the Butcher stomped toward him, preparing its axe-hand to strike.

Hayden retrieved the transceiver and flipped the switch to turn it on. "Hold up there, pardner," he said into it. There was a small chance the battery had died, and if so, his pain was about to get a lot worse.

Thankfully, the Butcher came to an immediate stop.

"Good boy. Follow me." He turned and retraced his steps back toward the elevator, the Butcher following dutifully behind. The walk felt shorter this time, every step bringing him closer to the surface and the raiders in the control room. He knew he would need to use the Butcher strategically; sending it in ahead of him would provide the distraction he needed to take out the so-called disciples and finish the job.

Back at the elevator, he pressed the call button and waited, his anticipation building with every second that ticked by. With a clang, the elevator doors finally slid open, and Hayden stepped inside. The Butcher moved in right behind him, their tight fit in the small car made the ride up agonizingly slow. He was pretty sure he had stopped bleeding, but his body still struggled to heal, slowing him down when he couldn't afford to lose any more time.

Hayden stepped out into the dimly lit corridor when the doors slid open. "Stay close in front of me," he ordered the Butcher. "And move as quietly as you can."

If the Butcher could answer, he imagined it would ask him if he were kidding. The damn thing made about as much noise as a herd of baby elephants. It did a pretty good job of moving as quietly as possible, though, barely lifting its feet as it shuffled along, advancing slowly through the chemical plant. The control room drew closer with each step. As they neared, Hayden could again hear the raiders' voices.

"How does it feel?" Breaker asked.

"Cold and hot at the same time," Carver replied. "But it doesn't sting. Feels kind of good. You said there are more of these things down there?"

"A lot more," Justice replied excitedly. "Thousands. The

scavvie we killed tried to bribe us into joining him and selling them. Said we could get rich that way."

"That's funny," Carver said. "Because Zed found a stamp in his pack. It looks like he can make his own notes. Who needs to sell shit when you can just stamp out currency at will?"

"Who was that guy anyway?" Zed said. "I still wish I had gotten to put the hole in him."

"How's your shoulder?" Justice asked.

"I think I can feel it getting better already."

Hayden stopped a short distance from the open doorway, spying the raiders from behind cover. He lifted the control box to his face. "Attack and kill the people in the room ahead, except the one with the light brown hair."

The butcher processed the command and moved toward the control room. Almost instantly, the raiders' conversation cut off, and they turned as one to see the Butcher approaching.

"Oh, hell," Breaker said, scrambling for his rifle. The others did the same.

Hayden moved into the open behind the robot, unable to see around it as it entered the control room. One of the raiders immediately began screaming in agony before suddenly falling silent.

By the time Hayden could see around the Butcher, Zed lay crumpled on the ground while the remaining raiders fired wildly at the Butcher, their shots barely slowing it down. Without warning, Breaker slammed into the side of the Butcher with his shoulder. The force of the impact sent the robot crashing to the floor, the vibration rippling up through Hayden's feet and into his legs.

He drew the microspear from his pocket and charged. Regaining his balance, Breaker's eyes widened in disbelief when he spotted Hayden. The raider tried to bring his rifle to bear, but Hayden was already on him. He stabbed at the raider with the microspear, only to have Breaker drop his rifle and grab his wrist, stopping him short of drawing blood. Bigger than Hayden, Breaker shoved Hayden back and looked down at him, sneering, the spear only inches from his chest.

"Good try, scavvie," he said.

Hayden cast the microspear upward. Catching it under-handed, he stabbed it deep into Breaker's gut, watching as the raider's face twisted in greater anger. For a second, Hayden thought he might shake off the deadly effects of the spear. Then Breaker's eyes rolled back in his head, and he collapsed to the floor.

Justice turned his plasma rifle on Hayden, the muzzle aimed squarely at his chest. "How are you still alive?" he demanded, disbelief and rage in his eyes. "I won't make the same mistake twice."

The Butcher, still struggling to reach its feet, finally managed it. Swinging its axe, it embedded the blade deep in Justice's back. The raider's shot missed Hayden by inches, his mouth wide open to emit a scream he didn't have time to follow through on as Hayden threw the microspear. The Axon weapon pierced Justice's chest with deadly accuracy. The raider collapsed, the life draining from his eyes.

Only Carver remained, cowering shirtless by the control panel, one of the medical patches affixed to his chest. He held Hayden's confiscated revolvers, the barrels trained on him.

"Who the hell are you?" Carver demanded, his voice and hands shaking with anger, pain and fear.

Hayden met his gaze, his resolve unyielding. "You know who I am. And you know what I'm capable of."

Carver's eyes narrowed, a flicker of uncertainty crossing his face. "You're not him. You can't be. He's just a character in cheap paper novels."

Hayden stepped forward, his movements deliberate and

calm. "I feel pretty real. You can shoot me if you want, but it won't stop me. I'll heal from the damage."

Carver's hands shook with uncertainty. "What do you want from me?"

"I want to know where the Fort is, for starters," Hayden replied. "I want to know what Clear is, too. Where you got it, how you know how to make it. I want to know—"

Carver's grip on the revolvers tightened, his knuckles white. The fear in his eyes was palpable. "For the glory of the Rebirth," he muttered, putting the barrel of one of the revolvers up to his temple.

"No!" Hayden shouted, but it was too late. Carver pulled the trigger, the gunshot echoing through the control room as the raider leader crumpled to the ground.

Hayden cursed. Not having the information he so badly needed would slow him down just as much or more than his healing wounds.

The Butcher loomed nearby, its mechanical form still and silent as Hayden pocketed the microspear and removed his coat, followed by his bandoliers and shirt. His shoulder was still a mess, the gash deep, but at least it hadn't reached beyond flesh and fat to muscle and bone. The hole in his chest from the plasma rifle was in better shape on the outside, but it had caused critical internal damage.

Hayden slipped the chain with the transceiver pendant over his head and stepped over Breaker to take one of the patches from the box. He used his teeth to rip the packaging open and then slapped it over his shoulder. He could heal fast on his own, but the patch would heal him even faster. He repeated the same process for his plasma wound before struggling back into what was left of his clothes.

With that done, he examined the canister attached to Justice's mask. He turned off the flow of the mysterious gas and figured out how to remove it from the raider. Obviously, the stuff could enhance a person's strength and reflexes, answering his question about how the Rebirthers had outfought a War Dog platoon. But he had plenty of other questions about the stuff, confident that the answers would lead him to Kady and the others, even if nothing else did.

Retrieving his saddlebags, Hayden packed them with as many medical patches as he could carry, sure they would come in handy soon enough. Last but not least, he recovered his revolvers, slipping them smoothly into their low-slung holsters.

"Pick up that box," he ordered the Butcher, pointing to the box of patches. It came out of its static posture and did as he instructed. "Follow me."

Hayden returned to the still-open door to the elevator leading down to the underground factory. The pain in his shoulder had already eased somewhat, and he no longer felt the plasma wound at all.

"In you go," Hayden said to the Butcher, motioning it across the threshold. The Butcher did as ordered. "When the elevator doors open, put the box down in front of them and return to your prior position. Then, enter standby mode. You have permission to recharge, but afterwards, return to me here. Acknowledge."

Hayden glanced at the robot. Its red eyes flashed green, signaling it understood the commands. He reached into the elevator and punched the down button, pulling his arm back before the doors closed. Then he waited for the Butcher to deliver the box of patches and return, following Hayden back through the entrance to the lower factory.

He used the transceiver's control panel to lock the entrance door and then push the shelving unit back into place, once more concealing the entrance to the lower factory. He removed the transceiver from around his neck and wound it around one of the butcher's fingers. The patches were too valuable to let just any old scavenger find. He would contact Nathan when he could so his friend could send a team to collect the patches and organize a plan for distributing them where they were most needed.

Going back outside, he checked the raiders' hoverbikes, finding them nearly as drained of battery power as the one he had ridden to the plant. He had hoped to skip Union and continue north, but that wouldn't be an option. He needed a fresh ride if he was going to catch up to the rest of the Rebirthers.

The pain in his shoulder finally subsiding, he climbed onto his hoverbike and sped away from the plant.

CHAPTER 12

Hayden gunned the hoverbike's engine, cruising along the road towards Union. The wind whipped through his hair, dust and grit stinging his eyes and his hat dangling from the string around his neck. His bloodied coat flapped behind him, a tattered banner of his recent trials.

He noticed as he rode that the route had been maintained, limiting the overgrowth and smoothing out large gaps in the centuries-old asphalt with dirt and gravel. Despite the relatively decent conditions, he still discovered evidence of the APC's passing in trampled weeds and tire marks. He also noted when he lost the trail, slowing the bike, doubling back, and checking the area to find the tracks again. The APC had come from the southwest, but had cut a more overland path north that he presumed circumvented the settlement. It was a curious development. Since the Rebirther's hoverbikes at the chem plant had been nearly out of charge, he wondered if they had bypassed Union because there was no opportunity to recharge them there. Or was it possible they were afraid of Tempest, the settlement's leader?

He doubted they would abandon the hoverbikes, which

meant they had to find a place to regain their range somewhere a little further north, no more than ten or twenty miles.

He also considered following the APC's trail and bypassing Union but ultimately decided against it. The last thing he needed right now was to run into more stragglers. His arm and chest no longer hurt, but the healing process always took a lot out of him. If these were ordinary raiders, maybe things would have been different. But the Rebirthers had proven to be hard kills.

Resuming his ride northeast, the compact settlement came into view soon after. The outskirts of Union appeared through the tall grass, flanking the roadway like a mirage. A ramshackle collection of dilapidated pre-war buildings spotted the terrain on both sides of the road.

Hayden slowed the bike as he entered the remains of the small town, scanning each street he passed for signs of life. When he spotted the exhaust of a modbox down one street, he made a left and followed it, keeping his distance.

He reached the occupied part of the town in no time, the center of it a large, stone building, its weathered, ornate facade announcing it as a courthouse. It acted as the centerpiece, occupying the middle of the square, the settlement radiating out from it. Different shops surrounded the central structure, the adjacent dirt roads lined with hitching posts where horses waited, mingled with a couple of modboxes, a wheeled motorcycle, and a handful of bicycles.

As Hayden slowed to enter the town proper, he immediately drew stares from the passersby. They eyed his battered hoverbike and ravaged appearance with suspicion, no doubt unaccustomed to hosting visitors arriving in such a battered state. Of course, the damage looked a lot worse than it was. The medi-patches, in combination with his healing factor, were making short work of his wounds.

He pulled the bike up to the side of the road, in front of a relatively new building with a freshly painted sign above the door proclaiming it to be The Sparkling Spur. The name of a saloon, if he'd ever seen one, and the smell of cooking meat confirmed it. A dusty, tired-looking horse was tethered to the adjacent post, its head hanging low as it dozed, knees locked. Hayden hopped off the bike, shaking his head. Some people either didn't know how to take care of a horse after a long, hard ride, or they didn't bother with the horse's comfort, being more in tune with their own.

He slung his saddlebags over his shoulder and positioned his hat back on his head before entering. The establishment's dim interior was thick with the scents of stale beer and unwashed bodies. A long wooden bar cut in half from a tree trunk stretched along one wall. Simple, unpadded tables and chairs were scattered haphazardly across the sawdust-strewn floor. A handful of rough-looking patrons nursed drinks, their conversations falling silent as Hayden approached.

The bartender, a grizzled man with curly black hair and a patch over his left eye, glared warily at him as he approached the bar. "What'll it be, stranger?"

"Information," Hayden replied, keeping his voice low. "I'm looking for a place to charge my hoverbike. Or maybe get some new transportation altogether. Is there a place in town where I can find something like that?" He removed a wad of notes from his pocket and, unrolling it, dropped one marked with fifty stamps on the bartop.

The bartender's eyebrows went up in response to his wealth. He smiled wide as he pulled the currency from the counter and shoved it into his pocket. "There's a mechanic down at the end of the street. Goes by the name of Rusty. He's got a knack for fixing up old tech. If anyone in Union can help you, it'd be him. If it's a horse you're after, which I personally recommend, you can head about a mile east of here, to Daly's farm. He breeds the best plough horses this side of the Ole Miss, and I think he has a couple of nags he's looking to sell.

Though, with your means, you could probably convince him to part with his prized stallion."

"Thank you kindly," Hayden said. He put another fifty on the bartop. "I have a few other questions, if you don't mind me asking."

"Why would I mind?" the bartender replied, smiling as he reached for the note. He paused suddenly, losing his smile as his eyes shifted to the door.

The sound that had returned to the saloon after Hayden's entrance fell silent again. Hayden didn't turn around, instead watching the bartender's expression. He looked nervous, and from how his eyes shifted, Hayden knew whoever had just entered was coming his way.

"It ain't every day a man comes riding into Union on a hoverbike," a woman said behind him, her voice a husky drawl. "Especially a man whose coat is dark with blood."

"Don't worry," Hayden replied. "It's all mine." He turned to face the newcomer.

"Now that's one I haven't heard before," the woman laughed, eyes bright. She was tall and lean, with short-cropped blonde hair and a face that might have been pretty if not for the hard lines etched around her mouth and eyes. She wore a duster not unlike his own, though hers was in much better shape. A USSF Marine base layer covered her beneath the coat, while a heavy plasma rifle was strapped to her back, the business end visible over her right shoulder. A pistol rode her hip, and two burly men, similarly equipped, flanked her, their expressions stony.

Her mirth vanished as quickly as it had arrived, her expression going cold again. "I'm Tempest. I run things in Union. And I don't take kindly to strangers in general. I especially don't take kindly to strangers who so clearly look like they're going to be a problem."

Hayden met her gaze steadily, refusing to be cowed. "I'm not here to be a problem. I'm actually here so I can move on.

My ride is out of charge, and I need to either fix it or ditch it and find something else."

Tempest's eyes narrowed. "Is that so? Then you won't mind telling me who you are, where you came from, and where you're headed."

Hayden presented his most charming smile while removing his hat. "Name's Hayden, ma'am. Originally from the territories in the west. Came east via New Eden, passed through the Arches, and took a charter boat down the Ole Miss to the Greens. As for where I'm headed, I'm on the trail of some raiders that attacked the Greens and razed half of it. They took something from me, and I aim to get it back."

"Raiders, huh?" Tempest looked him up and down, taking in his battered appearance. "From the looks of you, I'd say you already ran afoul of some troublemakers, especially since you say that blood on your coat is yours. Which I'm not fixing to believe, considering you're still upright. So, what's to say you're not some kind of bandit or killer yourself?"

Hayden bristled at the accusation. "I'm no raider, bandit, or otherwise. And I don't appreciate the insinuation that I might be one."

Tempest smirked. "Around here, we've got a saying. If it looks like bad news and smells like bad news…" She snapped her fingers and her cronies moved forward, grabbing Hayden's arms.

Hayden glared at her. "What do you think you're doing? I haven't done any harm to you or yours."

"Just a precaution," Tempest said. "Check his bags."

One of the men released Hayden and grabbed his saddle-bags, carrying them over to a nearby table. The other one, grabbing his free arm, held him by both arms now. Tempest watched as the contents of Hayden's saddlebags—medical patches, bullets, torn paper and his USSF logo stamp, plus the drug canister and the War Dog tags he'd taken off the dead raider—spilled out.

Tempest immediately scooped up the tags, turning to dangle them in front of Hayden's face. "Well, well. What have we here? These definitely don't belong to you." She looked them over, reading the inscription. Her eyes hardened. "Corporal Adrian Diaz. His great-great-grandson carried these tags. Damian Diaz. He never would have given these to you willingly. Not bad news, my ass." She clutched the tags tightly in her fist, using it to punch him in the gut. Hayden grunted as the air was expelled from his lungs. "You son of a bitch," she snarled. "Where did you get these?"

He glared at her. "Not from Damian Diaz. I took them off a dead man. The same raider whose hoverbike I'm riding."

"A likely story," Tempest scoffed. "You know, I could have you locked up on general principle. Just look at you. I'm sure you've done something to warrant it."

"On what charge?" Hayden demanded. "I haven't broken any laws."

"Around here, I am the law," Tempest said coldly. "Judge, jury, and executioner, when necessary. And I say—"

"Hold up," Hayden interrupted. "You knew Damian Diaz, didn't you?"

"I served with him in the 36th Regulars, based out of Fort Campbell, about a hundred klicks east of here. I left the Regulars about a year ago, and not on the best of terms. But I still consider those Dogs my family, and nobody messes with my family."

"Good," Hayden replied, surprising her. "These raiders I'm after. They call themselves Rebirthers. They wear white robes and breathe some kind of gas that makes them stronger and faster than normal men. I'd bet my life they hit the 36th."

"Right now, you are betting your life on it. Go on."

"Like I said, the Rebirthers raided the Greens and burned half of it to the ground. That thing they took from me? A young girl named Kady, along with almost a dozen other children. They're part of my family. And nobody messes with my family, either."

Tempest studied him for a long moment, her gaze inscrutable. Finally, she sighed and waved off the man still holding him. "Let him go."

The man released his hold, and Hayden rubbed his arms, eyeing Tempest warily. She gestured to his belongings. "Put his stuff back in the bags. Give them back to him."

As her men complied, Tempest turned back to Hayden. "Okay, let's say I believe you. What do these Rebirthers want with a young girl?"

"I'm not sure," Hayden admitted. "But the kids they took, they're special. They have…abilities. Or at least, Kady does. I think the Rebirthers know these abilities and want to exploit them somehow."

"What kind of abilities are we talking about?" Tempest asked dubiously.

"Kady has psychic abilities. Telepathy, for one."

Tempest laughed. "You almost had me convinced you were an honest man."

"I am," Hayden snapped. "More than any other soul in this room, I'd wager. You don't believe in supernatural abilities?"

"Why would I? Sounds like those tall tales about the Sheriff people like to throw around. It's all bull."

"Do you have a knife on you?"

Tempest pulled it from a sheathe against her thigh. Hayden smiled and put his hand down flat on the bar. "Stab me with it, all the way through."

She eyed him as if he were crazy. "I don't think—"

"You were ready to kill me, but you won't stab my hand?" Hayden pressed.

She smirked at that and, in a flash, slammed the blade down through his flesh, all the way through, so it stuck into the table, standing up straight when she let go.

Hayden gritted his teeth against the pain. Wrapping his other hand around the blade's handle, he pulled the knife out and dropped it next to his bloody hand. He put his palm up on the table, sliced open by the blade, and left his other hand where it was.

"Okay, Hayden. You proved you have a screw loose, but..." She trailed off when she saw his skin begin to knit back together, quickly recovering from the wound. "That... that's impossible."

"Supernatural," Hayden answered. "Not impossible. My DNA was cleansed by the Relyeh. The enemy who delivered the trife to Earth. Kady and those kids, their DNA was altered, too."

Tempest continued staring at his hand until both sides of the wound had closed over. She looked him in the eye. "You...you're the Sheriff."

"Pozz," Hayden agreed.

"Why...why didn't you just say so?"

"Would you have believed me?"

She laughed. "No, probably not. I won't say I'm a fan of yours, but even I can't deny your reputation. And if what you say about the Rebirthers is true—"

"It is," Hayden interrupted.

"Then I guess the enemy of my enemy is my friend." She paused, then asked gruffly, "When's the last time you ate something? You look like hammered shit."

CHAPTER 13

Hayden blinked, taken aback by the sudden shift in Tempest's demeanor. "It's been a while since I've eaten," he admitted. Now that she'd mentioned food, the gnawing hunger in his gut made itself known.

Tempest nodded curtly. "Come on, then. Let's get some food in you. I've got some questions of my own." She turned and strode out of the saloon without waiting for a response.

Hayden hesitated, glancing at the bartender. The man just shrugged as if to say, "What can you do?"

Slinging his saddlebags back over his shoulder, Hayden followed Tempest, wondering what sort of interrogation awaited him. But for now, it seemed he'd found an unlikely ally in his quest to save Kady and the others.

Tempest led him around back to a small courtyard, where a heavyset man stood over a sputtering grill, flipping cuts of unidentifiable meat.

The man looked up as they approached, his face splitting into a gap-toothed, slightly nervous grin. "Boss Tempest! I wasn't expecting you. Who's your friend?"

"This is…" Tempest paused, letting Hayden decide how to introduce himself.

"Hayden," he filled in.

"This is Hayden. He's not a friend. But he's not an enemy either, so I guess that makes him a guest. Rustle up two plates of whatever you've got going there."

"Yes, ma'am!" The cook set about preparing her order, his heavy focus on the meal suggesting Tempest liked her food just so.

She jerked her head towards a rickety table sitting against the saloon's back wall, a tarp strung overhead to keep the sun or rain off. "Have a seat."

Hayden settled across from her, the wooden bench creaking under his weight.

"So. These Rebirthers. What else can you tell me about them?"

Hayden leaned forward, elbows on the table. "Not much, I'm afraid. I've only run into them a couple of times, and I never heard of or crossed paths with them before the Greens. But from what I've learned so far, they believe in some prophecy of rebirth, a new world order rising from the ashes of the past."

Tempest snorted. "Sounds like a load of horseshit to me. Just an excuse for them to rob and kill and lord it over the rest of us."

"You're not wrong," Hayden agreed. "But I think there's more to it than that. The ones I've encountered, they had access to tech and gear that most raiders can only dream of. Military grade weapons, combat armor. Some of it, I'm sure they stole from the War Dogs, hence the tags. I'm concerned the 36th no longer exists. Which is something I never thought I would say."

She huffed a laugh. "And you said they use some kind of drug to make themselves stronger than normal folk?"

"They call it Clear. I fought a couple of them hand-to-hand. I don't usually lose a fight like that. They hit hard. Very hard. And when I shot at them, they were practically able to dodge the bullets."

"Supernatural," Tempest said.

"Pozz. I kept one of the canisters of the stuff, in the hope I might be able to track down the source, before or after I find the kids. This kind of stuff shouldn't be out in the wild. Plus, I reckon whoever is supplying it to the Rebirthers is supporting their cause. Doubly dangerous."

Before Tempest could ask any more questions, the cook appeared at the table, setting two plates heaped with charred meat, mashed potatoes, and a steaming cob of corn. Hayden tore into it enthusiastically, his hunger asserting itself with a vengeance. Across the table, Tempest dug in with almost equal gusto.

"Compliments to the chef," Hayden said around a mouthful. "This isn't half bad."

"First thing I did when I took over this town was make sure we had a decent cook," Tempest replied. "Good for morale."

"Folks I talked to further west made you sound like a monster," Hayden said.

"Don't get me wrong, I can be a hard master. But it's all in the name of keeping this place safe. That's why I couldn't stay with the War Dogs. They didn't care about collateral damage, or anything or anyone that didn't align with their views."

"You didn't know a former War Dog named Oz by any chance, did you?" Hayden asked.

"The name sounds familiar, but I didn't personally know an Oz. Is he a friend of yours?"

"He was. He died defending the Greens. What you said reminded me of him."

Tempest didn't reply, and they ate in silence for a few minutes, each lost in their own thoughts. Finally, Hayden set down his fork and leaned back, regarding Tempest with a steady gaze.

"I'm sorry about the 36th," he said quietly. "I know that doesn't change anything, but for what it's worth, I truly am."

Tempest looked at him, her eyes rigid and assessing. "You really are going after them, aren't you? Even knowing what they're capable of?"

Hayden nodded, his jaw set. "I don't have a choice. Those kids they took, they're counting on me. I'm the only one who can bring them home."

"And what will you do if you catch up to the Rebirthers? How do you plan to beat them, all by your lonesome?"

Hayden's hand drifted unconsciously to his revolvers, fingers brushing the worn grips. "Not if. When. I'll do whatever I have to. Whatever it takes."

Tempest studied him for a long moment, then sighed. "I guess there isn't much for the man who cleansed the world of the trife to fear, is there, Sheriff?"

"That's where you're wrong. If I weren't afraid, I'd be dead ten times over. I've had some good luck and some good companions is all."

"Are you looking for companionship, then?" she asked suggestively.

Hayden didn't hesitate. "Not the kind you might be thinking about. Don't get me wrong, you're a pretty lady. But my heart's spoken for, and everything else follows it."

Tempest didn't seem at all bothered by the rebuke. "Your loss," she said with a shrug. "But I do appreciate the kindness of your rejection. I suppose I shouldn't expect anything less from a man like you." She pushed back from the table, rising to her feet. "All right. I've decided to help you out. I'll get Rusty to take a look at your bike right away, see if he can't get it fixed up and ready to ride. I'll get you some new clothes, too. You need them. Also, if you need guns, ammunition, or any other weaponry, I've got some Centurion tech in my armory in the old courthouse."

"Thank you, kindly, Tempest. I'll take the clothes and

maybe a new bandolier if you have one, but other than that, I have all I need right here." He patted his saddlebags. "Except transportation."

"Sure thing. In the meantime, you can rest up here, get your strength back. You're gonna need it if you're serious about taking on the Rebirthers."

Hayden stood as well, gratitude welling in his chest. "I...thank you, Tempest. I won't forget this."

Tempest waved him off gruffly, but her eyes showed a hint of warmth. "Yeah, well. Don't get all sentimental on me. I'm not doing this for you. I'm doing it for those kids. Only a monster messes with kids. And for Damian and the 36th."

They finished eating and walked back to the saloon, an understanding forged between them. Tempest's two guards waited inside, ready for new orders.

"Gary, I need you to bring Hayden's bike over to Rusty. Tell him he's got two hours to let me know if he can recharge it or not."

"Yes, ma'am," one of the guards said, looking at Hayden. "Do you got the keys?"

"Key's in the starter," Hayden replied.

"You ain't afraid someone will steal the bike?"

"Should I be?"

Tempest glared at Gary, annoyed that he'd insinuated Union wasn't safe.

"Not here, of course," Gary said, trying to get his foot out of his mouth. "I meant other places."

"When I get somewhere I think someone might steal it, I'll take the key with me."

"Right." Gary laughed nervously and slinked away.

Tempest turned to her other guard. "Barry, show Hayden to a room in the courthouse, and make sure he has anything he asks for."

"Yes, ma'am," he replied. "This way."

Hayden moved to follow when Tempest grabbed his arm.

"Now, don't go leaving town without saying goodbye, Hayden," she said. "I want to see you off."

"Yes, ma'am," Hayden replied in the same tone the two guards had used, drawing a laugh from her. She released his arm, and he followed Barry out of the saloon and across the street, up two sets of steps, and into the courthouse.

On entering, Hayden was surprised to find the place had been transformed from its original purpose, now serving as a mansion for the head of Union, though he doubted Tempest had been the one to convert it. He immediately noticed the bars on the windows and the gates placed on the inside of the doors, testament to the building's use as shelter against the trife. Judging by the fine rugs on the floor and paintings adorning the walls, only one family had hid out here, leaving any other desperate souls to fend for themselves.

The thought sent a chill down his spine.

"The guest rooms are this way," Barry said, waving him toward a stairwell to their left.

"Hayden!" Kady's voice hit Hayden so hard he doubled over, clutching at his head as it exploded in pain. "Help us!"

Hayden gritted his teeth against the force. "Kady," he thought, "I'm coming. If you know, tell me where you are."

The pain in his head subsided while he waited for Kady to reply, with no idea whether or not she could hear him. Barry looked at him as if he were crazy.

"I don't know!" Her reply bent him over again. "I know we crossed a river! I felt us floating."

"Good girl," Hayden thought back. "If you get more, you try to contact me again. I'm on my way. I'm going to find you. I promise."

He waited nearly five minutes for Kady to respond, but nothing came.

"Sir?" Barry said. "If you'll follow me."

"Neg," Hayden replied. "Some new clothes and a good horse are all I need. I don't have any more time to waste."

CHAPTER 14

Hayden strode purposefully back into the Sparkling Spur, searching for Tempest. He approached the bar, where the grizzled bartender was wiping down the bartop with a rag. He looked up as Hayden approached.

"Back already, stranger? Fixin' for a mug of sarsaparilla, perhaps?"

"Neg. I'm looking for Tempest. Has she come back through this way?" Hayden asked.

The bartender shook his head. "Ain't seen her since she took you out back. Maybe try her mansion, right smack dab in the center of town."

"I just came from there. Any other places she likes to go?"

"If I had to guess, I'd say the training grounds to the west."

"Training grounds?" Hayden asked.

"Yup. That's where her militia's stationed. Up to nearly two hundred of 'em now, I think."

Hayden considered the response. Had the Rebirthers known about the militia? Was that why they had avoided Union? But what did a small town like Union need with a force that large?

"Is she still recruiting?" he asked.

"Do you want to join up? Recruiting station's three doors down on your left."

"Maybe some other time," Hayden answered. Something about the situation tugged at his gut, instinct telling him there was more to the militia than it seemed. He also thought it strange that Tempest hadn't mentioned her army to him during their conversation and that they were stationed outside town, where passersby wouldn't immediately know they existed.

It was a mystery for another time.

"Thank you for the information," he said. He turned on his heel and stalked out the back door into the courtyard where he and Tempest had shared their meal. The cook was still there, scrubbing the grill with a wire brush. He looked up as Hayden approached, his face creasing into a tired smile.

"Back for more?" he asked.

Hayden shook his head. "I'm looking for Tempest. Have you seen her?"

The cook scratched his chin thoughtfully. "Not since she left with you earlier. She didn't say where she was going."

"Thank you, anyway," he said, turning to leave.

He couldn't afford to waste more time searching for Union's leader. He needed to get moving, which meant he needed a ride. The bartender had told him earlier where he might be able to get one.

The road to Daly's farm was well-worn and easy to follow, winding through gently rolling hills dotted with patches of scraggly trees. It wasn't long before a simple farmhouse appeared.

As Hayden approached, he saw a young boy, no more than twelve, sitting on the front porch, reading a book that had seen much better days. It appeared to be missing its cover and maybe some pages, too. The boy looked up as Hayden drew near, his eyes narrowing cautiously at the sight of his long, blood-stained shirt and duster, each side of the duster hooked behind the butt of a low-slung revolver.

"Howdy there, son," Hayden called out, keeping his voice friendly. "Is your pa around? I just came from the Sparkling Spur. The barkeep told me he has some horses for sale."

The boy nodded, his posture relaxing as he hopped to his feet. "Sure thing, mister. He's in the stable. I'll take you to him."

He led Hayden around the side of the house and across a small pasture where a few horses grazed contentedly. Fields of corn, oats and wheat occupied the area behind the pasture. The stable was a simple affair, a long, low building that looked recently erected. More a shedrow than a stable, it had six stalls with a roofed walkway along the front. The top half of each stall door was open, and two bay horses had their heads out, eyes alert for anything interesting. Both were chewing contentedly on hay, some of the dried foliage poking out from between their lips. One nickered to the boy.

"Hey, Sadie." The boy walked up to the mare and scratched under her hairy chin just as the clang of iron on iron emanated from one of the stalls. "Pa!" the boy called out as he smoothed his hand down Sadie's sleek, dark brown neck and then patted her. "Got a man out here looking to buy a horse!"

The door two stalls down opened, and a tall, lanky man wearing a leather farrier's apron over his dirty shirt and pants emerged. He had shaggy, unkempt black hair and a jagged scar running from the bottom of his left ear to the corner of his wide mouth. Set in a weathered, sun-beaten face, it made him look ominous. Yet, his brown eyes were kind as he appraised Hayden.

"Howdy, stranger," he said, extending a hand. "Name's Ben Daly. So you're in the market for a horse?"

Hayden shook his hand firmly. "That's right. I'm headed west and I need a strong, fast mount."

"You aren't looking to make a getaway from something... untoward, are you?" Daly asked, eying his shirt and duster.

"The blood is all mine," Hayden replied. "I had an accident on my way through the wilds a week or so ago."

"Looks like enough blood to kill you three times over, if you don't mind me saying."

"It would've killed me, but I have these." He opened a saddlebag and lifted out a couple of the medi-patches. "Left over from the war. Put one of these on almost any wound, it'll heal within days and without scarring. Even if it would have otherwise been a mortal wound."

Daly eyed the patches with interest. "No kidding? Do they work on horses?"

"I've never tried, but I don't see why they wouldn't."

"I see. You a scavenger, then? Most scavvies already have transportation. Carts full of junk, mostly."

"Not a scavenger. Just a traveler, trying to get west as quickly as possible."

"Well, I deal in draft horses, so they're plenty strong, but not always the fastest. They're all accustomed to plowing and pullin' logs, not runnin'."

"I understand, but I imagine they can still cover considerable ground in a day."

"As long as you don't push them too hard, they'll keep going for hours," he agreed.

"Show me your best."

Daly smiled. "Ah, sir. My best isn't for sale."

Hayden retrieved the wad of notes from his coat pocket. "I can pay in considerable notes or medi-patches."

Daly grinned. "Well, then, follow me." He led Hayden down the row of stalls. All the horses in them were sturdy-looking draft horses, their muscles rippling under shaggy coats, but he took Hayden to the last stall. The massive chestnut stallion inside it had to be over eighteen hands tall at the withers, dwarfing even Zorro.

"This here's Big Red," Daly said, patting the horse's flank. The horse swung his head around at the sound of his name to fix intelligent eyes on his owner and then Hayden. "He's experienced under a saddle," Daly continued, "but he won't come cheap."

Hayden eyed the horse appraisingly. It was a fine-looking animal, with a glossy dark red coat, a white slash running down his broad forehead, and two white stockings up front. But what really mattered was his powerful haunches and deep chest. Hayden had no doubt he could handle the rough terrain ahead. "How much?" he asked.

"How many of those patches you got?"

"I can spare five."

"Then five patches and two hundred notes. And I'll throw in the tack and a feed bag full of oats. The tack ain't new, but I keep my tack up. It'll get you where you want to go and then some."

Hayden raised an eyebrow. He figured Daly had high-balled him, prepared for him to try haggling him down some, but Hayden wasn't in the mood to waste time bargaining. He needed a horse, and he needed it now.

"I'll take him," he said, reaching into his saddlebags to get more patches before counting the notes.

Daly's eyes widened slightly as he took the money. "Dang,..." He grinned. "...I guess I should have asked for more. He's well worth it."

'You still got a deal." Hayden smirked.

Daly laughed. "That I did, and I thank you."

While Daly went to fetch the tack and filled a feed bag, Hayden opened the gate and stepped in to lift one of Big Red's front hooves, confirming what he'd expected. The farmer had cared for his hooves; his shoes almost looked new.

When Daly returned, he helped Hayden saddle up Big Red, ensuring the girth was tight and the stirrups were adjusted properly. "I hate to give you up, Red," he said to the horse, scratching between his ears. "But two hundred will replace you twice over. Thanks for giving me some good foals." He patted the horse, who seemed ambivalent to the change in ownership. "Take care of him," Daly added as Hayden swung into the saddle. "He's a good horse. If you ever want to sell him, I might be in the market to buy him back."

"I'll keep that in mind." Hayden nodded his thanks and gathered up the reins. With a click of his tongue and a gentle nudge of his heels, he set off at a trot, the powerful horse responding to his commands without hesitation.

Hayden guided Big Red through downtown, collecting more looks as he continued to where the barkeep had said to find the training grounds. He had to travel nearly as far as he'd gone to Daly's farm to reach it, but at least it was along the route he now needed to take. West instead of North.

Cresting a small hill, he spotted Tempest's training grounds in the hollow below. A few dozen canvas tents lined one corner of a large field. An obstacle course of logs and ropes occupied another area, a firing range another. Men and women, all dressed in simple brown uniforms, practiced at each location, their commanders barking orders at them. Hayden quickly noticed the rifles were all plasma, which was why he hadn't heard the crack of conventional long-range rifles echoing through town. At the rate they fired, Tempest didn't seem concerned about running out of cell charges for the weapons.

Seeing the army convinced him this was why the Rebirthers had steered clear of Union. The assembly below almost put a platoon of War Dogs to shame.

He found Tempest behind the shooters, observing. Nudging Big Red back into motion, he rode down the hill toward her, making it halfway before the first soldier noticed him. He immediately sounded the alarm, and before Hayden knew it, a dozen militia members were rushing him, rifles shouldered and ready to fire. Bringing Red to a stop, he put up his hands.

"Are you lost, mister?" One of the soldiers asked. "This area is off-limits."

"No offense intended," Hayden replied. "I was looking for Tempest. Came to say goodbye, like she asked."

The first soldier said something quietly to another, and she ran off, headed for Tempest, who had yet to notice his arrival. Hayden watched as the woman got Tempest's attention. She looked at Hayden, smiled, and called out to her troops. "I recommend letting the Sheriff through, before he decides he doesn't like the looks of your smarmy faces."

Hayden winced to have his identity so publicly revealed. The soldiers around him shifted from wariness to awe. "You're the Sheriff?" the man who'd confronted him asked.

"Pozz," Hayden replied. "I know, no metal arms. It's a long story."

The militia parted to let him through, and he rode the rest of the way down the hill, meeting Tempest near the tents.

"Leaving so soon?" she asked as he drew Red up in front of her. "I thought you were going to get your bike looked at and rest up for the night."

"So did I, but I can't wait any longer," he said. "Kady reached out to me again. She said they crossed a river, heading west. She's getting desperate, which means I need to get after them as soon and as hard as I can."

Tempest eyed his battered coat and dusty hat with a critical eye. "I promised you new clothes and a bandolier. I planned to bring them back with me, but since you're here…" She whistled to a couple of nearby recruits. "Find Sergeant Brand and tell her I need that requisition filled immediately. Hurry up and don't come back without it."

"Yes, ma'am," they replied, rushing to one of the tents.

"What do you think?" Tempest asked, turning and swinging her arm toward the training grounds.

"It's impressive," Hayden replied, dismounting, reins in hand, to talk to her more privately. "But you said you didn't know about the Rebirthers, so what do you need such a large militia for?"

"There's too much division between people today, wouldn't you agree?"

"Pozz. I do."

"The way I see it, there are two ways to bring people together. Commonality or force. You eradicated the trife nearly four years ago, and look at us. We're still scattered. Still trying to make our own way. Still dealing with raiders like the Rebirthers. It shouldn't be like that."

"So you're using force to fix the issue," Hayden said.

"That's right. The way I see it, I can start consolidating these scattered settlements with Union at the center. As my territory grows, my army grows, and I can expand more."

"Plenty of other warlords have thought the same. It hasn't panned out for them. Force is a bad way to bring people together."

"I figured you would say that, Sheriff. You're the hero of the masses, always there to help those in need. I commend you for your efforts, but I don't see the world the same way you do. We need more focus and a faster consolidation of resources. That's how we rebuild what we lost."

"I've come across folks who have said the same thing. They mean well in the beginning, but the power always gets to them. What makes you any different?"

She shrugged. "I don't know, Sheriff. I guess we'll find out. I suppose if I don't stay in line, I'll get another visit from you, and it won't be as friendly."

"That just might be. You treat people fair, you'll have no problem with me."

Rushing back with a bulky, oddly shaped pack, the recruits interrupted before she could say anything more. Tempest took the pack and handed it up to Hayden. "Here you go, handsome. A change of clothes and a few other things you might need on the road."

Hayden took the pack, surprised by the gesture. "More than I asked for. Thank you kindly, Tempest. I appreciate your aid."

"I can't make any promises for the future, Sheriff. But I owe those bastards for the 36th, and for those kids. I hope the next time we meet, it's still on good terms."

"Me, too," Hayden replied.

"Maybe I can talk you into spending the night with me next time. I have an idea that not too many women can claim to have done that."

"Only one, Tempest," he said sadly. "My one and only." With that, he secured the pack behind his saddle and swung back up onto Big Red's back.

With a final nod to Tempest, he wheeled the horse around and set off at a gallop, following the road the way he had come. Back toward the river and one step closer to finding Kady.

CHAPTER 15

As darkness deepened across the wilds, Hayden guided Big Red back to Lonnie's isolated farmhouse. The old woman's silhouette appeared in the doorway as he approached, her weathered face a mixture of surprise and wariness in the fading light.

"Didn't expect to see you again so soon," she called out, her voice carrying a hint of suspicion. "That's a fine horse. Much better than that metal monstrosity you left on."

Hayden dismounted, grinning as he approached. "Just passing through, ma'am. Thought I'd drop something off for you before I continue west."

He reached into his saddlebags, retrieving two of the precious medi-patches.

"These will help with any injuries you might face out here on your own," Hayden explained. "They're not a cure-all, but they'll give you a fighting chance if something goes wrong and you get hurt."

Lonnie took the patches with trembling hands, clutching them to her chest. "I... I don't know what to say. Thank you. There's an awful shortage of good folks like you around."

Hayden tipped his hat. "Just doing what I can to help, ma'am. Take care of yourself."

"Be safe out there," Lonnie replied.

Hayden nodded, returning to Big Red and swinging back into the saddle. The powerful horse's hooves pounded the earth as they set off once more.

They rode hard, heading west to the banks of Ole Miss. It chafed him to know the Rebirthers had crossed the river without his notice on the way north. He had kept a close eye on the shoreline nearly the entire trip and hadn't spotted anything.

Following the riverbank north, he kept his keen eyes scanning the terrain for any sign of the Rebirthers' passage. He kept Red's pace sedate to both rest the big horse and to make sure he wouldn't miss any signs of the Rebirthers' passage as he had from Hank's boat.

It was well past midnight when Hayden thought he spotted something. Dismounting, he crouched low to examine the shore. Two deep ruts had formed in the dirt, about twelve feet apart and stretching back from the water. Not APC tracks, but still a clue. Looking across the Ole Miss, he saw the shore was tantalizingly close. He could picture the scene in his mind's eye—the Rebirthers using their hoverbikes to lift the massive APC and ferry it across the water—in a feat of ingenuity. The extra counter-push of the repulsors had condensed the ground there, creating the ruts.

Hayden patted Big Red's neck, leaning close over the horse's ear. "What do you say? Think you can make it across?" The horse snorted, pawing at the ground as if eager for the challenge. Hayden gathered the reins and urged Big Red forward.

The water was shockingly cold as they plunged in, the current immediately tugging at them. Hayden leaned low over the horse's neck, whispering encouragement as the horse's powerful legs churned through the river.

For a heart-stopping moment, it seemed the current might sweep them away, but Big Red was strong. He fought his way across until his hooves found purchase on the opposite bank. With a heave, they scrambled up onto dry land.

Hayden gave Big Red an appreciative pat. "Good work, Red," he murmured. "You've more than earned your cost tonight."

Big Red shook his head, water droplets flying off his mane as Hayden surveyed their surroundings. Fortunately, the moon was nearly full, and he could see that the ruts continued as expected. He urged Red up the bank and slid from the saddle, dropping the reins to ground tie him as he followed the ruts into a copse of trees. He found a heavy chain net with evenly spaced crossbars, evidently the cradle used to carry the APC across the river.

And that wasn't all.

The moonlight glinted off something metallic. Drawing his revolvers, he approached cautiously and discovered a handful of abandoned hoverbikes. Checking one confirmed his suspicions. The batteries were dead.

"So they're on foot now," Hayden mused. "Or packed into that APC like sardines." He could imagine how eager the Rebirthers were to return the children to the Fort, wherever it was, that they'd planned to abandon such rare and high-tech machinery so readily.

They obviously didn't want to waste time waiting for batteries to be brought to them. Did that also mean they knew he was on their trail and was close to catching up to them? They knew where the children had originated. It was reasonable to suspect they also knew he had rescued them from Grimmel's facility. Alina had verified the general accuracy of his dream. If Kady had revealed her psychic abilities to the Rebirthers as he'd dreamt, they may have guessed she had reached out to him.

Maybe they weren't so much in a hurry as they were running scared.

He returned to Red and climbed back into the saddle. The tracks left by the APC were clear, even in the dim light, leading away from the river and into the western wilderness. Hayden urged Big Red onward, following the trail at a trot.

They rode through the night, the landscape gradually changing around them. The trees along the river quickly turned to open plains which gave way to more trees, then former farmland where the weeds had grown uncontested for years. A packed dirt road too dense for the weeds to take root in cut through it all. The APC's tracks ended on that packed dirt, but the vehicle no doubt followed the dirt path as it angled southwest.

As dawn began to break, Hayden spotted something on the horizon.

A town, or what remained of one.

Nature had reclaimed much of it, ivy and weeds crawling up the sides of crumbling buildings. Trees pushed through cracked pavement, their roots slowly demolishing what man had built. It was a ghost town, abandoned long ago and left to rot.

The APC's trail returned in the trampled overgrowth and broken-down asphalt, leading straight through the center of the town. Hayden's instincts prickled. Assuming he was right and the Rebirthers believed he was tracking them, this would be the perfect place for an ambush.

He slowed Big Red to a walk and pulled a revolver with his left hand, every sense on high alert as they entered the outskirts of the forgotten settlement. The silence was oppressive, broken only by the soft clop of Big Red's hooves on the overgrown street.

A flicker of movement—barely more than a shadow shifting behind a grimy window—caught Hayden's eye. But it was enough. In a single quick motion, he aimed and fired.

The bullet shattered the window and hit its mark. A Rebirther fell through the weakened glass, a hole in his forehead.

Hayden dug his heels into Big Red's barrel, wheeling the horse away as plasma sizzled through the air from both sides of the street. They quickly made it to cover between two buildings, the gunfire stopping almost as quickly as it had started, the ambush revealed.

He could have sent Big Red galloping through the town, continuing west without confronting the Rebirthers. Except, he wasn't built that way. Besides, he didn't need them at his back, following him close enough to put a bullet in his back.

He rode into an alley with scattered debris. "Wait here," he said to the horse, stepping down from the saddle and looping the reins through the handle of a rusty dumpster.

He inched back to the corner where the alley met the street, eyes shifting to search for signs of the Rebirthers. He located a few of them right away, moving behind empty window frames or crossing from one side of the street to the other. He counted six right away, almost certain there were more.

A plasma bolt whizzed past his ear, close enough that he felt the heat of its passage. He ducked back. They had spotted him, but he'd also spotted them.

"Come on out, Sheriff," one of them shouted. "We've got you surrounded."

Hayden was right. They knew who he was. Good. His response was to poke his head out around the corner and fire a single shot at the speaker, hitting him in the gut. He tumbled from his perch on an apartment balcony, screaming until the ground silenced him. The air immediately filled with a renewed barrage of plasma fire, forcing Hayden to keep his head back behind the corner, close to the ground and the building.

He needed to move. Staying in one place would only end

with them flanking him. Hayden took a deep breath, steeling himself for what came next.

In one fluid motion, he rose and sprinted toward the tumbled down store across the street. Plasma bolts sizzled past him as he hit the ground running, zigzagging between piles of rubble and abandoned vehicles.

A Rebirther leapt out from behind a rusted-out truck, swinging the butt of his rifle at Hayden's head. Instinct had him ducking under the blow and coming up inside the man's guard. His fist connected with the Rebirther's solar plexus, driving the air from his lungs. As the man doubled over, Hayden grabbed him by the back of the neck and slammed his face into the side of the truck. The Rebirther crumpled to the ground, unconscious or dead. Hayden didn't stop to check.

He dove behind what was left of a wall just as another volley of plasma fire cut through the air where he'd been standing. The acrid smell of ozone filled his nostrils as he pressed his back against the weathered stone.

"You can't win this, Sheriff!" The shout came from somewhere above him. Hayden risked a glance upward, catching sight of a Rebirther on a nearby rooftop. "Our cause is a just one! The Rebirth cannot be stopped!"

Hayden answered with a pair of bullets that caught the speaker center mass, knocking him back and out of sight. Hayden pushed off from the wall, sprinting toward a nearby alleyway. Plasma bolts scorched the ground at his heels as he ran, the Rebirthers struggling to draw a bead on his weaving form.

The alley was choked with debris and overgrown weeds, forcing Hayden to slow his pace. He could hear footsteps pounding behind him. They were giving chase like he'd hoped.

He rounded a corner and found himself face-to-face with a Rebirther trying to outflank him. The man fired his plasma rifle point-blank into Hayden's chest, the superheated bolt burning a hole right through him. Hayden's revolver barked twice in return. The first shot shattered the Rebirther's mask, the second punched through his chest. He fell backward without a sound, dead before he hit the ground.

More shouts echoed from behind him. Hayden gritted his teeth against the pain, crouching to snatch up the fallen Rebirther's plasma rifle before continuing down the alley. He emerged onto what had once been the town's main street, a wide boulevard now choked with years of accumulated detritus.

Hayden ducked behind an overturned car, barely recognizable between the vegetation and rust covering it. He holstered his revolver, checking his wound. It was already healing and certainly wouldn't kill him, but damn it hurt. Shouldering the plasma rifle he'd picked up, he popped up from cover long enough to shoot at the raiders chasing him.

Two more Rebirthers fell, their white robes blackened and smoking. The others scattered, seeking cover wherever they could find it. Hayden used the momentary lull to catch his breath.

"How many more of you do I need to kill?" he shouted as he crept to the edge of his cover, peering out at the street. He could see three of the remaining Rebirthers, their white robes stark against the drab grays and browns of the decaying town. They were moving cautiously, trying to flank his position.

"Five!" the shout came back. "You're still outnumbered, Sheriff!"

Hayden leaned out and fired, hitting one of the careless Rebirthers in the head with a plasma bolt. "Make that four!" he replied, backing away as the remaining enemies returned fire.

Rather than sit behind the car, he backed up to the alley and through the open portal of a mostly collapsed building.

Scaling over some rubble, he moved to the intact corner of the old shop, the racks long emptied. He could see the Rebirthers in the street through the filthy window, using hand gestures to move from cover to cover. They hadn't figured out that he'd abandoned his position yet.

His gaze stretched across the street, to the alley where Big Red remained hitched. One of the Rebirthers was getting close to the alley and would have to be blind to miss the large draft horse standing there. He couldn't afford to lose his ride.

He checked the charge on the plasma rifle. Sixty shots. Plenty. Switching it from single bolt to burst mode, he sprinted forward and threw his shoulder into the window. Glass shattered around him, and he hit the ground rolling, coming up to a knee and squeezing the trigger as he swept the rifle across the street, multiple bolts spewing out of the weapon. Two Rebirthers went down, and he rolled aside, Resetting the rifle to bolt mode and turned the gun on the raider near Big Red.

Just as the Rebirther reached the alleyway, a plasma bolt caught Hayden in the hand. He dropped the rifle, cursing as he rose and charged the man, who was already turning his plasma rifle on the horse. Hayden hit him before he could fire, his tackle sending them both tumbling. When they stopped rolling in the middle of the street, Hayden was trapped under the raider.

"I'm going to crush you," the Rebirther said through his mask, eyes narrowed in anger as his fingers tightened around Hayden's throat, crushing his windpipe closed. Hayden refused to panic. He reached behind the man, grabbing the line to his canister and ripping it out.

Without Clear, the man's strength faded in a hurry. Hayden hit him twice in the face before throwing him off. The man tried to get up, but Hayden's quick draw of his right-hand revolver put a bullet between his eyes.

The Rebirther was still collapsing as Hayden rolled out

from under him and into a crouch. He fired again, his round smashing through the mask of the last Rebirther, but not before the marauder unleashed a plasma bolt at Hayden. It barely missed his right shoulder, but a miss was a miss. He put one more bullet in the man who'd fired the bolt. Hit in the heart, he dropped in a heap.

Hayden walked over to him and stood there, less than ten feet from Big Red, looking down at the dead Rebirther. His chest hurt. His hand had a hole in it. But the streets were silent.

He had won.

He walked over and retrieved his hat where it had come off in the street. Picking it up, he slapped it against his thigh to rid it of dirt and settled it back on his head. Dropping his chin to his chest, he closed his eyes momentarily as exhaustion swamped him. When he looked up again, Big Red was staring intently at him. "What do you say, big fella?" he asked as he walked over and unhitched Red. "I think we could both use a rest. Maybe a change of clothes. For me, anyway."

He led Big Red out of the alleyway and across to one of the more intact storefronts, guiding the horse to the rear, where he found a patch of long grass ripe for equine munching. He hobbled Red in the middle of it, noting the barrel of collected rainwater by the back entrance. By the time he had the horse unsaddled, the saddle and reins slung over the only remaining section of a porch railing, Red was ripping off long grass stems and chewing to his heart's content.

Hayden grabbed his saddlebags and the pack Tempest had gifted him from where he'd laid them on the single step and went inside. He found a spot under a set of stairs to settle into in relative security. Taking off his coat, the one remaining bandolier, and then his destroyed vest and shirt. He patched his wounds before opening Tempest's pack.

Laying on top of a pair of pants, a shirt and a new duster was a Centurion Space Force Marine issue protective base layer, thin and rubbery. A brand new bandolier and a plasma rifle rested beside it, and underneath it all, some ration bars and of all things, a jar of honey. He hefted the jar in his hand and smiled at it.

"Son of a gun," he said, more than surprised. Not so much because he hadn't tasted honey in a long time, but because he would have saved himself some pain had he checked the pack sooner and put on the CSF base layer. It was also a shocker that Tempest had access to the new Centurion kit, which meant either she had direct communication with the CSF or she had connections to someone who did.

And they were helping her build an army to conquer the wilds without informing Nathan. Why?

More questions for another time.

He didn't put the base layer armor on right away. Better to let the patches do their work and change later. He settled in and lowered his hat over his face, quickly falling asleep.

CHAPTER 16

Hayden awoke with a start, his hand instinctively reaching for his revolver. For a moment, he was disoriented, the unfamiliar surroundings of the derelict storefront taking a moment to register. The previous day's events came rushing back—the ambush, the firefight, and the Rebirthers he had killed.

He sat up, wincing slightly as his newly healed wounds pulled. The medi-patches had done their job well, knitting flesh and bone back together as he slept. He felt refreshed, his mind clear and focused on the task ahead.

Rising to his feet, Hayden quickly donned the Centurion base armor, the thin, flexible suit molding to his body like a second skin. Over this, he pulled on the new clothes—sturdy pants, a plain shirt, bandoliers, gunbelt and a duster not unlike his old one, but without the bloodstains and blackened laser holes. No vest, but he could do without that.

Fully dressed, he packed the rest of Tempest's gifts in his saddlebags, picked up the plasma rifle, and stepped out into the rear of the store where Big Red waited patiently. The horse snorted a greeting, stamping his hoof as Hayden approached.

"Ready to go, big fella?" Hayden asked, dropping his saddlebags and laying the rifle against them. He patted the horse's neck, and Big Red tossed his head as if in answer.

Retrieving the saddle and bridle from where he'd left them, he eased the bit into Red's mouth and slipped on the bridle, followed by the saddle. The hobbles went back into his saddlebags. Remaining on foot, he guided Big Red out onto the deserted street. The town was as silent as a grave, the bodies of the Rebirthers he had killed still lying where they had fallen. He spent some time collecting their weapons and checking their gear. All the Clear had spilled from their open canisters while he slept, and he didn't discover anything else useful on their bodies.

After stashing their plasma rifles and stowing as many cell charges as he could carry, his saddlebags were stuffed, and every tiedown on his saddle was in use. He climbed back into the saddle and urged Big Red into a trot, again following the tracks of the APC southwest out of town, leaving the corpses for the buzzards.

The sun climbed higher in the sky as they rode, the heat radiating off the cracked asphalt. Hayden kept a wary eye on his surroundings, alert for any sign of another ambush. But the landscape remained silent, broken only by the steady rhythm of Big Red's hooves.

They rode for hours, briefly stopping to rest, feed and water Big Red at a small stream. The horse grazed and drank deeply, his flanks heaving, but there was no sign of flagging in his stride when Hayden remounted.

It was late afternoon when Hayden first spotted the smoke on the horizon, a thin black line staining the clear blue sky. His heart sank at the sight, a sense of dread settling in his gut. He urged Big Red into a gallop, the horse surging forward as if sensing his rider's urgency.

As they drew closer, the source of the smoke became clear. It was a town, or what was left of one. Buildings smoldered, their roofs caved in and walls blackened by fire. The streets were littered with debris.

Hayden reined in Big Red at the edge of town, eyes scanning the devastation. The survivors were spread among the ruins, sifting through the wreckage and cleaning up the mess. They looked up as Hayden approached, hope and fear warring in their eyes.

He dismounted, leading Big Red on foot as he approached a small group huddled near the remains of what might have once been a general store. A simple cart behind them had at least a dozen bodies piled on top of one another, each wrapped in blankets to help keep the flies out and the smell in.

"What happened here?" he asked, fearing he already knew the answer.

A man stepped forward, his face haggard. "Raiders in white robes," he said, his voice hollow. "They came demanding food. We gave them what we had, but it wasn't enough." He swallowed hard, his eyes haunted. "Their leader, he claimed we were holding out on them. That we had more hidden away. We swore we didn't, but they wouldn't listen."

The man's voice broke, and a woman put a comforting hand on his shoulder, taking up the tale. "They tore the place apart, searching. And when they found our emergency stash..." She shook her head, tears welling in her eyes. "They took that too, and set fire to the town. Killed anyone who tried to stop them. The leader, he said our lives were meaningless. That we had no need of food because we were food. That the Rebirth would fix the world in a way the Sheriff couldn't."

Hayden's jaw clenched, a cold fury building in his chest. The callousness, the cruelty of it was almost too much to comprehend. At the same time, the hairs on the back of his neck rose at the woman's words. "Are you sure that's what he said? That you're food?"

"That's what he said all right," the man replied. "We all heard it."

"He also said the Rebirth is only weeks away," a second woman said. "And that we should make peace with whatever we believe in because our end is coming. Only the strong will survive."

Hayden considered the statement, his already bad feeling intensifying. Carver and the other Rebirthers hadn't heard of Iagorth or Idhra, but that didn't mean there wasn't some other Relyeh these zealots were hoping to lure to Earth.

"How long ago did the white robes pass through?" he asked.

"Two days," the man replied.

"And how many did you see?"

"About thirty on foot, and a group in the biggest modbox I ever did see."

"They're not on foot now," the woman said. "They took all our wagons except that one." She motioned to the cart with the bodies in it. "And all our horses. Luckily, we have an ass to take the dead out for burial."

"How many did you lose?"

"Twenty-two in all," the second woman said, tears in her eyes. "My son…" She trailed off, breaking into sobs.

"I'm sorry, ma'am," Hayden said, his anger intensifying. "I've been chasing these Rebirthers across the wilds. They hit my settlement, too. The Greens, on the other side of the Ole Miss. But they didn't take food. They took children."

"Did you say children?" the second woman said, lifting her head from her hands.

"Pozz. Why?"

"A child," the man said. "A boy, he escaped from their machine during the attack. Ran off into the trees."

Hayden's heart skipped a beat. "What did this boy look like?"

"Young. Maybe ten? Blonde hair, fair skin. Looked scared out of his wits, poor thing."

"Which way did he run?"

The man pointed a trembling finger to the nearby tree line. "That way. They went after him when they realized he was missing, but I don't think they ever found him."

"What makes you say that?"

"A group of ours went into the woods the next day to hunt and forage, so we could eat. They came back not long after, saying they spotted a few of the white robes still out there, probably looking for the boy."

"I see. If the boy's still out there, I'll find him. Do you have wounded?"

"Too many, I'm afraid. Burns mostly, but a couple of gunshots, too."

Hayden reached into his saddlebags, pulling out a handful of the medi-patches. He pressed them into the second woman's hands. "Here," he said gently. "Tear off the wrapper, take out the patch, and put it on the worst of the wounds. It'll heal them in no time. I'm sorry I couldn't get here before this ever happened."

The woman clutched the patches to her chest, tears spilling down her cheeks. "Thank you," she whispered. "Thank you."

Hayden nodded, turning to remount Big Red. With a tongue click, he urged the horse toward the forest at a gallop. The trees swallowed them up in moments, the ruined town disappearing behind them.

Hayden slowed Big Red to a snail's pace, allowing the horse to pick his way under limbs and through the underbrush at his own pace while he scanned the underbrush for any sign of the boy or his pursuers. Two days was a long time for a child to be alone in the woods, but he knew how resourceful Alina's charges could be. It was just as likely the boy was still out here as it was that he'd been captured. The only question was how he would find him. The forest was dense here, and the sun was barely able to penetrate. At least it would be just as hard for the Rebirthers to locate the boy as it was for him.

Of course, a child could only get so far on foot, limiting the search area to within a few miles of the razed settlement. Odds were he would ride right past the boy's hiding place. He could only hope the child would recognize him and come out on his own.

They had been riding for nearly an hour when Big Red suddenly stopped and pawed the ground, snorting as he shook his head, long mane flying.

"Easy, boy," Hayden murmured, looking warily around as he patted Red's twitching withers. "What's got you so spooked?"

Then he heard it, too. A shout, followed by the unmistakable sound of a child's terrified scream.

Hayden kicked Big Red into swift action, his massive body crashing like a battering ram through the underbrush. Red jumped over exposed roots, and Hayden ducked low-hanging branches, the vegetation whipping at them as they surged through it.

Another scream followed the first, echoing through the canopy and helping guide Hayden toward its source. Holding the reins in his left hand, Hayden drew a revolver with the other. They burst into a small clearing just in time to catch a flash of blonde hair as a small figure darted between the trees on the far side. Two men in white robes closed in behind him.

Hayden didn't bother aiming; he popped off a shot at them just to draw their attention from the boy. The Rebirthers spun toward him, their plasma rifles coming up to bear. But Hayden was faster. His first shot took the closer man in the head, sending him sprawling. The second dove for cover behind a large oak, his plasma bolts sizzling through the air toward Hayden.

Hayden threw himself from the saddle, rolling to come up in a crouch behind a fallen log. He watched Big Red disappear into the trees on the far side of the meadow. Bark exploded near his head, jerking his attention off Red as a plasma bolt struck the log. He ducked his head as splinters showered his head.

He glanced over the log, spotting the Rebirther leaning out from behind the tree to take another shot. Hayden fired, his bullet catching the man in the shoulder and spinning him around. The Rebirther fell, his rifle tumbling from his grasp.

Hayden vaulted over the log, running towards the fallen man. The Rebirther struggled to rise, his hand scrabbling for his dropped weapon. Hayden reached him before he could get a good hold on the rifle, kicking it out of his hand and pressing the barrel of his revolver to the man's forehead. "Look at you, chasing after a child like that. I ought to put a bullet through your skull, but I won't shoot an unarmed man."

The Rebirther spat a glob of blood at Hayden's feet. "Who says I'm unarmed?" The man's arm flashed toward Hayden, the knife punching through his duster and smacking harmlessly against the Centurion base layer.

Hayden's shot echoed through the trees at the same time, sending birds bursting from the treetops in a flurry of flapping wings. Hayden straightened, scanning the surrounding forest.

There was no sign of the boy.

CHAPTER 17

"Hey, kid!" Hayden called out, pitching his voice to carry. "It's alright, you can come out now! I'm here to help you!"

For a long moment, there was nothing but silence. Then, a small, dirt-smudged face peeked slowly from behind a tree. Wide, frightened eyes stared at Hayden, the boy's small body trembling. Hayden holstered his gun, holding his hands placatingly as he took a slow step forward.

"It's okay, son," he said softly. "I'm not going to hurt you. I'm a friend." He paused, recognition dawning as he got a better look at the child's face. "James? Is that you?"

The boy's eyes widened, a spark of hope kindling in their depths. "Sheriff?" he whispered, his voice small and scared. "Is...is it really you?"

Hayden nodded. "Pozz. It's me. You're safe now, kiddo."

James burst from his hiding place with a strangled cry, running straight into Hayden's open arms. He buried his face against Hayden's chest, small shoulders heaving with sobs.

Hayden held him tightly, one hand cradling the back of the boy's head. "Shh, it's alright," he murmured. "I've got you. You're safe."

James clung to him like a lifeline, his small hands gripping

Hayden's duster. "I'm s-sorry," he hiccuped. "I t-tried to be brave, like you taught us. But I was s-so scared."

Hayden's heart broke at the child's words. He pulled back slightly, tipping James' chin up to look him in the eye. "You have nothing to be sorry for," he said firmly. "You were very brave, James. Braver than most grown men would be in your shoes."

James sniffled, rubbing at his nose with the back of his hand. "R-really?"

"Really," Hayden confirmed. "Now, can you tell me what happened? How did you end up here?"

The boy's face crumpled, fresh tears welling in his eyes. "They came at night," he whispered. "The men in white. They burned everything, and they..." He swallowed hard, his voice breaking. "They killed Sam. And Oz. They tried to protect us, but there were too many."

Hayden closed his eyes for a moment, grief and rage once again warring in his chest. He had known, from his dream and what Alina had told him, but hearing it again, this time from a child's mouth, made it that much harder.

Hayden opened his eyes, forcing his voice to remain steady. "What about the other children? Kady and the rest?"

"They took them. Took us all," James said. "Put us in the big machine and drove away. I tried to fight, but one of the men hit me." He touched his temple, where a livid bruise had formed. "I woke up inside the machine. It was dark and smelly and everyone was crying. I was s-s-so scared."

Hayden hugged him tighter. "You're very brave, James. How did you get away?"

"T-they didn't pay much attention to me, be-because I'm small. When they stopped and opened the back, t-they didn't even look at me. So...so I ran." He looked up at Hayden, his bottom lip trembling. "Did I do the right thing, Sheriff? Should I have stayed with the others?"

Hayden's throat tightened at the question. What a burden for such small shoulders to bear.

"You did exactly the right thing," he said. "If you hadn't escaped, I wouldn't know which way they went. Now, thanks to you, I can keep following them. We'll get the other kids back, James. I promise."

The boy nodded, some of the fear leaching from his eyes at Hayden's words. He believed because he believed in Hayden. The Sheriff had never let them down.

Hayden straightened, taking James' small hand in his own. "Come on," he said. "Let's get you out of here."

They walked back to where Big Red was poking his big head out of the underbrush, huffing softly. He stepped out of the vegetation at their approach.

James' eyes widened at the sight of the massive animal. "Wow," he breathed. "He's huge."

Hayden chuckled. "His name's Big Red. And don't worry; he's a gentle giant. You just wait here with him a minute while I collect the rifles from those men. The folks back in that town I just came through could sure use them."

He grabbed the knives and rifles from the dead Rebirthers, tying them to the saddle with his plasma rifle before mounting Red and then reaching down to help James up, both his hands wrapping around Hayden's wrist as he lifted him up and swung him into the saddle in front of him. The boy settled comfortably against his chest as Hayden clicked his tongue and kneed Red, urging him into a walk. The horse picked his way carefully through the trees, back the way they had come.

They rode in silence for a time, James' small body gradually relaxing against Hayden as the adrenaline of his ordeal wore off. He finally nodded off, obviously done in, his head resting against Hayden's forearm. As the boy slept, Hayden kept a watchful eye on their surroundings, alert for any sign of more Rebirthers if they had split up to search. But the forest remained still and quiet.

James stirred as the trees began to thin, twisting in the saddle to look up at Hayden.

"Where are we going, Sheriff?" he asked.

"I'm bringing you back to the settlement where you escaped. I'm going to ask them to watch over you for a spell while I find the others."

"B-but I want to come with you," James replied, fresh fear setting on his face.

"I know you do. But where I'm going it's too dangerous for you, and the people back at the town are good folks. They'll protect you while I'm gone."

"What if the men in white robes come back to the town?"

Hayden squeezed James' shoulder reassuringly. "They won't. They've already stripped it clean. Besides, they'd have to get through me first, and that won't happen." When James didn't argue, he continued. "How are the others holding up? Are they being treated well?"

"I guess," James replied. "They fed us, and stopped every few hours so we could go to the bathroom and stretch our legs. But it's hot in the machine, and they're all so scary."

"Did they say what they're planning to do with you and the others?"

"No, Sheriff. Just that we're the key to the Rebirth. Well, one of us is. They just don't know which one."

Hayden was sure he did. Kady. But why didn't the Rebirthers know that? She was the only one who had shown any special abilities. Unless...

He didn't continue the thought. He hoped it wasn't true but feared his instincts were right.

"Are you okay, Sheriff?" James asked, somehow sensing his discomfort.

"I'm worried about the others."

"Me too."

They reached the ruined town soon after. The townsfolk were surprised to see him again but kept to themselves. Hayden sought out the woman he had spoken to earlier, the one who had lost her son. He found her in front of one of the few upright structures.

"Ma'am," he said, getting her attention.

"You're back," she replied, smiling when she saw James. "And you found your boy, like you said you would."

"Pozz. I have a favor to ask. I need to continue on after those raiders, but that's no place for a boy."

She nodded. "I'd be happy to watch him, if it means you can avenge my Billy." She looked at James. "I'm Margie. What's your name?"

"James," he replied.

"So happy to make your acquaintance, James," she said, beaming. "Would you like to stay with us for a few days, while your pa chases after those bad men?"

"Oh, this isn't my pa," James replied. "This is Sheriff Duke. He's a good man. The best there is."

Everyone in earshot suddenly stopped what they were doing, turning to gawk at Hayden.

"Well I'll be," Margie said. "I didn't know I was talking to the Sheriff." She bowed her head. "It's an honor, sir."

"Please," Hayden replied. "I'm just doing the work I was made to do, ma'am. And fulfilling a promise." He patted the rifles on his saddle. "I brought these for you, to help you defend yourselves. They belonged to the men hunting for James after he ran away. They won't be needing them anymore."

"Thank you, Sheriff," the man he had spoken to earlier said as he approached. "For this, and for all you do."

Hayden nodded. "Off you go, James." He lifted the boy from the saddle, passing him down to Margie, who wrapped her arms around him and held him close. She looked overjoyed to have a child to care for again.

"You'll be back soon, won't you, Sheriff?" James asked.

"Pozz. And the others will be with me," he replied. He untied the rifles and passed them to the man. "The woods should be safe for hunting and gathering. If you can spare anyone, I took care of some other white robes in an abandoned town about a day's ride east of here. I stashed their weapons in a rusted dumpster."

"We'll send the cart after we finish burying our dead," the man said. "Thank you again, Sheriff."

"You can thank me by taking good care of James."

"We will," Margie promised.

"I'll see you soon, James."

"Okay, Sheriff."

He waved as Hayden turned Big Red around and headed out once more.

CHAPTER 18

For nearly five days, Hayden followed the tracks of the Rebirthers' APC and evidence of the passage of horse-driven wagons, the trail clear through the overgrowth lining the long untraveled asphalt roads. He stopped only long enough to allow the big horse to rest, graze, and drink while he remained awake, calling out to Kady in his mind and hoping she would respond.

So far, she hadn't.

On the morning of the sixth day, Hayden reached a section of the wilds recently scorched by wildfire. Charred grass fields flanked both sides of the highway, where the weeds and overgrowth were burned away, and signs of the APC's passage faded completely.

He followed the road through the area, bothered by the devastation around him. It was a part of nature, he knew, but still difficult to look at.

Continuing past the scorched earth, Hayden thought he would pick up the APC's trail again without issue, only to quickly discover that he was wrong. Backtracking, he spent another half-day searching the area he had passed through, certain he could pick up the trail. He didn't, even more dismayed when it failed to materialize. Somehow, the Rebirthers had gone through the area without leaving any tracks. Or maybe, knowing he was following them, they had gone through greater efforts to conceal the tracks and throw him from the trail. Either way, in the end, Hayden admitted defeat.

The Rebirthers had vanished.

Lacking any other leads, Hayden turned Big Red to the west, urging the horse into a trot. He had no way of knowing if he was still on the right track, but he figured if the raiders had continued on a similar tack, he would either stumble across them or a settlement where he might be able to ask about them. Or perhaps he'd locate the Fort where they were headed.

"Kady..." he murmured, sending his thoughts into the vast emptiness again. "Kady, can you hear me?"

As usual, for a long moment, there was nothing but the wind in his ears and the steady rhythm of Big Red's hoof-beats. Then, like a whisper at the edge of his mind, he felt it. A presence, faint but unmistakable.

"Sheriff?"

The voice was distant and strained, but it was undeniably Kady's.

"Kady! Are you alright?" he said out loud. "Where are you?"

"We're... we're in a building. An old one. They've locked us in a big room, all of us together." Her mental voice was shaky, laced with fear. "Sheriff, please. You have to help us."

"I'm coming, Kady," Hayden assured her, his voice a fierce promise. "I'm on my way. Can you tell me anything about where you are? Which direction did they take you?"

But there was no response, just a fading sense of her presence, like a candle flame guttering in the wind.

Hayden gritted his teeth. He'd hoped to get some direction from her. At least he knew she was still alive and relatively safe. He kept calling her in his mind in case she might respond again. But nothing came.

It was late afternoon when he finally spotted something in the distance, a small, moving shape that resolved into a man on horseback as he drew closer. The horse was a scrubby, swaybacked nag, plodding along and pulling a small modbox with its roof cut off and engine removed, the space filled with a motley assortment of scavenged goods.

Hayden reined in Big Red as he approached, hailing the man with a raised hand. The scavenger looked up, wariness and curiosity on his weathered face.

"Howdy, pardner," Hayden called out. "A moment of your time?"

The scavenger pulled his horse to a halt, one hand resting casually on the butt of a rusty pistol at his hip. "What can I do for you, stranger?"

Hayden dismounted, keeping his movements slow and unthreatening. He dropped Red's reins, ground-tying him as he approached the man. "Name's Hayden. I'm looking for some people. A group traveling in a big vehicle. They would have passed this way in the last day or two."

The scavenger scratched his chin, squinting at Hayden appraisingly. "Can't say as I've seen anything like that. Been out here for near a week, and you're the first soul I've come across."

Hayden's shoulders slumped, disappointment a bitter taste in his mouth. Another dead end.

The scavenger must have seen something in his face, for his expression softened slightly. "Where you headed, if you don't mind me asking?"

Hayden hesitated, debating how much to reveal. But a rough sort of honesty in the man's manner made him decide to chance telling him. "I'm trying to find a place called the Fort. Heard of it?"

The scavenger's eyebrows shot up, surprise and fear flickering across his face. "The Fort? Yeah, I've heard of it. It's south by southwest of here, maybe a day, day and a half, ride. But you don't want to go there, friend. Trust me."

Hayden frowned. "Why not?"

"Place is bad news. Used to be a military base, back before everything went to hell. Now? It's been taken over by some kind of cult. Call themselves the Reborn, or something like that."

Hayden's blood ran cold at the words. The Reborn. The Rebirthers. It had to be the same group.

"What do you know about them?" he asked, his voice tight.

The scavenger shook his head. "Not much. They keep to themselves, mostly. But I've heard stories from folks who've gotten too close. They're fanatics, every one of them. Worship some kind of prophecy about the end of the world and a new beginning. And they don't take kindly to outsiders who don't believe in their bull."

"I have to go there," he said, more to himself than the scavenger. "I have to get inside."

The scavenger looked at him like he'd grown a second head. "Didn't you hear what I just said? It's suicide, going there. You'd be better off just turning around and heading back the way you came."

But Hayden was already shaking his head, his resolve hardening like steel in his veins. "I can't do that. There are lives at stake. Children's lives."

The scavenger's expression shifted, understanding and a hint of respect dawning in his eyes. "I see. Well, I won't try to talk you out of it then. A man's gotta do what a man's gotta do. But that's a real pit of vipers if I ever saw one. You best be careful. Anyways, if you're determined to go, you'll know when you're close because you'll need to cross a river to get there. It's not hard, there's an old train trestle you can use. Just follow the tracks around to the Fort. You can't miss it."

"I appreciate the directions," Hayden said, a sudden idea forming. "You know, that's a fine horse you've got there," he said, nodding towards the scavenger's nag. "Sturdy. Reliable."

The scavenger glanced at his horse, then back at Hayden, confusion wrinkling his brow. "She gets the job done, sure. Why do you ask?"

Hayden gestured to Big Red. "I was thinking we might make a trade. My horse for yours, straight up."

The scavenger's eyes widened, surprise and naked longing written across his face as he took in Big Red's powerful frame and glossy coat. "You serious, mister? That's a damn fine animal you've got there. Worth ten of Daisy here, easy."

Hayden shrugged. "Call it a fair exchange for the information. And the horse. She'll serve my purposes better, where I'm going. A nag like yours won't draw much attention. Big Red here, on the other hand...the Rebirthers will take notice of a horse like him."

Understanding dawned on the scavenger's face. "I see. You're planning to go in quiet like. Smart."

Hayden dismounted and picked up Big Red's reins. "So, do we have a deal?"

The scavenger hesitated for only a moment before a grin split his face. "Mister, you've got yourself a trade."

They quickly swapped horses, saddles and gear, the scavenger bouncing excitedly as he hitched his cart up to Red and prepared to mount him.

"Thanks for the ride west, big fella," Hayden said, patting the side of Big Red's head. "I'm sure my new friend here will take excellent care of you." He glanced at the scavenger with a pointed look.

"Sure will," he agreed.

As Hayden swung onto his new horse, settling into the creaking leather saddle, he paused, looking down at the scavenger.

"One more thing. When you head east, make sure you stop by Union. Tell them Hayden sent you."

The scavenger nodded, still grinning from ear to ear. "Union. I'll remember that. Thank you, Hayden. And good luck. I hope you find what you're looking for."

With that, he swung up onto Big Red and, with a whoop of joy, urged the big horse away. They disappeared into the distance, leaving Hayden alone with his new mount and his thoughts.

He looked to the south, where the Fort and the Rebirthers awaited. He was close now and wouldn't be denied.

CHAPTER 19

Hayden rode on, the sun sinking lower on the horizon as he followed the scavenger's directions toward the Fort. The landscape slowly began to change, the endless grasslands giving way to scattered copses of trees and the occasional rocky outcropping. He paused to rest his new horse in an old gas station on the side of the road, keeping out of sight just in case anyone happened to wander past. A few hours and they were on the road again, but he had to stop much more often for the old nag than he had Big Red.

What the scavenger had called a day's ride turned into two, leaving Hayden and Daisy hungrier than he would have liked. He thought about getting out what was left of his honey jar, but he had nothing to put it on. He'd already eaten the ration bars, and he had no more oats for Daisy. She had to rely on grass only.

Finally, as the light began to fade on the second day, he found what he had been looking for. A river, wide and swift, cutting across his path like a ribbon. And spanning it, a train trestle, its rusted girders and weathered wooden ties a relic of a bygone era.

Hayden dismounted, letting Daisy get a drink and graze

before leading her onto the trestle. The structure creaked and groaned but held firm. On the other side of the river, Hayden spotted a small, fenced-off area just off the tracks. A cemetery, its tombstones tilted and moss-covered with age. He guided Daisy over a rusted gate lying in overgrown grass. Locating a memorable spot, he tethered the old girl to a tree. She dove greedily into the tall grass while he began digging with a flat rock and his bare hands. The ground was hard and unyielding, but Hayden was relentless.

Finally, judging the hole deep enough, Hayden unslung his saddlebags, and carefully removed his revolvers and bandoliers. He ran a loving hand over the worn grips of his guns, feeling the weight of all they had seen and done. Then he placed them into the hole, along with the saddlebags. He kept only his microspear, tucked into the pocket of his trousers. A weapon of last resort.

Refilling the hole, Hayden carefully noted its location relative to the tree and the nearest tombstone, for a man named Paul Getty who had died nearly three hundred years ago and whose name was barely legible beneath the wear of time and the elements. He would remember this spot and return for his belongings when his mission was done.

With that finished, Hayden untethered Daisy and climbed back into the saddle. They set off again, following the train tracks as they wound through the gathering dusk.

Darkness had fallen when he passed through what had been a thriving town before the war. Now, it was nothing more than a collection of burned-out husks and crumbling walls, the whole place had been set on fire at some point in its more recent history, likely to hold back or counter a slick of trife.

Hayden rode cautiously through the ruined streets, every sense on high alert. Shadows lurked in every doorway, danger seeming to hide behind each corner. He expected an ambush with every step, but the town was as silent as a tomb.

The only sound was the soft clop of Daisy's hooves on the crumbling asphalt.

As he rounded a bend in the tracks on the far side of town, Hayden saw what had to be the Fort, and pulled Daisy up to look the place over. It rose from the plains like a fortress of old, its walls a patchwork of rusted cars and scavenged metal.

He picked out details. Guards in combat armor beneath white robes, plasma rifles held at the ready. A single, heavily fortified entrance. And beyond the walls, the shapes of buildings and vehicles, tantalizing hints of what lay within.

Hayden urged Daisy back into her lazy rolling gate, approaching the entrance. Two guards stepped forward, their weapons trained on his chest.

"Hold!" one of them barked, his voice muffled by his breathing mask. "State your name and business."

Hayden raised his hands slowly, keeping his expression neutral. "My name is Sam. I've heard of your cause," he said. "The Rebirth. I want to join you. I want to be part of the remaking of the world."

The guards exchanged a glance, suspicious yet excited at the same time.

"Is that right?" the second guard asked. "And what makes you think you're worthy?"

Hayden met his gaze. "I believe in the prophecy. I believe the world is broken, and that it needs to be remade. I want to be a part of that. I want to help foster a new era."

The first guard stepped closer, his head cocked to the side. "Do you believe the destruction of civilization was humankind's rightful fate?"

"Yes," Hayden replied without hesitation, remembering Carver's words. "The balance was upset. Our future denied. But the Rebirth will make right what is wrong."

Slowly, the guards lowered their weapons. "Welcome, brother," the first one said. "You've come to the right place."

They led Hayden through the gates, into the heart of the Fort. He looked eagerly around, taking in every detail.

The APC sat just ahead, its armored bulk looming like a slumbering beast. Hoverbikes and motorcycles were parked nearby, alongside a fleet of modboxes laden with heavy machine guns mounted to turrets.

Barracks buildings lined one side of the compound. On the other side, additional fortifications had been erected, as well as makeshift watchtowers where additional guards kept a lookout. They had undoubtedly seen him coming long before he spotted the Fort.

At the far end, the main building was a sturdy, two-story brick and stone structure. It had been the centerpiece of the Fort a long time ago. In front of it, a tall flagpole was adorned with a limp red flag, its pattern hidden from view.

Hayden's gaze locked onto the building, his heart racing. Kady was in there. He could feel it in his bones. But the guard wasn't leading him that way. Instead, he guided Hayden to one of the barracks, pushing open the door and ushering him inside.

The interior was spartan, with rows of bunks lining the walls and a few rough-hewn tables and chairs scattered about. A group of Rebirthers looked up as they entered, curiosity and wariness in their eyes.

The guard led Hayden to a man who sat apart from the others. His posture was ramrod straight, and his eyes were closed as if he were lost in meditation.

"Commander Fang," the guard said, snapping a salute. "This man wishes to join our cause."

The commander's eyes slowly opened. He looked Hayden up and down, his gaze sharp and assessing. "Does he now? And what's your name, recruit?"

"Sam, sir."

"Well, Sam, you've come at a most opportune time. The Rebirth is close at hand. The prophecy will be fulfilled very soon." The commander leaned forward, his eyes gleaming with enthusiasm. "But if you wish to join us, to be a part of this glorious future, you must first prove yourself worthy."

Hayden's stomach tightened with unease, but he kept his expression carefully blank. "Of course, Commander. How do I prove myself to you?"

A slow, predatory smile spread across the commander's face. "Trial by combat. Hand-to-hand. No weapons. Only the strength of your conviction and the power of Clear."

Hayden's blood ran cold at the mention of the drug. He had seen firsthand what it could do, the unnatural speed and strength it granted, but he didn't want any part of it. He'd never heard of a drug that wasn't addictive or didn't come with side effects. And he had no idea how it might interact with his Relyeh-cleansed DNA.

But he had no choice. Kady and the others were counting on him. He had to do this. "I accept," he said, his voice steady.

Fang's smile widened. "Excellent. Come with me." He got to his feet, calling out to the Rebirthers in the barracks. "Attention brothers! We have a new potential! Run and tell the others to come outside for the trial."

The other Rebirthers jumped to their feet and excitedly hurried from the barracks ahead of Hayden and the commander.

"Do you know how to fight, recruit?" the man asked as they walked.

"A little," Hayden replied.

"Normally, I would go easy on you. But our most recent potentials have been…less than ideal. With the Rebirth so close at hand, we need true strength among our ranks. Our enemies will stop at nothing to prevent our destiny."

"They can't stop it," Hayden answered. "It's destiny, like you said."

Fang laughed. "Exactly so, recruit."

He and Hayden returned to the courtyard, where a crowd

was already gathering, forming a rough circle. They moved aside to let Fang and Hayden enter.

"This is Sam," Fang said, introducing him. "He'd like to become a brother."

The Rebirthers all made a hissing sound that sent a chill down Hayden's spine. They sounded just like trife.

"I need a volunteer to assist Sam in his trial. Who will step forward?"

Over two dozen Rebirthers answered the call. Most were average in size and build. A couple stood out as real bruisers, large and muscled. Hayden already knew who the commander would pick based on his earlier comment.

"Brother Lion," Fang said, pointing to one of the brutes. "The honor is yours!"

Lion, one of the brutes, raised his fist while the other Rebirthers cheered. He moved to the middle of the circle, opposite Hayden.

"Welcome, Sam," he said, no hint of malice in his voice. "I hope you can beat me, but I doubt you will."

Hayden nodded, flinching as hands grabbed his coat and pulled it off him. A pair of Rebirthers approached both he and Lion, carrying breathing masks and canisters.

"Put these on," the Rebirther instructed.

Hayden hesitated momentarily before complying, securing the mask over his face. The canister hissed as it began to feed Clear into his lungs.

Immediately, the world seemed to slow down. Hayden's senses sharpened, his muscles thrumming with sudden energy. But even with the drug coursing through his system. Within a few seconds, the effect lost its intensity, his body filtering it from his system almost as quickly as it entered, the same as it did with alcohol. His senses remained enhanced, but not to the same degree as his first breath of the stuff.

Fang stepped between them, looking from one to the other. "The rules are simple. The fight continues until one of you yields or can no longer continue." He paused as Lion dropped into a fighting stance. Hayden did the same. "Begin."

Hayden's opponent wasted no time, lunging forward with blinding speed. Hayden barely dodged the first blow, feeling the wind of its passage against his cheek.

He danced back, trying to find an opening, but his opponent pressed the attack, fists flying in a dizzying blur. It was all Hayden could do to evade and block, the impacts jarring his bones. He needed to end this quickly before his opponent's superior strength and speed won out.

Feinting left, Hayden ducked under a haymaker, driving his fist into the man's gut with all his might. His opponent grunted, doubling over, but only for a moment. He straightened with a feral grin as he again came at Hayden. They traded blows back and forth, the crowd cheering and jeering with each landed hit.

Hayden took a punishing series of strikes to the ribs that left him gasping, the Centurion armor beneath his shirt the only thing saving him from broken ribs. He pushed through the pain, the Clear dulling its edge.

He waited for his moment, letting his opponent overextend on a wide swing. Then, with a surge of adrenaline and Clear-fueled strength, Hayden caught the man's arm, twisting and pulling simultaneously. There was a sickening pop as the joint dislocated, and his opponent howled in agony.

Hayden pressed his advantage, driving a knee into the man's face once, twice, three times. On the third strike, he felt cartilage crunch and saw blood spray from a shattered nose. His opponent crumpled, his scream cut off as he hit the ground in a boneless heap.

For a moment, there was silence, save for Hayden's ragged breathing. Then Lion raised an open palm. "I yield."

Fang stepped forward, clasping Hayden's arm and raising it high.

"We have a winner!" he declared, his voice ringing across

the courtyard. "Welcome Brother Sam, to the Disciples of the Rebirth!"

The crowd erupted in cheers, surging forward to clap Hayden on the back to welcome him as one of their own. Hayden was thankful for the mask so he didn't need to force a smile. He did his best to ignore the way his stomach churned with disgust.

He had done what he'd had to do. He was in. Now, he just needed to find Kady and the others and get them out.

Somehow.

CHAPTER 20

Hayden joined the other disciples as they returned to the barracks following the trial. Now part of their so-called family, the Rebirthers around him were surprisingly welcoming, eager to meet their new brother and offer encouragement.

Commander Fang walked beside him and as they neared the barracks buildings, he pointed to the second one down. "You've proven your skill in combat," he said. "An impressive display, and more than I expected from you. I'm placing you with Sergeant Steel and his platoon. They're one of my top units. I think you'll fit nicely with them."

"Thank you, Commander," Hayden replied. "I'm honored."

"As you should be."

Fang led him into the building, still buzzing with activity while the other Rebirthers resumed their prior tasks. Fang's eyes scanned each room they passed until he found Sergeant Steel in the mess hall. The man sat alone at a table, his back to the doorway, his position evident from the red armor visible beneath his white robes.

"Sergeant Steel," Fang said, approaching him. "You

witnessed the trial, I'm sure. I'm assigning Brother Sam to your platoon."

The other man swallowed one last bite of the stew on the table before turning around.

"Brother Sam," he said, eyes boring into Hayden. "You did well out there. Where did you learn to fight?"

Hayden barely heard him. He could feel his eyes narrowing, his heart pounding with furious anger. Sergeant Steel was the man who had attacked the Greens and taken Kady. The man he'd spent the last two weeks chasing across the wilds.

"Is there a problem?" Steel asked when he didn't respond.

"No," Hayden spat out. "No problem at all. I'm honored to serve you, Sergeant." The words tasted like acid.

"I asked you where you learned to fight, brother," Steel repeated.

"The same place most folks do, I reckon," Hayden replied. "Out in the wilds, where only the strong survive."

"That was true once, before the Sheriff came along. But we will make it true again, won't we? The Rebirth is at hand."

Hayden forced a smile. "Yes. I can't wait."

"You won't have to wait much longer." He rose to his feet. "Thank you, Commander. I'll show Brother Sam to his cot."

"Welcome Sam," Fang said one last time before turning and leaving the room.

"Let's get you set up," Steel said, clapping Hayden on the shoulder like old friends. He led Hayden out of the mess hall to one of the long, rectangular rooms where nearly two dozen Rebirthers sat on their cots engaged in various activities.

"Brothers," Steel said, even though there were females in the room. "Welcome, Brother Sam."

"Welcome, Sam," they each said in their own way, some louder than others.

"Joshua, Lacey, you're in charge of getting Sam set up with everything he needs."

"Yes, Sergeant," two disciples replied, rising from their cots and rushing from the room.

"Now, I have other matters to attend to," Steel said, clapping Hayden on the back before leaving.

Joshua, a young, lanky man with short red hair and a freckled face, and Lacey, also young, with a rounder face and dark hair, returned a couple of minutes later. Looking more closely at Joshua, Hayden recognized him from his dream as one of the hoverbike riders.

"That's your cot there," Joshua said, pointing to the one between his and Lacey's. "It belongs to Breaker, but he hasn't come back from the last mission."

"He's dead," Lacey said. "The Sheriff caught him and killed him."

"You don't know that," Joshua said.

"He would have been here by now if he was still alive."

"I suppose. Here's your gear," Joshua said, turning to Hayden.

They gave him a robe, the white fabric coarse against his skin, and a pair of simple sandals. Hayden took it with a nod of thanks, trying not to let his revulsion show as he clipped the canister to his belt.

A plasma rifle was pressed into his hands, the weapon heavy and cold. Hayden turned it over, examining it with a critical eye. It was Centurion-made, just like the ones he'd seen the Rebirthers using in their ambush.

"You can stow the rifle and the Clear in your footlocker here," Joshua said, tapping the top of the metal box. "Don't ever let Steel catch you vaping in here. The Clear's only for active use, not recreation."

"The withdrawal is tough to deal with sometimes, but you'll get used to it," Lacey added.

"The Clear is amazing," Hayden said, removing the mask and canister and stowing it in the locker. "Do you know what it is, or where it comes from?"

"Somewhere far up north, or so they say," Joshua said. "We get fresh deliveries every week, regular as clockwork. Plane flies over and drops it out of the sky."

"You don't know who's making it?"

"Don't know, and don't care. They believe in the cause, like you and me. That's all that matters."

It wasn't all that mattered to him, but he didn't press it. "What about the rifles and the hoverbikes? And that military APC you have outside? I've been scavenging the wilds for years. I know how hard it is to come across gear like that. Most of it's already spoken for. In the hands of War Dogs, in my experience."

Joshua grinned. "You aren't wrong about that, brother," he said. "Spoils of war, you might say. We've been taking them off the bodies of those so-called War Dogs. They're well trained, but the Clear gives us an edge. Makes us faster, stronger. They never stood a chance against the righteous fury of the Reborn!"

"Taking out War Dogs. I'm impressed. You aren't worried they'll come after you?"

"Nah. You saw the fortifications. Nobody's getting in here without our say-so. Besides, the dead can't fight." He laughed. "The Rebirth will have happened by the time they organize enough to be a serious problem. And then they'll have other things to worry about."

Hayden wanted to ask what the Rebirth was, but it seemed too curious a question, as if he didn't fully believe. He shifted gears instead.

"I heard about this place from a scavenger I crossed paths with. He thought you were crazy, but everything he said, I've felt the same way. It takes a strong man to start a movement like this. Is there any way I might have a chance to meet whoever started all this?"

"Zephyr," Lacey said, her voice hushed, almost worshipful. "He's our leader, our prophet. He's the one who heard the call, who saw the truth of the Rebirth when the rest of us were still stumbling in the dark."

"He's incredibly inspiring," Joshua added. "A real visionary. And you will meet. Zephyr speaks to all of us. Guides us on the path to salvation. You'll see, soon enough. And when you do, you'll never forget the moment."

Hayden was about to ask more when Steel's voice rang out from the doorway, cutting through the chatter like a knife. "All right, you lot! Lights out! Get some shut-eye, brothers. We've got a big day ahead of us tomorrow, and you'll need to be rested and ready."

There was rustling and shuffling as the Rebirthers made their way to their cots, settling in for the night. Hayden laid down on his back, staring up at the dark ceiling. He tried reaching out to Kady, to tell her that he was here at the Fort, less than a few hundred feet away, working on getting her and the other children out. If she could hear him, she didn't respond.

In the meantime, his mind whirled with plans and possibilities. He needed to find Kady and the other children, and get them out. But he couldn't just grab them and run. There were too many Rebirthers, all of them too well-armed. He needed a distraction, a way to draw their attention elsewhere.

Perhaps he could sabotage their vehicles, or stage some kind of attack from outside the walls. If he could just create enough chaos...

He was still turning over ideas, discarding one after another, when a sudden clanging jolted him from his thoughts. A bell, ringing loudly in the night, urgent and insistent. Around him, the Rebirthers began to stir, excited murmurs running through the barracks.

The lights flicked on, harsh and blinding after the darkness. Hayden blinked, shading his eyes as he sat up.

"What's going on?" he asked Lacey. "Is something wrong?"

She grinned at him, her eyes bright with fervor. "Wrong?

No, brother. Just the opposite. Zephyr has called a gathering. Dress yourself and come, quickly now."

Hayden rose and put on his own robe, settling the mask over his face. But he left the canister off, unwilling to cloud his mind with the drug. He followed the flow of bodies out of the barracks, into the cool night air.

They gathered in the main courtyard, a sea of white robes and masks, the sounds of their breathing like a single rhythmic hiss. Glancing around, Hayden estimated their numbers at close to a thousand, a formidable force by any measure.

He had gotten into the compound, but how would he get out past this with a bunch of children in tow? He didn't let the despair of the question overwhelm him. He would find a way. He always did.

At the top of the steps leading to the main building, a group of figures stood apart. Their robes were the same colorless white, but their armor was a deep, blood red. Higher-ranking disciples, Hayden guessed, Zephyr's inner circle. Commander Fang and Sergeant Steel stood among them.

Fang stepped forward, raising his hands for silence. The crowd's murmurs died away, and a hush fell over the assembled Rebirthers.

"Brothers and sisters," Fang said, his voice ringing out across the courtyard. "We are gathered here tonight to bear witness. To hear the words of our prophet, our guide on the path to truth."

The crowd cheered, a roar of anticipation and devotion that quickly shifted into a unified cry for their leader. Hayden joined in, raising his fist and shouting with the rest, though the words tasted like ashes on his tongue.

Fang didn't wait for the noise to die down before continuing. He knew it wouldn't until the disciples got what they wanted. It was so loud, that Hayden couldn't hear whatever he said next.

The doors to the main building swung open, and a figure emerged. He was tall and lean, his robe a pristine white, and his combat armor seemed to glow in the moonlight. As he walked to the edge of the steps, the crowd fell silent, every eye fixed on him in rapt attention.

"My children," Zephyr began, his voice rich and resonant, carrying easily over the assembled crowd. "My fellow seekers on the path to enlightenment. I stand before you tonight with joyous news that will set your very souls alight."

He spread his arms wide, his face rapturous. "The time of the Rebirth is at hand, my brothers and sisters. The prophecy is nearing its fulfillment. Soon, very soon, we will witness the dawning of a new age, a new world rising from the ashes of the old."

The crowd erupted in cheers, the fervor of their belief a palpable thing, a living, breathing entity. Hayden cheered along with them, though for him, it was all show. His insides burned with anger.

Zephyr continued, his voice rising above the din, commanding attention. "But as with all great changes, there will be obstacles in our path. Those who cling to the old ways, to the corrupt and broken world that was. They will seek to stop us, to deny us our destiny, to keep us from our rightful place as the inheritors of the earth. Even now, the Sheriff hunts us, hoping to prevent that which cannot be denied."

Boos and jeers arose from the Rebirthers, their faces twisted with anger, with righteous indignation. Zephyr let it go on momentarily before raising his hand for silence, the gesture simple but powerful.

"But we will not be deterred, my children. We will not be denied. For we have the truth on our side. We have the power of the Clear, the strength of our conviction. And most importantly..."

He paused, his gaze sweeping over the crowd, seeming to

linger on every face. "We have the Children of Grimmel. We have the One."

The resulting cheers were deafening. Chants rose from around him. "One. One. One. One."

A group of Rebirthers emerged from the main building as if on cue, each leading a child by the hand. The kids looked scared and confused, their faces streaked with tears, their small forms dwarfed by the burly zealots gripping their arms. But where was Kady?

The Rebirthers lined the children up on both sides of the steps, holding them fast.

"The Children of Grimmel," Zephyr repeated. "The Chosen, who will form the backbone of the world's reshaping. And with them, the One."

Sergeant Steel appeared in the doorway, his hands on Kady's shoulders, guiding her forward. She had a mask over her mouth, but it wasn't attached to a canister. It was there to keep her from screaming. To prevent a psionic attack.

"The One has sensed the queen. She lives!"

The crowd cheered while Hayden remained silent, his suspicious fear realized. Heart clenching, he looked up and back as a sudden wind swept through the compound, lifting and spreading the Rebirther flag, visible in the light of the buildings. Stylized but unmistakable, the curled form of a trife queen greeted him.

"No," he whispered, drowned out by the cheering. It couldn't be that there was one left. That it had been too deeply in hibernation not to succumb to the plague he had unleashed on all the Relyeh on Earth. If these idiots managed to get to it, to wake it up...within weeks, the trife invasion and occupation would happen all over again, as if he'd never done anything at all.

"With the help of the One, we will locate our queen. We will revive her from her slumber. And the rightful inheritors of our planet will rise once more, in glorious rebirth!"

The crowd roared its approval, the sound like a physical force battering at Hayden, pressing in on him from all sides. He couldn't let this happen. Whatever had led these people to believe in this cause, they were wrong. Dead wrong. He clenched his fists, fighting the urge to charge forward, to cut down anyone who tried to stop him.

He couldn't. Not yet. There were too many of them, and he was just one man. He needed a plan, needed...

His thoughts scattered like leaves in the wind as Zephyr's gaze suddenly locked with his own. Even across the distance, Hayden could feel the intensity of that stare, the weight of it, as if the man could see straight into his soul.

"Those aren't the only good tidings I bring on this night," Zephyr said, his voice suddenly softer, more intimate, yet still carrying to every ear. "Let us not forget that we have a new brother among us tonight. And he bested Lion in the trial."

Hayden's heart hammered as Zephyr beckoned to him with a single, imperious gesture. "Come forward, Brother Sam. Let your new family look upon you. Let them see the face of their new champion."

For a moment, Hayden was frozen, panic clawing at his throat, rooting him to the spot. But he couldn't afford to hesitate or show any weakness, not with so many eyes upon him.

Slowly, he stepped forward, the crowd parting before him. He could feel their eyes on him, feel the weight of their expectations, their hopes, their dreams of a new world. He could only hope none of them recognized him or knew who he was, the way Hank had when they met.

He reached the bottom of the steps, looking up at Zephyr. The man smiled down at him, expression almost paternal and loving.

"Welcome, Brother Sam," he said. "Welcome to your destiny."

He reached out a hand, and Hayden had no choice but to take it, to allow himself to be pulled up the steps to stand at

Zephyr's side, to feel the man's arm wrap around his shoulders like a vise.

The crowd cheered, their adulation washing over Hayden like a tide, threatening to sweep him away. But all he could focus on was Kady, her wide, frightened eyes meeting his across the sea of white robes, a silent plea, a desperate hope.

He had to get her out of there. Had to save her and the others. But how?

As Zephyr raised their joined hands high, the crowd's roar reaching a crescendo in a deafening cacophony of joy and madness, Hayden knew one thing for certain.

He had to end this, or die trying.

And soon.

CHAPTER 21

"Thank you, Brother Sam, for joining us," Zephyr said, his voice rich with approval. The roar of the crowd still rang in Hayden's ears as Zephyr released his hand. "You may return to the others now."

Hayden glanced at Kady one last time, her eyes wide and pleading above the mask that covered her mouth. He wanted nothing more than to rush to her, to gather her and the other children up and flee this madness. But he couldn't. Not yet. He had to be smart about this.

With a final nod to Zephyr, he descended the steps, the crowd parting before him as he returned to his place among the ranks. Joshua and Lacey grinned at him, their faces alight with fervor and excitement.

Zephyr continued speaking, his voice rising above the murmurs of the crowd. "Tomorrow, my children, we begin our march towards destiny. All but a few units will head out at dawn, setting forth to find our sleeping queen and bring about the glorious Rebirth!"

Another cheer went up, the Rebirthers' devotion palpable. Hayden joined in, raising his fist and shouting along with the rest, though he could no longer fake his zeal.

"Now, go and rest," Zephyr commanded. "Gather your strength, for the journey ahead will test us all. But we will not falter, will not fail. The Rebirth is at hand!"

With those final words, he dismissed them. The crowd began to disperse, the Rebirthers talking excitedly amongst themselves as they headed back to their barracks.

Hayden lingered, watching Steel lead Kady back inside the main building, the other children herded behind them by more red-armored disciples. His heart clenched at the sight of their small, frightened faces, some dragging their feet, others stumbling and unsure.

He had to get them out. Had to stop this insanity before it was too late.

Turning, he followed Joshua and Lacey back to their barracks, the two chattering non-stop about the upcoming march.

"Can you believe it, Sam?" Joshua said, his eyes shining. "We're going to be a part of history! The Rebirth of the new world...it's really happening!"

Lacey nodded eagerly. "And with the One to guide us to the queen, it's only a matter of time. Oh, I can hardly wait!"

Hayden forced a smile, making the appropriate noises of agreement, while inside, he had continued working on a desperate plan. There was only one way forward that he could see, and it was risky as all hell.

Back in the barracks, he lay on his cot, staring up at the dark ceiling as the other Rebirthers settled in around him. He could hear their breathing, the rustle of their blankets, the occasional whispered conversation. But he was a million miles away, his thoughts consumed by Kady and the others, by the terrible fate that awaited them if he failed.

Hours passed, the night deepening around him. Gradually, the sounds of the barracks faded away as the Rebirthers succumbed to sleep one by one. Hayden remained awake, every nerve tense and thrumming as he waited.

Finally, when he was certain that most of the compound was asleep, he rose silently from his cot and padded barefoot out of the room. Pausing in the hallway to listen for any movement, all was still and quiet.

He exited the barracks, keeping close to the walls to avoid the guards' attention on the watchtowers and near the gates. Other than the guards, the courtyard was empty.

Hayden crossed quickly to the main building. Instead of ascending the front steps, he circled to the side, searching for another way in.

"Kady," he thought desperately, reaching out with his mind. "Where are you? Can you hear me?" But there was no response, no whisper of her presence at the edge of his consciousness. He was on his own.

Gritting his teeth, he approached a window and tested the frame. It was old, the wood warped and ill-fitting. He removed his shirt and wrapped it around his hand, and with a swift, decisive movement, he broke the glass as quietly as possible.

He remained in place, waiting for an alarm to sound or a guard to either walk into the room or come around the corner to check on the noise. After a few minutes passed without any sign of trouble, he reached through to unlatch the window from the inside.

He climbed into what appeared to be an office, filled with a strange assortment of trife-related objects—bones and claws, scraps of leathery hide—all displayed like macabre trophies. The centerpiece was a complete trife skeleton hanging from the ceiling by wires, its elongated skull grinning down at him in the gloom.

Hayden suppressed a shudder, moving quickly to the door. He opened it a crack, peering out into the corridor. As luck would have it, a guard was just outside, staring back at him in surprise. He didn't hesitate. In a single, fluid motion, he drew his microspear and lunged, the needle-fine point punching through the guard's armored chest before he could make a sound. The man dropped like a stone, his weapon clattering to the floor.

Dragging the body back into the office, Hayden quickly stripped off the man's armor and robes, donning them over his clothes. The breathing mask and canister came last, and he turned the canister off rather than inhale the Clear.

He started his search in the corridor, checking rooms as he went. At one point, the building seemed to have been some kind of museum, but its exhibits were now ransacked and half-destroyed. He passed shattered display cases, toppled statues, and torn and faded informational plaques.

He encountered another guard, but his disguise held. The man nodded to him, muttering something about the glory of the Rebirth as he passed, his eyes alight with the same fervor that gripped all the Rebirthers.

Hayden returned the nod, his skin crawling beneath the robes. He bypassed a cracked open door marked with Zephyr's name, catching a glimpse of an empty office through the gap. A large satellite map of the wilds was spread out on the desk. Where had the cult leader gotten such a thing? And where was the man himself?

Questions for later. He had to focus on finding Kady.

Reaching a junction near the middle of the building, a sidelong glance to the right revealed a set of double doors—the mess hall—flanked by two red-armored disciples. They stood at rigid attention, plasma rifles held across their chests.

The children had to be inside.

"Hail the Reborn," he said to the guards, pitching his voice low to disguise it. "Glory to Zephyr."

"Glory to Zephyr," they echoed, relaxing slightly.

"Such an exciting night, isn't it?" Hayden asked.

"It is," the guard on his left agreed. "Everything we've worked so hard for is finally coming to fruition. The world will be remade as it was intended."

Hayden stepped closer as if to continue the conversation. Then, in a blur of motion, he lashed out with the microspear, catching both men in the chest before they could react. They dropped soundlessly, their rifles hitting the floor with muffled thumps.

Quickly, pushing through the doors, Hayden found himself in a large room filled with long tables and benches. And there, seated at one of the tables in the corner, were the children from the Greens.

All except Kady.

Hayden hurried over to them. They cringed back, eyes wide with fear until he pulled off the breathing mask.

"Sheriff!" the oldest child, Charlie, whispered excitedly. "I knew you would come."

Hayden put his finger to his lips to keep them quiet. "I'm going to get you out of here. Where's Kady?"

"She never came back after the gathering," Charlie replied. "Their leader, Zephyr. I think he still has her somewhere."

Hayden's gut clenched. He had to find her, and fast.

He turned to the window, the glass reflecting the room behind him. "I'm going to find Kady," he said, "and then I'm going to get the APC and bring it around to this window. I need you all to be ready to climb out and get into the vehicle as quickly as you can." The commotion would no doubt draw the guards' attention, but if he could get the APC out of the gates and across the trestle bridge, he was sure he could collapse the bridge and buy them enough time to get far away from this place.

"We'll be ready, Sheriff," Charlie said. "I'll make sure of it."

Hayden clasped the boy's shoulder. "I know you will, son."

He turned to leave, to begin his desperate search, but froze as the mess hall doors swung open. Sergeant Steel stepped through, flanked by Joshua, Lacey, and a half-dozen other Rebirthers, their plasma rifles leveled at Hayden's chest.

Steel's eyes glittered with a cold, triumphant light as he took in the scene. "Going somewhere, Sheriff Duke?"

CHAPTER 22

"And here I thought you wanted to be a part of the Rebirth," Steel continued, his voice a mocking drawl. "Looks like you're nothing but a dirty lie, just like the old world you cling to."

Hayden glared at Steel. He had feared someone in the crowd might recognize him, and apparently, they had. Unless Zephyr had some other means to figure out who he was. He had forced Kady to contact the trife queen. Had he forced her to reveal him, too?

Either way, the jig was up, his true identity revealed. There would be no more pretense, no more hiding in plain sight. It was now or never.

"You caught me," he said, his voice steady despite the tension thrumming through his body. "But then, I suppose that was inevitable. You're a sharp one, Steel."

The Sergeant's eyes narrowed behind his mask, his posture tense and ready for action. "I knew there was something off about you from the moment you stepped into the compound," he growled. "You defeated Lion way too easily. And now here you are, trying to steal away with our future. Not that I'm surprised."

He gestured to the children huddled behind Hayden, their faces pale and frightened in the dim light. Joshua and Lacey flanked Steel, plasma rifles at the ready, while the other Rebirthers fanned out, cutting off any avenue of escape.

Hayden's hand went to the armor's pocket. He rested it on the comforting presence of the microspear, his gaze flicking to the window. He gauged the distance, calculating the odds. It was a long shot, but it was his only shot.

"I'll give you this, Steel," he said, his tone almost conversational. "You and Zephyr have built quite the little empire here. Got yourself a nice army of drug-addled fanatics, ready to die for your cause. You must be real proud of yourself."

Steel's lips twisted in a sneer. "Our cause, Duke. All of us. The cause of the Rebirth. You can't stand in the way of destiny. It will happen whether you like it or not."

"The only thing you're birthing is fear and death," Hayden snapped. "You're chasing a fever dream, a madman's fantasy. The trife are only the tip of a very large iceberg. Believe me, you don't want to see what's underneath. If you follow through with this, even the strong won't be safe. Even you won't be safe. You're leading these people to their doom."

"Liar!" Joshua snarled, his finger tightening on his trigger. "You're the one who doomed us! You took away our purpose, our future! But Zephyr showed us the truth. Showed us the way back to glory!"

Hayden shook his head, genuine pity mingling with his anger. "He's blinded you, kid. You and all the rest. But it's not too late. You don't have to do this. You can still walk away."

The young Rebirther's resolve seemed to waver for a moment, his eyes darting to Steel with uncertainty. But Lacey stepped forward, her voice ringing with zealous conviction.

"We are the Reborn!" she cried. "We will not be swayed by your lies, Sheriff. The prophecy will be fulfilled, and you will be nothing but dust beneath our feet!"

Steel nodded, satisfaction glinting in his eyes. "Well said, Sister Lacey." He glared smugly at Hayden. "Do you think we don't know what else is out there? You're wrong. The children…" he pointed to them, "…are the key to humankind's new beginning. Children of Grimmel, the Relyeh know them as their own. The trife won't harm them, or any of their companions or future offspring. As for you, Sheriff…your road ends here." He raised his plasma rifle, the muzzle aimed squarely at Hayden's chest. "Any last words?"

Hayden smiled. "Just five," he said. "Charlie…get them out now!"

With that, he moved, hurling himself sideways just as Steel's rifle spat blue fire. The plasma bolt sizzled past Hayden's ear, close enough for him to smell the ozone, but he was already on top of one of the Rebirthers, and a microspear jabbed into his chest.

Chaos erupted as the children scattered. Charlie desperately tried but without much success to herd them towards the window. The Rebirthers shouted, trying to grab them, but Hayden was among them like a whirlwind, the microspear flashing in the light.

Two more went down before they knew what hit them, the microspear stretching its fibrous tendrils to their hearts and dropping them in their tracks. Joshua tried to bring his rifle to bear, but Hayden was inside his guard, the spear punching through armor and flesh with sickening ease. He hated to kill the kid, but he didn't have a choice. It was either the Rebirthers or the whole world.

Lacey screamed, firing wildly, the plasma bolts stitching across the walls, threatening to hit the fleeing children. Hayden dove and rolled, feeling the heat of the bolts' passage. Then he came up behind her, one arm snaking around her throat, the other driving the spear up under her ribs.

She went limp in his grasp, life fading from her eyes, and Hayden let her fall, already turning to face the last threat.

Steel.

He stood in the doorway, rifle leveled, his face a mask of rage. "You bastard," he snarled. "I'll skin you alive for this!"

Hayden's smile never wavered. "You're welcome to try."

He lunged, ducking low, the plasma bolt hissing over his head. His shoulder caught Steel in the gut, driving the air from the Sergeant's lungs, and they both went down in a tangle of limbs.

The rifle skittered away, and then it was down to fists, knees and elbows—a brutal, no-holds-barred brawl. Steel was strong, the Clear lending him unnatural strength and vigor, but Hayden was relentless, giving as good as he got, his own enhanced body absorbing the punishment. They rolled across the floor, grappling, blood spattering the tiles. Hayden's heart fell as the microspear thumped on the tile. He tried to reach for it as it tumbled away, and Steel took the opportunity to pound his midsection. Hayden grunted as his fingers grazed the spear, managing only to stop its roll. His fingers slipped off it as a rib cracked under Steel's fist. He tasted copper as it pierced his lung, but he didn't let up, didn't give an inch.

Steel's hands found his throat, squeezing, crushing. Spots danced before Hayden's eyes. Hayden reached again for the spear, muscles stretching, straining until his fingers closed around the hilt. With a final burst of strength, he drove the weapon into Steel's chest. The Sergeant convulsed, eyes wide with shock, and then he went still, slumping to the side.

Hayden lay there momentarily, gasping for air, his body one giant ache. But there was no time to rest, no time to recover. The sounds of shouting echoed from outside, the compound waking and rushing into the fracas.

He staggered to his feet, snatching up Steel's fallen plasma rifle. "Charlie!" he called, his voice ragged. "The window! Go!

Get into the APC. There's a control panel on the back to open it. Wait there for me! I'll cover you."

"I got it!" he cried, grabbing the hands of the two littlest children and lifting them, one at a time, through the window to a girl waiting outside, before scrambling through himself.

Hayden stumbled over to the window, peering out into the courtyard. It was pandemonium. Rebirthers ran to and fro, roused from their sleep, kits hastily donned. The guards had abandoned their posts, rushing toward the building.

Hayden leaned out, sending a hail of plasma into their midst. Shocked cries rose into the night as bodies tumbled, the superheated bolts burning through flesh and bone. Once, he'd had a rule about shooting an unarmed man. But he'd been forced to break it to kill a copy of the woman he loved, and after that, the belief had seemed so antiquated. The eager naïveté of someone who wanted morality to equal justice.

Sometimes, justice had to be enough.

He didn't stop shooting, pouring on the fire, giving the kids as much cover and time as he could.

Suddenly, Charlie appeared out of the darkness, a rifle in his hands. "C'mon, Sheriff! Let's go! I'll cover you," he shouted over the din as he knelt beside the window.

"Go!" He grabbed the boy under his arm and tugged him up. "I'll find another way!" Shoving him into action, Hayden sent a few more bolts flying out toward the APC before turning back to the room and sweeping it for any stragglers. It was clear.

He allowed himself a moment of satisfaction. The children were in the APC, reckoning that was the safest place for them since the Rebirthers didn't want to harm them. Now, he just had to find Kady, deal with Zephyr and the rest of his fanatics, and escape with the kids.

Simple.

Shaking his head at his own dark humor, Hayden checked

the charge on the plasma rifle before cautiously approaching the door leading back out into the hallway. The initial shock and confusion had faded as the Rebirthers regrouped. He needed to move. Fast.

He stepped out into the hallway, rifle at the ready, senses straining. No one was in sight, but he could hear the pound of booted feet drawing closer from the other end of the building. He turned away from the sound, sprinting toward the main foyer. The big double doors stood ajar, and beyond them...

Rebirthers.

At least a dozen were fanned out in a semicircle, weapons trained on the entrance. No way he was getting through there without being turned into Swiss cheese.

Hayden sprinted past them like a bolt, the disciples crying out when they spotted him. Plasma bolts chewed up the wall at his back, and he could hear some Rebirthers following. Reaching the trife room, he slammed the door shut and dived to the floor and crawled toward the window as a hail of plasma bolts burned through the wood. One hit him in the back, but thankfully, the bolts couldn't penetrate the door and the armor he'd taken from the guard.

Reaching the window, he looked out, finding the immediate area clear. Behind him, as he threw a leg over the sill, the door slammed open, and another bolt slammed into his back, lighting his robe on fire. It flamed up around Hayden as he threw himself out of the window, rolling on the dewy grass to extinguish flames.

He came to his feet, ready to circle the building and make a break for the APC, when an all too familiar voice echoed through the compound. Zephyr.

"Brothers! Sisters! Be at ease! The Sheriff may have interrupted our much needed slumber, but he has not won the day. No, my flock, he has only hastened his own demise!" A ragged cheer rose from the assembled zealots, quickly silenced as Zephyr continued. "He has forgotten the most important piece. The key to the prophecy itself! Behold!"

Hayden moved to the corner of the building to peer out toward the courtyard, his blood turning to ice. The cult leader stood in the center of the crowd of white robes, his features shadowed by the blazing torches his zealots held to ward off the darkness. With one arm wrapped around Kady, he clutched her tightly to him. Her mouth was taped over, her hands tied behind her back. Her face was streaked with tears.

"The One!" Zephyr cried. "She who will lead us to the Queen! She who will usher in the new age! And now, she will serve a greater purpose." He leaned down, his voice lowering to a purr that carried to Hayden's ear. "Isn't that right, child? You're going to bring the Sheriff to us. Bring him to his knees, where he belongs."

Kady shook her head mutely, her eyes wide with terror. Zephyr only smiled.

"Oh, but you will. You have no choice. For he will come for you, as surely as the sun rises. His love for you will be his undoing. And when he lies broken at my feet, then, my dear...then you will show me the way. And the Rebirth will be at hand."

The crowd roared deafeningly, a tidal wave of fanatical devotion. They stamped and howled, their fever pitch rising with every word from their prophet's lips.

And through it all, Hayden could only watch, helpless, trapped behind the bars of his own cage. Despair rose like bile in his throat, threatening to choke him, but even as it did, a cold, unstoppable rage flared to life in his chest. A bottomless well of fury and determination, the same fire that had driven him across a ruined world through horrors untold, all for the sake of a promise. A vow made in love and sealed in blood.

"Zephyr!" he shouted, stepping out from behind the

building. Hundreds of rifles turned on him in an instant. A word from their leader and his life would be snuffed out.

But he already knew Zephyr wouldn't end it that way. The man was too much into theatrics to gun him down without putting on a show for his followers.

As expected, instead of giving the order to kill him, Zephyr began to clap.

CHAPTER 23

Zephyr's slow clap echoed through the compound, silencing the Rebirthers' clamor and quickly becoming the only sound in the Fort. Hayden walked forward, his steps steady and purposeful, even as hundreds of plasma rifles tracked his every move. The air crackled with tension, the crowd's blood-lust palpable.

"Well done, Sheriff," Zephyr called out, his voice dripping with mock admiration. "Truly, a valiant effort. Sneaking into our midst, disguised as one of our own. Striking down poor Sergeant Steel and his team. And very nearly absconding with our precious charges. An effort worthy of your reputation, though I'm sure at least some of it has been exaggerated to nearly comical levels."

He tightened his grip on Kady, the girl wincing as his fingers dug into her shoulder. Hayden's jaw clenched at the sight, his hands tightening on his rifle.

"But alas," Zephyr continued, "you seem to have forgotten one crucial detail. The most important piece of the puzzle. Our dear little Kady here, the key to the Rebirth itself. And now, your ill-conceived rescue attempt has only sealed your fate, and hers."

Hayden stopped, staring up at Zephyr with cold fury in his eyes. "Let her go, Zephyr," he growled. "This is between you and me. Leave the children out of it."

Zephyr laughed, the sound harsh and grating. "Oh, I think not, Sheriff. You see, the children are everything. They are the future, the very lifeblood of the new world to come. And Kady, sweet Kady, she is the lynchpin. She will guide us to our destiny, to the glorious Rebirth!"

The crowd roared their approval, playing right into his theatrics. Hayden shook his head, disgust mingling with his anger.

"You're insane," he spat. "You're chasing a nightmare, Zephyr. The trife, the Relyeh, all of it...it's death incarnate. You wake that queen, you unleash that horror back on the world, and there won't be a Rebirth. There will only be squalor and fear."

Zephyr's eyes glittered with a fanatic light. "You lack vision, Sheriff. You always have. You cling to the old ways, the old world, not realizing it's already dead. We are the inheritors now, the chosen few who will reshape the very fabric of the world. And you...you're a relic. An obstacle to be removed."

Hayden's lips twisted into a grim smirk. "Is that so? Then why don't you remove me yourself? Just you and me, Zephyr. No guns, no tricks. Let's see who the real relic is."

For a moment, Zephyr looked taken aback. Then he threw back his head and laughed, long and loud.

"Do you take me for a fool, Sheriff? Even with the power of the Clear flowing through my veins, I'm not so deluded as to think I could best you in single combat. No, your end will not be so quick, so clean."

He leaned forward, his eyes boring into Hayden's. "You see, I have a far better fate in mind for you. You, who have been such a thorn in our sides, will bear witness to the dawning of the new age. You will watch as we awaken the queen, as we unleash the Rebirth upon the world. And when the queen begins her reproduction, when the first of the trife set out into the world, then you will know that you failed. That all your struggles, all your sacrifices, were for nothing."

Zephyr straightened, his voice rising to a fever pitch. "The Sheriff will live to see his precious world crumble! Take him!"

The Rebirthers surged forward as one, their plasma rifles raised, savage glee lighting their faces.

Hayden watched them come, resigned, letting his weapon hang slack at his side. By his reckoning, he could take down perhaps a dozen of them before they overwhelmed him through sheer numbers. But to what end? He was hopelessly outnumbered, and even if, by some miracle, he fought his way free, Zephyr still had Kady. The cult leader had masterfully played his hand, using the girl as shield and bait.

No, the only path forward was to bide his time, to let himself be taken, and to pray that an opportunity would present itself. At least then, he would be close to Kady and the other children. If the fates were kind, he could still protect them and find a way to get them to safety.

The first of the Rebirthers reached him. Rough hands seized his arms, wrenching them behind his back. He didn't resist as they forced him to his knees.

"Look upon your savior now!" Zephyr crowed to the assembled horde. "See how the mighty Sheriff kneels before us! See how—"

The rest of his words were lost in a sudden, deafening roar. The ground shook beneath Hayden's feet, and for a moment he thought it was an earthquake. Then flashes lit up the dark sky, blinding pulses pushing through the makeshift walls at the edge of the compound, followed immediately by gouts of flame as the stacked wrecks and metal exploded inward, lifted and torn by whatever had hit them.

Rockets.

More streaked overhead, leaving trails of smoke as they

slammed into the compound's barracks with thunderous impact. Masonry crumbled, metal shrieked and buckled, and Rebirthers suddenly scattered like frightened rats.

Hayden felt the hands holding him slacken as his captors instinctively ducked, their attention ripped away by the unexpected assault. He wasted no time taking advantage of the distraction.

Wrenching free, he drove an elbow back into the throat of the Rebirther behind him. The man gurgled and collapsed, his windpipe crushed. Hayden was already moving, snatching up his fallen plasma rifle to spray bolts into the confused crowd.

Zephyr's voice rose above the clamor, shrill with rage and fear. "To arms! Defend the compound! Defend the cause!"

But his cries were half-drowned by a new sound, a rising thunder that sent chills down Hayden's spine.

Engines. A lot of them. Roaring closer by the second.

He swiveled toward the ruined gates just as the first motorcycle burst through, its rider crouched low over the handlebars, a plasma rifle clinging to a mount to make it easy to fire with one hand. More bikes followed close behind, some sporting sidecars from which armored soldiers fired with ruthless precision.

Close on their heels came a phalanx of modboxes, heavy machine guns roaring from their turrets. The modified cars smashed through the Rebirthers' scrambling defenses, trampling fighters beneath their armored bulk.

Hayden's heart soared. Reinforcements. It seemed impossible, but someone had come to his aid. He had a pretty good idea who. A moment later, he found her standing tall in one of the sidecars, her short blonde hair whipping in the wind, a fierce, almost savage joy on her face as she directed the unfolding carnage.

Tempest. The leader of Union.

The Rebirthers reacted with commendable speed, their

initial shock giving way to the iron discipline instilled by their zealotry and augmented by the Clear. They rallied quickly, taking up defensive positions and returning fire with a ferocity born of fanatical devotion.

Plasma bolts crisscrossed the compound, searing the air and leaving glowing trails in their wake. Modboxes shuddered as their armor drank the barrage, their gun turrets swiveling to spit deadly replies. Rebirthers fell like dominoes.

But they gave as good as they got. Rocket-propelled grenades streaked from launchers, slamming into the attacking vehicles with devastating force. Two bikes cartwheeled through the air, trailing fire, their riders burning effigies. A modbox shuddered to a halt, its front end a twisted wreck, smoke gushing from rents in its hull.

The battle quickly devolved into a savage, chaotic melee. Hayden threw himself into the thick of it, plasma rifle growing hot in his grip. He blasted two Rebirthers rushing him, then pivoted to drop three more with precise shots to the head.

Out of the corner of his eye, he saw Tempest leap from her sidecar, rolling to her feet with fluid grace. Her plasma rifle spat a constant stream of death as she charged fearlessly into the thick of the enemy, teeth bared in a feral snarl.

A rocket streaked past Hayden's head, close enough to singe his hair. He dove behind the burnt-out husk of a modbox, sharing cover with a Union soldier bleeding from a dozen wounds. The man grinned at him manically, blood-flecked teeth shockingly white against his soot-smeared face. Hayden recognized him as the barkeep.

"It's an honor, Sheriff," he rasped before popping up to unleash a long burst from his rifle.

Hayden didn't reply, too busy putting plasma bolts through the bodies of the Rebirthers trying to flank their position. The cultists charged heedless of losses, firing from the hip, screaming incoherent battle cries. They fell in droves, but always more came, a tide of white-robed bodies that never seemed to slacken.

And through it all, a single, overriding thought pounded in Hayden's skull.

Kady. He had to reach Kady.

He vaulted over the wreckage, sprinting across the bullet-swept ground. A Rebirther rose up before him, swinging a baseball bat with unnatural strength and speed. Hayden barely ducked the swipe of it before smashing the butt of his rifle into the man's face. He reversed the weapon in a lightning motion and put a bolt through the batter's chest before he could scream.

Ahead, Zephyr's mob of personal guards was thinning, forced to split their attention between Hayden and the greater battle raging around them. The cult leader himself was using the confusion to make a break for the hoverbikes, Kady slung over his shoulder like a sack of grain.

Hayden redoubled his efforts, plasma bolts cutting down the foes in his path. But there were too many, and he was just one man. He saw Zephyr swing astride a bike, Kady crying out in terror as she was roughly deposited on the seat behind him and forced to hang onto him.

The bike's engine flared to life, repulsors glowing a baleful blue. It shot forward, the downdraft of its passage flattening the grass around it. Zephyr's elite guard and dozens of others took off after him, surrendering the compound for their mistaken greater good.

Despair and fury warred in Hayden's heart as he watched them vanish through the remains of the compound's entrance, Kady's small form, clinging to Zephyr for dear life, vanishing into the night's embrace.

Around him, the battle still raged, but the tide had undeniably turned. The remaining Rebirthers fought with the desperate ferocity of cornered beasts, but they were outmatched and overwhelmed by the firepower the former

War Dog had brought to bear. Firepower Hayden could hardly believe she possessed. Three more disciples succumbed for every one of Tempest's soldiers that fell.

Tempest herself was a maelstrom of destruction, her rifle spitting a ceaseless stream of death. She waded through the chaos like an avenging angel, flanked by her guards from the saloon, dressed in bulky Marine combat armor last worn over two centuries earlier.

And yet, it wasn't all a one-sided slaughter. Here and there, knots of Rebirthers held out, exacting a savage toll on their attackers. A modbox belched flames as a rocket found its ammo store, setting off a rippling series of explosions. Three more bikes careened into each other, a tangle of screeching metal and howling riders that skidded across the courtyard in a shower of sparks.

For long minutes that felt like hours, the fighting raged on unabated. The compound echoed with the unceasing thudding of gunfire, the screams of the maimed and dying, thick smoke choking the air.

And then, as suddenly as it had begun, it was over. The last few surviving Rebirthers threw down their weapons, hands raised in surrender. Union soldiers swarmed over them, roughly herding them together to keep them surrounded.

Hayden staggered through the sudden, eerie calm, his ears ringing, his skin caked with blood and grime. He'd been in plenty of fights before, but this had to be one of the most bloody and violent displays he'd ever witnessed. He reached Tempest's side, finding her leaning heavily against the flank of a battered modbox, her face ashen beneath the mask of soot and sweat.

"Zephyr got away," he rasped, the words bitter on his tongue. "With Kady."

Tempest turned to him, her eyes hard. "Damn it. I'm sorry, Sheriff. I tried."

Hayden looked around at the devastation, the bodies strewn like broken dolls, the writhing piles of wounded. The compound was a charnel house, a scene from a nightmare. But amid it all, he saw signs of life, of hope. The rescued children stood near the APC, dirty and frightened but alive. Charlie caught his eye, his young face displaying both exhaustion and relief.

"You sure did," Hayden replied. "I've never seen anything like this. If nothing else, we've weakened them considerably." He paused, raising a curious eyebrow. "But what are you doing here? You never gave me any indication you intended to provide more than just supplies."

Tempest met his gaze steadily. "You know I owed these bastards for the 36th. But I also have an annoying soft spot for children, and for men who are willing to go solo against odds like these to protect them."

Hayden smiled. "Well, I'm glad you came. Thank you, Tempest." He paused. "Just to be clear, I can't give you what you might be looking for."

"I know," she replied. "You lost someone you loved, and you'll never stop loving her. I can see that in your eyes. I have a soft spot for that, too." She grinned. "I imagine you don't want to linger here too long while Zephyr is getting further and further away."

"Pozz," Hayden agreed. "But I need to get the other children back to the Greens, too."

"You can let me worry about protecting the kids. I have someone who can drive the APC, and I know where the Greens is."

"You already helped me out here, I can't ask you to—"

"Don't be ridiculous, Sheriff. I came here to see this through."

"Well, then, thank you again."

Tempest scanned her group, whistling to one of the riders on a motorcycle with a sidecar. "Corporal, come here."

He hopped off the bike, approaching Tempest and saluting. "Ma'am?"

"Find Colonel Maven. Tell him I want all the Rebirthers rounded up and set in a line for execution. I—"

"No," Hayden interrupted. "No more killing."

"Sheriff, these people are dangerous," Tempest argued.

"Not for long. Once Zephyr is gone, once the Rebirth fails, they'll lose their programming real quick. You can hold them in the museum until then. Please."

Tempest's face twisted while she considered his request. Finally, she nodded. "Tell Colonel Maven to hold the Rebirthers in the main building. I want the injured sent back to Union if they're well enough to travel."

"I can help you out with your wounded," Hayden interjected, garnering her attention. "I buried my saddlebags in a cemetery just past the train trestle," Hayden explained. "Between a tree and the grave of a man named Paul Getty. There are medi-patches in it that will help heal the wounded."

"Pass that on to Colonel Maven as well," Tempest told the corporal. "He's also to maintain and defend this compound until two weeks passes or I come back."

"Yes, ma'am," the corporal replied.

"And if Maven is dead, find whoever is next in command who's still standing."

"Yes, ma'am."

Hayden waited until the corporal saluted Tempest and took off at a dead run to carry out her orders. "Get back from where?" he asked her. "Where are you going?"

She raised an eyebrow. "Seriously?" She crossed to the motorcycle and dropped into the sidecar. She patted the motorcycle's seat. " Let's ride."

CHAPTER 24

The stench of plasma-scorched flesh and smoldering metal hung thick in the compound's courtyard, the taste of death and destruction clinging to the back of Hayden's throat. Around him, survivors had already begun organizing triage and cleanup. The wounded were being assessed and brought for treatment while the dead were being stacked in the center of the courtyard for burial.

Hayden turned away, his jaw clenching. There would be time to mourn them later. Right now, every second counted. Zephyr had a head start, and the longer they delayed, the colder the trail would grow.

"Sheriff, are we going, or what?" Tempest asked impatiently from the motorcycle's sidecar.

He glanced at her, ready to affirm the question, when a sudden thought arrested him. The map. The one he'd glimpsed in Zephyr's office during his infiltration. With no idea which way the Rebirthers might have gone now, it might offer some kind of clue. An overview of their surroundings, if nothing else.

"Hold up a minute," he replied. "There's something I need to check."

Without waiting for a reply, he jogged back into the main building, retracing his steps to Zephyr's office. The room was just as he'd left it, the map still sitting on the desk. Hayden snatched it up, his eyes immediately drawn to a bold red circle inscribed on its surface that he hadn't noticed earlier.

The circle was west of their current position, encompassing a sizable swath of territory. Mountains, valleys, sprawling wilderness. He had no proof, but every instinct screamed that this was an estimated location for the trife queen's resting place.

He folded the map, his mind already spinning with possibilities and angles for catching up to Zephyr as he strode out, purpose lending fresh urgency to his steps.

When he got back to the bike, Tempest looked impatient enough to chew nails. "Whatever that is, I hope it's important enough to delay our departure."

"It is." Hayden said, spreading the map out on the seat of the bike. He jabbed a finger at the ominous red circle. "I think this is where Zephyr's heading. Where he thinks he'll find the trife queen."

"Trife queen?" Tempest asked, her face paling as she unfolded her arms. "Is that what this is all about?"

"Pozz. Zephyr needed Kady to help him locate the queen. He's hoping to wake it up."

"That's bad."

"Very bad. Just the fact that there's a queen out there, asleep or not, is stomach churning."

"Now, I'm even more glad I came to rescue you." She offered a weak grin before leaning in on the map, her eyes narrowing as she took in the details. "That's a lot of ground to cover," she said. "And not much to go on."

"It's more than we had a minute ago," Hayden countered. "And it makes sense. Remember what Zephyr said about Kady being the key to finding the queen? I'd bet my last bullet that she can sense the queen, but can't pinpoint her." He straightened, his gaze locking with Tempest's. "So that's where we're headed. West. As fast as these wheels can carry us."

Tempest nodded, grim determination settling over her features. "Let's ride, then. We're already nearly half an hour behind them."

Hayden mounted up, engine growling to life as he started up the bike. He wished he could have enjoyed it more. He preferred the rumble and vibration of an engine to the whine of repulsors any day. He cast one last look over the compound, the scene of so much violence and death, now eerily still in the predawn gloom.

Then he gunned the engine, and they roared through the shattered gates, leaving the carnage behind, chasing the fading starlight to the west.

Hayden's mind churned as he rode, trying to plot the Rebirthers' likely course. The hoverbikes were a key advantage, allowing the battle's survivors to strike out over any terrain, heedless of obstacles that would otherwise slow them down or force them to backtrack. Assuming they'd been fully charged before the attack, they likely had a range of around three hundred miles. Probably just about enough to reach the far side of the red circle by his quick estimate.

Ahead, the road split, one fork veering north, the other continuing west. Hayden slowed, frowning. The westward route would take them most directly toward the search area marked on the map. But there was a problem.

"River up ahead," he called out over the thrum of engines. "Looks like the bridge is out." He could see the expanse in the distance, the bridge plates little more than a jumbled pile of rubble sticking up out of the water.

"Not a problem for the hoverbikes," Tempest said. "Do you see another bridge in either direction?"

"Neg," Hayden replied, scanning as far as he could see. "If there is, it's some ways away."

"What do you suggest?"

"We'll have to backtrack to the trestle. Means we'll lose even more time, but we don't have a choice. We double back, cross at the trestle, then make up the lost ground as best we can."

The motorcycle kicked up a rooster tail of dust as he turned to the east and cracked the throttle almost wide open. Locating the train tracks, he retraced the path to the trestle with a renewed sense of urgency. Every minute lost was another minute for Zephyr to widen the gap between them as he drew closer to his nightmare goal.

The train trestle came into view in no time, its rusted girders and weathered timbers spanning the width of the river far below. Rather than head straight for it, Hayden veered off to the cemetery, guiding the bike to where he had left his belongings.

"What are we doing here?" Tempest asked as he stopped the motorcycle and jumped off.

"Figured since we had to come back this way, I would grab my gear."

"Do we have time for this?"

"We're already going to be a couple hours behind. A few minutes more won't hurt, but it could help."

Tempest climbed out of the sidecar to follow him. It didn't take long for him to locate Paul Getty's grave. Too little time had passed for the dirt he'd disturbed to resettle. He knelt beside the loose earth, his armored fingers scrabbling in the dirt until they closed around the strap of his buried saddlebag.

He hauled it free, shook the dirt off, and pawed through its contents. His hand closed around the familiar grips of his revolvers, the cool metal a comforting weight. He laid them on the grass, quickly pulling off his combat armor.

"Are you crazy?" Tempest asked.

"If I'm going to beat Zephyr and his guards, I need to be quicker than them. I can't do that wearing this."

"I saw you fighting back there. You could've fooled me."

Hayden half-smirked as he picked up his gun belt and cinched it around his waist. "Most of those Rebirthers were terrible fighters. The Clear makes them fast and strong, but it doesn't make them calm or brave. I don't know if we would have won, otherwise."

"We would have won," Tempest replied confidently.

Hayden pulled a few medi-patches out of the saddlebags, along with his note stamp. Given a choice, he didn't want to leave it to Tempest's crew. He was about to drop the bags back into the hole when the roar of an approaching engine announced a new arrival. Tempest swung her plasma rifle toward the sound, only to lower it at the sight of one of her own.

A burly man with a ruddy face and bristling beard drew to a halt next to their motorcycle by bringing the rear wheel around in a spray of loose gravel. "Boss lady," he said, giving her a smart salute.

"Grunk," she replied, saluting back. "You're here for the patches?"

"Yes, ma'am," he replied. "Colonel done says I can find them here. Didn't expect to find you here too, ma'am."

Hayden tossed the saddlebag to the man. "Take them all," he said.

The rider caught the bag, surprise and gratitude mingling on his craggy face. "Much obliged, Sheriff. Sure you don't want to keep a few, just in case?"

Hayden patted his pocket. "I've got what I need."

"Get those back to our wounded," Tempest said. "As fast as you can."

"Yes, ma'am," Grunk replied, laying the saddlebags across his gas tank. and gunning his engine before roaring back the way he'd come.

"You need a duster," Tempest said as they hurried back to their ride. "It completes the look."

"It's too warm for it," Hayden answered, looking down at it, folded in the bottom of the hole, "and sometimes it just gets in the way. I'll get another one later." If he had a later.

He scooped the dirt back into the hole and started their motorcycle. Ripping away from the cemetery, they reached the trestle in about a minute.

Uncertain if the ancient structure would hold them, Hayden twisted the throttle wide open as they approached it. The motorcycle with its sidecar and two people had to be heavier than Daisy, and he wanted to spend as little time on the dilapidated structure as possible. If it gave way, let it give way behind their wheels.

The bike hit the edge of the trestle hard enough to bounce, the front wheel threatening to skid out from under them and off the side of the bridge. Hayden held it steady, and they streaked across the bridge. The river churned below, hungry to swallow them if the structure didn't hold. It groaned beneath the weight of their passage but held fast.

Their wheels thumped back onto solid ground on the far side, and Hayden turned north, following the old train line, now a narrow dirt road. When they came to a decaying highway running east to west, he didn't bother slowing much as he turned onto it. The sidecar rose up and then bounced down as they headed west. Despite the bulk of the sidecar, the bike's smaller size allowed Hayden to navigate dozens of pot holes and rusted vehicles abandoned long ago.

"So," he began, talking loudly to overcome the noise of the engine and the wind. "You showed off some pretty impressive firepower back at the compound. Made me curious where you got the munitions."

Tempest glanced over, one eyebrow arched. "What are you implying, Sheriff?"

"Centurion plasma rifles aren't exactly easy to come by.

Neither are heavy machine guns or the kind of rockets you used to blast open the Rebirthers' walls. Even War Dogs don't generally have a stockpile of ordnance like that."

Tempest was silent for a long moment, the engine's rumble filling the void. Then, almost reluctantly: "There's a woman. A weapons dealer from Proxima. She approached the 36th a few years back, looking to establish a supply line."

Hayden's eyes narrowed. "So you know about Proxima?"

"I know they have enough firepower to do exactly what I told you I want to do, but they have for reasons unknown decided not to do it."

"I know the reasons. It's policy for them not to get involved with Earth affairs."

"Seriously?"

"Pozz. Most folks on Proxima don't know Earth still has people on it, and the ones who do couldn't care less about the humans they left behind on their original home world."

"That's sick."

"I agree. And I've told them as much. But I'm an Earther, too. I don't have much clout."

Tempest laughed. "Maybe you need to save a few more planets, first. Like theirs."

"Already did."

Her jaw dropped. "I haven't read about that one in the books."

"Max isn't subtle, but I suppose he's decided to keep quiet about Proxima. Most folks on Earth don't know there are other humans out there."

"Max? You know the author?"

Hayden laughed at the idea of Max sitting down to draw and write Sheriff comic books. "Pozz. We've been on a few adventures together. Anyways, do you know if this dealer works for the Organization or the Trust?"

"Who are they?"

"Black hats and white hats. Though their hats swap places

depending on the situation and time of day. At least in my experience with them."

"Neither, as far as I can tell. At least, she never mentioned it. Then again, she's a real secretive, paranoid type. She's never even told me her name."

"I'll tell you, it isn't easy for someone to travel to and from Earth on their own. And if General Haeri doesn't know about it, then that makes me more concerned. Anyway, what does a Centurion arms dealer want in exchange for her wares? Can't imagine she's taking payment in notes or TP."

Tempest shrugged. "There's a mine, not far from Union. Old steel mill, from back before the trife. We've been pulling ore out of there, stuff I've never seen before. Not iron. It doesn't rust, and we can't melt it down. Believe me, we tried. The dealer seems to think it's valuable."

Hayden frowned, turning this new information over in his mind. An unknown ore, rare enough to serve as currency for advanced weapons. And a mysterious benefactor, eager to arm a ramshackle militia in the middle of nowhere.

He didn't like it. It stank of hidden agendas, of schemes within schemes. "The whole thing smells bad," he said. "But then, most things having to do with Proxima do. I don't suppose I can convince you to kill the deal?"

"And cut off the arms shipments?"

"Pozz. Whatever that ore is, I promise it won't be put to good use."

"Sorry, Sheriff. I can't do that. I used half my cache helping you out, and the wilds will always be wild unless I can put my plan into action."

"I sure hope that won't be the case. People are consolidating in settlements every day, without being conquered. They just need safe, thriving areas to move to."

"I don't want to get into this with you again."

"Something for another day," Hayden agreed. "Right now, Kady's the only thing that matters."

They rode hard through the morning, stopping to gas up the bike from a tank attached to the rear of the sidecar, have a drink of water, relieve themselves, not to mention stretch the stiffness out of their joints. Of course, there was no sign of the Rebirthers anywhere along the route. And despite efforts to contact Kady, she'd remained completely silent.

Wanting to check their location, Hayden unfolded the map on the seat of the motorcycle, estimating their position by the landmarks they had passed.

"I think we're about here," he said, pointing to a spot on the map. "If I'm right, we should pass through a larger settlement within the next hour. If anyone lives there, maybe we can ask them if they're familiar with these parts." He traced the highway they traveled on with his finger. "We'll need to switch roads here…" He tapped the spot, just ahead of what appeared to have once been an airport, "…but it should be a fairly straight shot southwest from there."

"I'd say another three hours or so," Tempest agreed.

"If we assume the trife queen is dormant, hibernating, then she's likely to be underground," Hayden said. "Deep underground, in a place that's remained undisturbed for a long, long time."

"Here, maybe." His finger tapped a series of jagged lines, a small mountain range nestled in the southwest corner of the circle. "Or here." Another tap, further north. "Old mine shafts, natural caves. Places where a creature could slumber undisturbed, for decades or even centuries."

Tempest leaned in, her brow furrowed. "Even if we can narrow it down to a mine, that's still a lot of ground to cover. And we're racing against the clock."

Hayden's jaw clenched. "I know. But without more information, we're shooting blind. Our best bet is to keep moving, keep looking for signs of Zephyr's passage. I don't know if getting closer will help Kady zero in on the trife queen. And even if it does, she's a smart kid. She might try to keep

Zephyr off the mark to buy us back some time. Failing that, let's hope she reaches out to us and gives us something more to go on."

But a cold dread settled in his gut even as he said it. So far, his connection with Kady had been tenuous at best, sputtering and inconsistent. If she couldn't make contact, if Zephyr found a way to block or keep her under control...he shook his head, forcibly banishing the thought. He couldn't afford doubt, not now. He had to trust in Kady's strength and courage.

He had to trust that she would put them on the right path when the time came.

For all their sakes.

CHAPTER 25

The sun beat down on the cracked and weathered asphalt as Hayden and Tempest continued along the abandoned highway through the remains of a larger town. Rusted hulks of cars littered the roadway, and he had to slow to continually guide the motorcycle around the abandoned junkers.

His keen eyes scanned the area, alert for signs of an ambush or evidence of the Rebirthers' passing. Gaze sliding across the buildings flanking the roadway, he was surprised by the minimal damage to the structures. Most had intact walls, windows, and doors. A few had even managed to keep their paint, though it had faded a long time ago. Weeds and overgrowth surrounded the structures, but he felt as though he could trim them all back and move right in. He wouldn't have even been too surprised to find furniture in the houses.

"I don't get it," Tempest said, her voice muffled by the engine's roar. "This place is practically untouched. Why hasn't anyone tried to resettle here? There's got to be plenty of resources, maybe even some government stockpiles squirreled away."

Hayden shook his head. "Too exposed. The open plains all around, no natural barriers...it would've been easy pickings for trife swarms. And old habits die hard. Folks aren't eager to go poking around in open places like this. I don't even think many scavvies, if any, have passed through here."

Tempest grunted in acknowledgment. "That makes sense. I haven't seen many places as unprotected as this one."

Leaving the silent city behind, they traded one highway for another that curved southwest and stretched on for miles like an endless ribbon of sun-baked asphalt. Heat shimmered off the pavement, distorting the horizon into a blurry haze, the few abandoned cars left on it appearing to float on the heat waves as if the highway were a river.

Hayden's eyes continued sweeping back and forth, never focused only on the road ahead, always ready for trouble. He didn't think the Rebirthers had come this way. There would be no reason for them to stick to the highways and byways when they had hoverbikes.

But Rebirthers weren't the only threats out here.

Finally, Hayden pulled over at a lonely gas station, its windows shattered, its pumps long since run dry. He killed the engine and dismounted, once again unfolding the map across the motorcycle's seat.

"Judging by the terrain, we should be about here," he said, tapping a spot well within the boundaries of the red circle. "We're close, but we could use some help. I'm going to call out to Kady again."

He closed his eyes, reaching out with his mind, casting about for some flicker of Kady's presence. But there was only silence. A cold knot of dread tightened in his chest.

"Still nothing?" Tempest asked, seeing the look on his face.

Hayden shook his head. "Not a peep. I'm not usually one to worry, but this one has me concerned. What if we're too late? What if Zephyr's already found the queen, woken her up and set her free? She could be laying her eggs as we speak, spawning a whole new horde of nightmares."

"Hey…" Tempest laid a hand on his arm, her grip firm

and reassuring. "You know we can't think like that. We've got to stay focused, keep pushing forward. Now, assuming Kady can't guide us, then how the hell do we find this mine? That circle covers a lot of ground."

"It sure does," he replied, staring at the map. There were enough hills within the circle for a dozen mines. And of course, none of them were labeled. They could be anywhere.

"Aren't you the Sheriff?" Tempest asked. "I thought sniffing out trouble was your specialty."

Hayden knew she was trying to lighten the mood, but he was beyond responding to humor. The consequences of failure were beyond consideration. The thought that kept circling in his mind was that if they failed, if the trife returned, then Natalia's death would have been for nothing.

He didn't know if he could live with that.

"I'm sorry, Sheriff," Tempest said. "I was just trying to pick your gloomy ass up out of the dirt."

He almost smiled. "I know, and I appreciate it," he replied without looking away from the map. "But if we have to fight the trife again..." He couldn't bring himself to finish the sentence.

Tempest sighed, hands on her hips as she surveyed the vast, empty landscape around them. "So, what do we do next? Comb the hills, mile by mile, hoping we stumble across some sign of Zephyr's bunch? That could take weeks, months even. And the whole time, they're getting closer to their goal."

Hayden's eyes hardened, his jaw setting in a stubborn line. "If that's what it takes, then that's what we do. We keep searching until we find them, until Kady tells us which direction to go, or until...until it's too late to matter anymore." He looked at her, his gaze level. "I'm not giving up. I can't. Not while there's still a chance. Probably not after that, either. But I know I'm asking a lot of you, dragging you with me. The motorcycle, the gear, it's yours if you want it. No hard feelings if you'd rather cut loose, head back—"

Tempest cut him off with a sharp bark of laughter. "And miss all the fun? Not a chance in hell, Hayden. I'm in this till the end, wherever it takes us. Besides, you know I've got my own score to settle with those Rebirth bastards."

Hayden nodded, a flicker of gratitude in his eyes. He knew the value of a friend and staunch ally, especially in times like these. Returning to the map, he scanned it with renewed intensity, looking for anything that might help narrow the search.

"There," he said suddenly, jabbing a finger at the southern edge of the circle. "Judging by the satellite view, that's got to be some kind of old military base. Probably long abandoned. As far as I know, the army wasn't into mining, so unless they have a USSF lab with the queen in it under the base, we can rule that one out."

"What if they do have a USSF lab with a trife queen in it?" Tempest questioned.

"Not impossible, strange as it seems. But also not likely. If the USSF was operating here in any big capacity, we would have seen evidence."

He traced a line from the military base to a faded roadway that snaked northwest into a range of jagged hills. "I say we try this route. Skirt the base, head into the high country. Maybe get to high ground so we can see out a ways. If we're lucky, maybe we'll pick up a repulsor-created dust cloud or spot one of their outriders."

Tempest leaned in, studying the proposed path. "About as good as following your nose, but it's as good a plan as any. Let's do it."

Minutes later, they were back on the road, the motorcycle thrumming as they chased the sun westward. The landscape gradually began to change, the flat plains giving way to gently rolling hills, with steeper terrain visible in the distance.

"If we can get up on top of that hill there," he shouted at her, taking his left hand off the hand grip to point at it, "we can scan for a good fifty miles around. That'll help cut the search time a bit."

Tempest nodded when he looked over at her rather than shouting over the rumble of the engine.

Hayden turned onto a road heading directly for the mountain, gaining speed as he opened the throttle. He had just passed a dilapidated old building with a rusted water tower beside it when he spotted a little girl huddled up against one of the tower's support legs, shoulders shaking with what could only be sobs.

A little girl, alone and crying, in the middle of nowhere?

Every instinct screamed at him that it had to be some kind of trap. But he couldn't just leave her there. Couldn't take the chance that this one time, it was real. Plan for the worst and hope for the best. At least he had backup.

He slowed the motorcycle, pulling up a cautious distance from the girl. Tempest tensed beside him, raising her plasma rifle, ready to use it if need be. She felt it, too, the wrongness hanging thick in the air.

Hayden swung his leg over the bike seat. "Hayden, I don't know about this. Be careful."

He didn't acknowledge Tempest; he didn't have to. Approaching the child slowly, he held his hands at his sides to show he meant no harm. "Hey there," he called softly. "Are you alright? Are you hurt?"

The girl looked up, her tear-streaked face breaking into a timid smile. "I... I'm okay now," she sniffled. "Now that you're h-here."

The crack of a high-powered rifle split the air, and suddenly Hayden was falling, a searing lance of agony burning through his back and into his chest. He hit the ground hard, the breath driven from his lungs, hot blood already soaking through his shirtfront.

Tempest leaped from the side car, her weapon at the ready as she sprinted toward Hayden's fallen form. But before she could close half the distance, a second shot kicked up a geyser of dirt at her feet, forcing her to skid to a frantic halt.

Rough voices rose in triumph as figures emerged from the building on their flanks and from concealment behind boulders and withered trees. A motley assortment of bandits, ragged and filthy beneath the hodgepodge of armor and weapons they sported. They moved with the dangerous swagger of predators, confident in their numbers and the shock of their ambush.

The leader swaggered up to Hayden's prone form, a gap-toothed grin splitting his grizzled face as he prodded Hayden with the toe of his boot. No response. The Sheriff was out cold, maybe even dead, a widening pool of crimson staining the dirt beneath him.

Chuckling nastily, the bandit turned his eyes to Tempest, raking his gaze up and down her form with undisguised hunger. "Well, now," he drawled, "ain't this just my lucky day. Fine motorcycle, some mighty fine hardware..." His tongue darted out, licking at cracked lips. "And quite the pretty little bonus, too."

Raucous laughter erupted from the surrounding bandits, vicious and cruel. The bandit leader's eyes cut to the side, to the little girl still huddled by the water tank.

"Good job, squirt," the leader said. "Played your part real well." She sniffed, her sobs transforming into a forced smile. "Now scram before I forget what a good mood I'm in."

The girl hurried off without a backward glance, vanishing into the building on the right side of the road.

The leader turned back to Tempest, smirking as he saw her hands tense on her rifle. "Go ahead, darlin'," he sneered. "Try it. See how far you get before we pump you full of holes."

Rather than raise the rifle, Tempest dropped it. The leader, distracted by the motion, reacted way too slowly when she lunged at him, her fist crashing into his nose with a sickening crunch. The bandit reeled back. She would have pursued him with a punch to the throat, but a muzzle pressed into the side of her head, bringing her to a total standstill. Another man grabbed Tempest's arms from behind, restraining her.

The injured leader clutched his ruined nose, blood seeping between his fingers as his initial shock gave way to a look of black fury. "Oh, you're gonna regret that, girlie," he snarled, his fists balling at his sides. Stepping forward, the leader spat a gobbet of blood in the dust at Tempest's feet. "I like my fillies with some fight in 'em, but that's a line you really shouldn't have crossed."

Tempest glared defiantly back at him, still straining against the hands holding her. "You started this party, asshole," she growled. "Don't cry to me if you don't like the dance. I've got a mean right hook, but you're welcome to see my left any time you're feeling frisky."

"Gag her," the leader grunted, waving a hand. "And stick her in the sidecar. She'll learn to mind her manners soon enough."

As Tempest bucked and swore, one of the bandits bent to rummage through Hayden's saddlebags, pawing carelessly through the contents. He held up one of the medi-patches with a perplexed frown before tossing it aside. But then his eyes fell on the note stamp, and they went wide with astonished greed.

"Boss!" he called. "You need to see this!"

The leader stomped over, a dirty red bandana mopping at his still-gushing nose. He snatched the stamp from his lackey's hand, turning it over with an unholy light kindling in his eyes. "Sweet mother of sin," he breathed. "Do you know what this is?"

The other bandit shook his head in awe. "It looks like—"

"It's a Space Force stamper," the leader gloated, stroking his thumb almost lovingly over it. "The real deal," he said, stuffing the bloody bandana back into his back pocket. "All we need is paper and we can make as many notes as we could ever want. Forget taking little girls hostage, we're about to become the richest bastards in the wilds."

He slipped the stamp into his front pants pocket. "C'mon…" He swung his arm toward the sidecar. "…get that bitch loaded up!"

Tempest, bound and gagged, was roughly bundled into the motorcycle's sidecar. He mounted the motorcycle and looked over at her.

"You and me, we're gonna have some good times later." He laughed as he started the bike and jerked his chin at his men. "Alright! Let's get out of here before the local wildlife starts to circle!"

The other bandits hurried into the building, emerging moments later on horseback, the little girl riding double with one of the men. The leader tore out on the motorcycle, leaving the horses laboring in his exhaust.

With the bandits pulling out, Hayden shifted, coughing up blood as a brutal spike of pain lanced through his chest. He lifted his head with superhuman effort, straining to catch one last glimpse of Tempest. before the bike and horses vanished from sight. Hayden collapsed back, his meager strength draining from his limbs, his vision dimming.

An ordinary man would have been dead already. Even Hayden's Relyeh-perfected physiology was straining to cope with the trauma and blood loss, his flesh struggling to knit itself back together around the gaping exit wound to his chest. An involuntary shudder wracked his frame, and he tasted fresh copper on his tongue.

He could barely contain his anger and frustration despite the pain. He'd been a damn fool, stopping for the little girl. As sure as he knew his own name, he'd known it was a trap. But there was no way he could have ridden right past her. He just wasn't wired that way. Besides, he hadn't expected roadside bandits to have a high-powered sniper rifle, never mind someone competent enough to use it.

A pervasive coldness seeped into his extremities as his lifeblood continued draining away, shock setting in. He tried to rise, his hands pawing weakly at the ground, trying to claw his way forward on sheer grit and determination. His traitorous body just wouldn't respond.

The world narrowed to a blurry tunnel, darkness bleeding in at the edges, and in that endless, fading moment between heartbeats, Hayden saw them all. The faces of the fallen, of the lost. Oz and Sam, their lives snuffed out in defense of innocents. Max, laughing as usual. Natalia, the love of his life, transcending death itself. All the other nameless, numberless casualties in his long-running war for justice and peace.

Their sacrifices couldn't be in vain. He couldn't fail them, not when it mattered most. Not like this. Maybe his body was ready to die. Maybe it was hurt enough to die.

But damn it, he refused.

Lifting his head once more, his eyes landed on the medi-patch the idiot bandit had tossed aside, thinking it was worthless.

With a final reserve of will, he dragged himself to the patch. Coughing up blood, his vision dimming, he rolled over on his back, both sides of his wound burning with agony. The bullet's entrance wound would heal fast enough on its own, but the exit wound had blown a hole bigger than his fist after tearing through his innards. He was lucky the bullet hadn't hit his spine.

Ripping his shirt open, he made the ragged hole in the armored underlayer bigger over the sucking chest wound and then ripped open the medi-patch packaging. He slapped the patch over the damage and collapsed back in the dirt. Relief wasn't instant, and It wasn't a cure-all. It wouldn't replace the blood he'd lost, and he'd be in pain for days, but it was a lifeline thrown to a drowning man.

A very angry drowning man.

Still operating on willpower alone, he dragged himself up out of the dirt and started to walk, shambling in the direction the bandits had gone. Unlike hoverbikes, motorcycles and horses left a pretty obvious trail.

The bandits' lucky day?

Not anymore.

CHAPTER 26

Hayden stumbled down the dusty road, his hand clutching the medi-patch adhered to his chest. Each step sent a fresh lance of agony through his body, but he gritted his teeth and pushed on.

The bullet's exit wound was already beginning to knit itself back together. But it was a slow process. While the hole in his back had stopped bleeding, his chest wound was still oozing blood that ran in rivulets from beneath the patch. He was probably still losing about as much blood as his body was making. He needed water and something sweet to eat to help in the process. Otherwise, it would be days before he was fully healed. He knew if he could lay down and rest for just a few hours, he'd heal faster, but that would take time he didn't have. Every minute spent on finding the bandits and rescuing Tempest was another minute Kady remained in Zephyr's clutches, another minute the madman drew closer to his goal of awakening the slumbering trife queen.

The sun sank lower on the horizon, shadows lengthening across the barren landscape as Hayden doggedly followed the bandits' trail. The motorcycle's tracks cut a clear path through the dirt and scrub, flanked by the hoofprints of the outlaws' horses. They were making no attempt to hide their passage, confident in their numbers and the area's remoteness.

And in his death.

Night had fallen in earnest when Hayden finally stumbled across a small spring and a scrawny bush of wild blueberries growing beside it. He drank his fill and ate the few berries the bush offered. There were also a few stalks of clover, Zorro's favorite, that he could eat. It wasn't enough to relieve his hunger, but it relieved his thirst and gave him enough energy to carry on.

When he crested a small rise a good hour later, he spotted the telltale flicker of firelight in the distance. He dropped into a crouch, a hand pressed to the medi-patch as a fresh wave of pain seared through his chest. Moments turned into minutes as he crept closer to the fire, hoping the darkness would be sufficient cover despite the now full moon.

The bandits had made their camp in an abandoned housing development next to a nearby lake. A dozen houses, little more than shells, ringed a central cul-de-sac. The structures looked to have been picked clean long ago, their glass-less windows gaping like empty eye sockets.

The firelight came from a bonfire set in the middle of the street, around which the raucous bandits passed bottles back and forth and ripped into hunks of meat that had sizzled on metal spits jammed into the dirt. Their guns lay close at hand, but their attention was focused on their leader as he regaled them with plans for the future.

"With this here stamper, boys, we're gonna be swimming in notes!" the leader crowed, waving the precious device over his head. "No more scraping by on scraps and leavin's. We'll ride into the nearest town like kings! Gonna enjoy all the whores, booze and card games we can handle!"

A chorus of cheers greeted this proclamation. The leader grinned, his teeth flashing in the firelight. But then his expression turned sly.

"'Course, that's for tomorrow. Tonight, I got me some private entertainment to attend to." His men hooted, laughed, and egged him on. "You boys behave. I'll be back when I'm good and ready."

With that, he strode off toward one of the houses, a definite swagger in his step. Hayden's gut clenched as he watched the man vanish inside. He had no doubt Tempest was in there, helpless, at the mercy of that bastard. He had to act, and fast.

He'd just risen from his concealed position when a small shape detached itself from the shadows behind him. He spun, hand darting for his gun, only to freeze as he found himself staring into a pair of wide, frightened eyes.

It was the little girl from the ambush, the one who had played her part in luring him into the sniper's sights.

Her mouth opened to scream, and Hayden moved, clamping a hand over her mouth and bundling her into his arms. She struggled wildly, but he was far stronger. Ignoring the searing pain in his chest, he carried her away from the camp, back into the darkness of the skeletal houses.

Only when he was sure they hadn't been observed did he set her down, crouching to bring himself to her eye level. She cringed away, tears streaking her grubby face.

"Shhh, easy there," Hayden said, keeping his voice low and soothing. "I'm not gonna hurt you."

She stared at him, her lower lip trembling. "Y-you're not?"

"No. I'm not like them." He jerked his chin towards the distant fire. "I'm here to help. I'm here to stop those men from doing to someone else what they did to me."

A spark of hope kindled in her eyes. "Really?"

"Really. Now, what's your name?"

"Mac," she whispered. "It's short for Mackenzie, but nobody ever calls me that."

"Alright, Mac. I'm Hayden. Can you tell me about that man? The leader?"

She nodded jerkily, casting a fearful glance over her shoulder. "His name's Rooster. H-he's real mean."

"Is he your pa?"

Mac shook her head vehemently. "No! I was... I was just passing through with my folks. We were going east, to the Arches, to live. Rooster, he... he killed my ma and pa." Fresh tears welled, spilling down her cheeks. "Took me and everything else. Sometimes I don't get to ride with them. I got to walk, don't get to eat until they're done, and I gotta help them steal from folks, or else they hurt me."

Hayden's heart broke at the desolate despair in her voice. Gently, he reached out, clasping her thin shoulder. "Not anymore, Mac. Not ever again. I promise. You wait right here, okay? I'm gonna deal with Rooster and his men."

She looked at him, a fragile hope dawning on her face. "You'll really stop them? You'll get me out of here?"

"I will. I swear it." He straightened, his face hardening into a mask of resolve. "Sit tight. I'll be back for you."

With that, he turned and stalked towards the house Rooster had entered. The pain of his wound had faded to a dull throb, subsumed beneath the cold, implacable fury building in his chest.

He slipped through the shadows, walking around the back of the dilapidated structure. The rear door hung drunkenly from one hinge. He eased it open, wincing at the faint creak. Gut tight with tension, he crept down the short hallway, following the thin thread of lantern light spilling from a doorway ahead.

Gun in hand, he edged up to the opening and peered inside. What he saw turned his stomach.

Tempest was spreadeagled on a stained mattress, bound hand and foot, a rag stuffed into her mouth. Her armor and clothing lay in a heap on the floor, leaving her in just her underwear. Rooster stood over her, slowly unhitching his gun belt.

"I promised you payback for breaking my nose, girlie," Rooster said, his voice nasally from his swollen nose. "It's time to settle up." He reached for the waistband of her underwear.

Hayden stepped into the room, his revolver leveled at Rooster's back, microspear in his other hand. "Get your hands off her, you son-of-a-bitch."

Rooster whirled, his face slack with shock. His mouth opened, but before he could utter a sound, Hayden was on him, stabbing him in the chest with the microspear.

Rooster's eyes went wide as the Axon weapon brought his heart to a sudden, complete stop. Then he toppled to the floor.

Tempest stared up at Hayden, her face a mask of mingled relief and humiliation. A livid bruise darkened her cheek, the blood had dried on her split lip, and her blackened left eye was swollen shut. Hayden cut her bonds, and she sat up, cringing with pain before she gave him a sour look.

"Took your sweet damn time, Sheriff," she rasped, gingerly rubbing her wrists.

"I had to walk seven miles with a hole the size of my fist in my chest."

"Like that's an excuse," Tempest grumbled, more in embarrassment than true criticism. She scooped up her armor and clothes, stiffly pulling them on, ignoring Hayden's politely averted gaze.

"At least he didn't get a chance to do...anything more than knock me around a bit," she said gruffly. "He was too busy crowing about his new toy and his big plans."

Hayden crouched next to Rooster, retrieving the note stamp from the man's pocket and tucking it into his own. "I'm glad I got here when I did."

"Me, too," Tempest whispered, putting a hand on his shoulder and squeezing. "Thank you for getting me out of this mess. I wish I could say it was my first time in this kind of situation, but…" She trailed off as Hayden put his hand on top of hers.

"It's over now," he said, drawing his second revolver and holding it out to Tempest. "You up for dishing out some payback?"

She released his shoulder and chuckled devilishly as she accepted the gun. "Damn right, let's make these bastards regret ever being born."

Together, they exited the house, moving with silent, deadly purpose. The bandits were still gathered near the cook fire, but they'd gone quiet, as if they'd smelled the coming storm. There was a moment of shocked stillness when they recognized the two figures striding towards them out of the darkness, and they reached for the weapons leaning against their seats.

Then all hell broke loose.

Hayden and Tempest opened fire as the bandits dove out of their seats, rolling to their feet and breaking every which way, desperate to escape the bullets flying at them. Two bandits fell right away, their chests blooming crimson. Hayden pivoted to track another, a single round through the neck knocking him down.

Tempest was a picture of perfect vengeance, her borrowed revolver thundering in time with Hayden's. The bandits dropped like a sack of bricks as she pressed forward, teeth bared in rage.

Though caught off-guard and without their leader, the outlaws weren't complete pushovers. Three remained alive, and they rallied quickly, falling back to better firing positions and pouring on a steady barrage.

Tempest dove to her belly and fired, taking one of them out before he could make it to cover behind a tree. Another hunkered down behind her motorcycle, tracking Hayden with his shotgun, finger tightening on the double triggers. He fired an instant before Hayden's round took him between the eyes. Hayden grunted as buckshot peppered his chest, some of the pellets plucking harmlessly at his sleeve. Though the pellets that did hit him stung like a swarm of bees, they failed to penetrate his underarmor.

Hayden lined up on another bandit, moving toward the rusted-out remains of a car parked on the street. He pulled the trigger, his target falling before he reached cover, a loud crack split the night, and a large round whistled past Hayden's ear, missing by centimeters. The sniper, of course. He'd gotten away and was out there in the darkness.

Hayden's head swiveled, searching frantically as he threw himself prone, trying to pinpoint the source of the shot. There! The orange cigarette flare in the house's second story at the far end of the cul de sac.

"Tempest!" he whisper-shouted. "Sniper, eleven o'clock high!"

The sniper fired again, the rifle's muzzle flash, pinpointing his exact position. Hayden rolled out of the sniper's line of fire just as the bullet whistled in, doing nothing but kicking up dirt.

"I've got him," Tempest said, getting up and running away from the fire into the darkness.

Hayden kept firing, emptying his revolver at the sniper's nest, reloading and emptying it again. The rounds punched into the sniper's position, forcing the sniper to drop down, out of sight.

He spotted Tempest then, a faint blur of motion in the moonlight as she approached the back of the house. He reloaded once more and fired at the distant window, bullets passing through the open space and smashing into the surrounding frame.

He caught sight of movement in the window. It had to be the sniper swinging around to shoot Tempest. Too late. Her weapon barked twice, and in the light of the twin flashes, Hayden saw the sniper's weapon tumble from the window.

Then he moved again, reloading on the run as he hunted the remaining bandits.

He found one crouched behind another derelict car, taking him in the head the moment he popped out to fire at him. He found another inside a house. A shot from the outlaw's hunting rifle failed to penetrate Hayden's armor. The bandit wasn't so lucky.

A third charged him from a dark corner, flashing a nasty blade. Hayden spun, throwing himself down on his back and firing up into the man as he dove at Hayden. Hayden rolled out of the way, the dead landing with a thud beside him.

Footsteps coming up behind him had him rolling again and bringing his revolver around as bandit number four came at him, knife blade gleaming the firelight. Hayden fired, but the only sound was a click of his empty gun. The outlaw dove at him. Hayden dropped his gun, reaching for the knife, ready to fight for it. A thunderclap sounded in the distance, followed by the whistle of a high-speed round, and the outlaw dropped to the dirt before he reached him, the top of his skull completely blown off.

In the silence that followed, Hayden released the breath he'd been holding. His head fell back to the ground, and he closed his eyes, totally spent and ravaged by pain. All he could hear was the crackle of the fire and the rasp of his own panting breaths.

Then footsteps. And here he'd thought the silence meant it was over. He gathered himself and rolled over to fire.

"Don't shoot, Hayden! We got 'em all," Tempest said, walking out of the night shadows, grinning, the strap of the sniper rifle slung over her shoulder. "I counted."

Relieved. Hayden dropped his gun hand, his finger coming off the trigger as he laid the side of his head down in the dirt and looked up at her. "You sure?" he asked as she walked into the light of the dying fire.

"Positive."

Hayden exhaled, slipping his revolver back into its holster and hauling himself up to his knees.

"Hayden!"

He turned as Mac came running. She hit hard enough to sit him back on his haunches. Throwing her arms around him, she held him as if he might suddenly disappear, a figment of her imagination.

"Is it... is it over?" she asked, her voice small.

Hayden squeezed her gently. "Yes, darlin'. It's over. You're safe now." He eased her back. "You aren't hurt, are you?"

"No. They never found me."

"Great work."

He looked up at Tempest. She looked as exhausted as he felt, but she wore a look of savage satisfaction. "Thank you for that shot, Tempest," he told her. "I don't know if I could have fought him off."

She looked around at the devastation, then fixed Hayden with a level stare. "You do look fit to collapse."

He wavered, nearly toppling, Mac's grip on him the only thing that kept him upright. Tempest was right. He was in bad shape. The bullet may not have killed him, but it had taken a serious toll. Even his genetically perfected body could only do so much, and he was reaching his limits.

"Much as I hate to do it, we'll rest here for a few hours. Then we'll continue on horseback. It's slower overall, but we can cover rougher terrain, go places the bike can't, and we don't have to worry about running out of gas." He turned to Mac. "Darlin', you don't know of any old mines in these parts, do you?"

She shook her head. "No, sorry. I been with Rooster and his bunch ever since they killed my ma and pa, and he ain't gone near no mines. Me and my folks, we was headed east, to the Arches. They was so excited to get there." Her expression shifted to sadness. "But they'll never get to see it now."

"I'm damn sorry, kiddo," Hayden said. "I wish I had

gotten here before you lost them." He turned to Tempest. "I need you to take her back to Union."

"What?" Tempest replied. "Hayden, you need my help."

"I admit, things would be a lot easier with you here, but we can't just abandon her, and we can't bring her with us."

"How old are you, Mac?" Tempest asked.

"Ten and a half."

"I was already being trained by the War Dogs at her age," Tempest argued. "We don't have to abandon her, but she's old enough to take care of herself out here for a few days. It's not like she has to worry about the bandits anymore. Or trife."

"And what if we don't make it back here to get her?"

"Then the queen will be free, and it won't much matter."

Hayden considered it. Tempest had a point. But leaving a child out here on her own felt wrong.

"It's okay, Sheriff," Mac said. "Ma and pa taught me to take care of myself, in case anything ever happened to them. I can wait here for you so long as you think it's safe."

"You know how to shoot?" Hayden asked.

"My pa taught me how," she replied. He stared at her, still conflicted. "I'll be okay. You saved me from Rooster. Nothing worse can happen in a few days. And if you don't come back, I can pilfer Rooster's notes and ride a horse. I'll make my own way to the Arches if I have to."

"My kind of kiddo," Tempest said with a grin. "What do you say, Sheriff?"

Hayden finally relented with a nod. "Pozz. If we don't come back, and you head for the Arches, make sure to visit Jack and Tabitha. They own a hotel there. It's called Hotel Colten. They'll take good care of you."

"I will," Mac said.

"Let's get you settled, Hayden," Tempest said. "You too, little miss. I'll take the first watch and clean up this mess while you're both resting."

"I have a mattress in the room next to Rooster's in his house," Mac said.

"I'll pull Rooster's body outta his room so you can sleep there," Tempest said to Hayden. "I'll enjoy dumping it in the fire."

Hayden nodded. Within twenty minutes, he was on his back on a relatively comfortable straw mattress, doing his best to relax and give his body a chance to heal.

It was easier said than done, and when he finally fell asleep, the darkness was filled with images of dark claws, sharp teeth, and the endless drone of hissing.

CHAPTER 27

Sheriff!

Kady's desperate scream jerked Hayden awake with a start, his heart hammering as it echoed through his mind.

He bolted upright in bed, the sudden motion sending fresh pain lancing through the wound to his chest, the one to his back pretty much healed already. The pain he did feel barely registered, drowned out by the icy certainty that something was horribly wrong.

Kady! He mentally cried out. *Kiddo, where are you? I'm looking for you, but I don't know where to go.* He waited for a reply as her voice faded from his thoughts, leaving him staring at peeling wallpaper and rotted drywall. *Kady!* This time, his silent call was so forceful he thought Shub'Nigu might hear it and deign to respond.

But there was nothing but silence, both inside his head and out.

Kady was already in trouble, but now there was something more. Something worse. Much worse.

He leapt to his feet, ignoring the protest of his sore, battered body, bursting out of the room and through the front door. The predawn gloom still clung to the abandoned housing development, but Tempest and Mac were already up and about, moving with a purpose that brought him to a quick stop.

To his surprise, they had saddled three of the bandit's horses, the animals pawing at the ground and snorting in the cool morning air, anxious to be on their way now that they knew they were going somewhere. Hayden frowned, confusion momentarily replacing urgency.

"What's going on?" he asked, striding over to them.

"Morning, Hayden," Tempest said, turning to meet his gaze. Her warm expression turned fearful at the sight of his tense jaw. "What is it?"

"Kady cried out to me," he replied. "Something bad is either going to happen soon, or has already happened."

"You don't know which?"

He shook his head. "She called out for me, and I could tell she was desperate, terrified. And then she was gone. She won't…or can't answer me now."

"Then I'm glad Mac and I have already fed and saddled the horses. Though I'd still rather bring the bike."

"I appreciate your moxie. But why three?"

"Mac's coming with us," she said simply.

Hayden shook his head instinctively. "What? No, it's too dangerous. She can't—"

"I want to help," Mac interrupted, her determined expression belying her age. "I remembered a place nearby. A hill with a good view of the surrounding area. I can show you."

Hayden hesitated, torn. The thought of bringing a child into the heart of danger went against his every instinct. "Mac, darlin', where we're going it isn't safe. We're hunting bad people. Worse than Rooster and his crew. Worse than you can imagine."

"I think the safest place in the world is with the Sheriff," Mac said firmly.

Hayden glanced at Tempest. "You told her?"

"To be fair, she asked me if you were the Sheriff. I just confirmed it. I didn't see the harm, and I didn't want to lie to her."

"The harm is that now she wants to come with us," Hayden argued, his worry for both her and Kady exhibited in his growly attitude and the scowl deepening the lines between his eyes into virtual trenches.

"Do you really think I'll be safer crossing the wilds on my own than I would be with you?" Mac asked. "I know some of the stories about you are tall tales, but you did kill the trife, didn't you?"

"Pozz, but—"

"How can riding with the Sheriff be more dangerous than being out here alone?"

Hayden frowned. The kid had a point. "What about supplies? Food, water? We don't have much, and I don't want you going hungry out here."

Mac grinned, a flash of pride in her eyes. "I found Rooster's stash of jerky and bottled water. I already emptied what we wouldn't need out of all their saddlebags and added it to two of them for me and Miss Tempest to carry. We got plenty now for all three of us."

"And I suppose you can handle a gun, too?" he asked the girl, only half-joking.

"I already told you I know how to shoot," Mac replied, "and Miss Tempest taught me how to shoot her rifle."

"Why don't you show him?" Tempest said, passing her plasma rifle to the girl.

The weapon seemed oversized and ungainly in Mac's small hands. But there was no hesitation in her movements as she brought it to her shoulder, sighting down the barrel at a distant tree. The weapon hummed, then spat a bolt of super-heated gas. It struck the trunk dead center, burning a deep hole in it. If the tree were Zephyr, she would have hit him center mass from fifty paces.

Mac lowered the rifle, turning to Hayden with a grin. "I like these better than regular huntin' rifles. A lot easier on my shoulder without the recoil."

Hayden stared at her, then shook his head, a rueful chuckle escaping him. "Alright, darlin'. You've made your case. Let's get moving."

They mounted up and set off, riding south around the lake before turning west. As they rode, Hayden dropped back to pace alongside Mac.

"Tell me about your folks," he said gently. "Where did you live before they decided to move to the Arches?"

A shadow passed over Mac's face, but she answered readily enough. "We're from down south. A place called Luk. It used to be a big city, but..." She trailed off, memories clearly painful.

Hayden nodded in understanding. "The trife," he said softly.

"Yeah. We survived by hiding out in this big ol' parking garage. A whole bunch of us. But after the monsters were gone, after a while..." She shrugged. "Raiders, bandits. They were bad. They killed and hurt people, and took all our food. Believe it or not, they wasn't even the worst. Some folks who were nice when they were afraid, they weren't so nice anymore once they were safe." She paused, looking over at him with a wisdom deeper than her years. "At least the trife didn't pretend to be human."

The bitterness in her voice made Hayden's heartache. She reminded him so much of his own children—may they rest in peace—and of Kady. "So your parents decided it was time to leave?"

"That's right. They said it was only a matter of time before Mayor Jones found fault with us and made us his next target, the way he did other folks in the settlement. Pa heard from a scavvie on his way through that the Arches were safe. That they had good folks there. People who look out for each other.

Not like Luk." She looked over at Hayden again, a fragile hope in her eyes. "Do you think you could go there someday? To Luk? Help make it better, like the Arches?"

Hayden met her gaze, wishing that he could promise her that. "I'd like to, darlin'. I surely would. But the wilds are a big place, and I'm just one man. I do my best, but it's hard, going everywhere that needs help."

Mac nodded, understanding and disappointment mingling on her face. "That's why we were going to the Arches. Ma said it was better to light a candle than curse the dark. That if enough people did that, the world wouldn't be so dark anymore."

"Your Ma sounds like she was a wise woman," Hayden said softly.

Mac smiled, a glimmer of unshed tears in her eyes. "She was. And brave. Like you."

A pang of guilt coursed through Hayden. If he hadn't taken those months to mourn Nat and hide from the world, might he have made his way to Luk before Mac's parents ever left? Or run into Rooster before they killed them on the road to Arches? Or better yet, engaged the Rebirthers before they attacked the Greens?

He had to force his mind off that road. He did the best he could, but he was still only human. And the world didn't stop turning just because he was off the trail. He couldn't be responsible for all of it.

However, that didn't stop him from feeling responsible.

They lapsed into silence then, the only sounds being the thud of hooves and the creak of leather. After a while, Mac perked up, pointing to a side road that switched back on itself up the steep hillside.

"There," she said. "That's the place I remembered. You can see for miles from the top."

Hayden followed her gaze, then nodded. "Alright. I'll ride ahead, take a look. You two stay here."

He urged his horse up the road. It took a good half hour to reach the summit, but Hayden felt every minute ticking by, an invisible clock counting down to disaster.

At the top, he reined in his mount, shading his eyes against the rising sun's glare. Mac had been right. The view was spectacular, and the surrounding countryside lay before him like a map. He could see the lake at the old housing development, the skeletal remains of old wind farms, and the vast expanse of plains and hills stretching out in every direction.

And there, off to the southwest, beyond a smaller body of water and a row of higher crags, a plume of dust, kicked up by something moving over the arid ground. It was distant, but it was there.

Hayden's jaw tightened. It could be anyone, anything. But even if it wasn't Zephyr, maybe whoever it was had seen them and could point them in the right direction. And if they were unfriendly...well, he would make them friendly. Or dead.

He wheeled his horse, galloping back down the hillside. Tempest and Mac looked up at his approach, questions in their eyes.

"I spotted a dust cloud to the southwest," Hayden said without preamble. "It's a ways off, but it's the only sign of life out here. It's likely them. We need to check it out. Maybe get to those hills between us and them first and surprise them. Cut them off if we can."

Tempest nodded. They both knew the stakes. Every minute counted.

As they set off again, riding hard, Hayden could only hope that they wouldn't catch up to them too late.

CHAPTER 28

Hayden, Tempest, and Mac nearly rode their horses into the ground, trying to intercept whatever was sending up the dust plume to the southwest. The rising sun beat down on their backs, the air shimmering across the barren landscape, but Hayden barely felt the heat from it. His mind focused solely on the distant sign of life and the hope it represented.

He held up a hand, slowing their pace as they approached the foothills ahead. Rocky outcroppings and scrubby vegetation were already replacing the flat expanse of plains. The dust cloud they were keeping track of was visible now. Whatever was creating it would soon come around the edge of the foothills.

"We need to hurry and find cover in those hills, wait for whatever's making that cloud to get here. If it's Zephyr, we don't want him to know we're already here. And if it's something else, maybe a stampede or a cattle drive, we don't want to be caught in the middle of it."

Tempest and Mac nodded, following his lead as they urged their horses toward the foothills. As luck would have it, Hayden quickly found a ravine deep enough to provide concealment from prying eyes. Taking refuge in it, they dismounted and crept up to the top of the ravine, peering cautiously over the top edge of it.

The dust cloud was closer now—a low, deep rumble in front of it, like distant thunder. Hayden's brow furrowed. Not hoverbikes. The sound was all wrong. For a moment, he wondered if he was right about it being a stampede. He could make out a cacophony of rapid and rhythmic hoofbeats. Wild horses, maybe, spooked by some unseen threat.

He hoped not. He needed answers. Direction. They were running out of time, and this was their only lead. He desperately wanted it to be the Rebirthers, but he knew it wasn't.

He breathed easy as the first horse crested a nearby rise, both animal and, thankfully, a rider silhouetted against the sky. Then another, until it seemed the very hills were disgorging a tide of humanity. They rode hard, crouched low over the necks of their lathered mounts, a ragtag assortment of men, women, and children on horseback and in covered wagons. Hayden counted maybe eighty people in all, their faces drawn and haggard, all appearing wild with fear.

They were running from something. Running like the devil himself was on their heels. Could it be the Rebirthers? No, he'd only seen one dust cloud. Whatever had sent them moving at their breakneck pace, it had given up the chase or fallen far behind.

Hayden rose from his concealment, stepping out of the ravine and waving his arms. "Hey! Over here!" he cried out, his voice lost beneath the thunder of hooves. He tried again, cupping his hands around his mouth to shout again, but the riders didn't hear or see him, focusing solely on the path ahead. Hayden tried again, waving his arms, but to no avail.

Frowning, he drew one of his revolvers and fired it into the air, the sharp report cracking like a whip. The lead rider's head jerked around, eyes widening as he saw Hayden, but he still didn't slow. Instead, he whipped his horse's withers even harder with the loose ends of the reins.

"I've got this, Sheriff," Tempest said, unslinging the sniper rifle from her back. She rested it on the ravine's edge and sighted it through the scope. The weapon cracked, and a puff of dust kicked up inches in front of the lead horse's hooves. The animal reared, screaming, the rider fighting to control it and stay in the saddle.

Behind him, the other nomads reacted, some swerving to avoid their leader, others drawing up short. "Stay here," Hayden told Mac over his shoulder, his voice low and urgent as he holstered his gun. "Cover me, but don't shoot unless I say so."

The girl nodded, her face pale but steadfast as she took up a position at the top of the ravine, her rifle aimed over the edge. Hayden raised his hands as the nomads with weapons wheeled and leveled them at him, ready for a fight.

Tempest re-slung the sniper rifle over her shoulder and joined Hayden. Keeping their hands up, they walked out to meet the nomads.

The leader spurred his horse toward them, his face a mix of apprehension and anger as he pulled his horse up in front of them. He drew his revolver, pointing it at Hayden through the cloud of dust kicked up by his horse's hooves. "What the hell do you think you're doing, shooting at us?" he demanded."You got a death wish, mister? Or are you just crazy?"

"Sorry to stop you the hard way, pardner," Hayden said evenly. "But we needed to talk to you, and you weren't slowing down."

"Talk?" the man spat. "Ain't got time for talkin', mister. Ain't got time for nothin' but runnin'."

"Running from what?" Hayden pressed. He nodded at the other nomads, at the terror etched on every face he could make out. "What's got you all so spooked?"

The man hesitated, his eyes darting to his people, then back to Hayden. His voice was little more than a whisper when he spoke, as if he feared the very word.

"Trife," he said, fear darkening his eyes. "It's the damned trife."

Hayden felt the blood drain from his face, a cold knot of dread forming in his gut. Beside him, Tempest stiffened, her eyes jerking up toward Hayden and then at the nomad leader, eyes narrowing warily.

"That's not possible," Hayden said slowly, shaking his head. "The trife are gone. Have been for five years."

The nomad leader barked a harsh laugh. "Yeah? Well, you can tell that to the trife behind us. 'Cause they sure as hell didn't get the message."

Hayden's mind raced, trying to make sense of it. "Tell me everything," he said. "Start from the beginning."

"I ain't about to stand here tellin' tales, mister. We need to get clear of this area, and I suggest you do the same."

"Please," Hayden said. "I'm looking for a young girl named Kady. She was taken by a group of masked cultists riding hoverbikes. They're somewhere in this area. I know that much. Have you seen them?"

"We ain't seen a thing out of the ordinary except the damn trife. Now, if you'll excuse us." He was about to turn his horse away when Tempest spoke up.

"Are you going to turn your back on the Sheriff?" she said. "If you're being chased by trife like you say, you'd best give him an account."

The man froze, glaring at Hayden, eyes shifting to his arms. "You're the Sheriff?"

"Pozz. I've got a healing bullet hole in my chest big enough to kill an ordinary man if you want proof," Hayden replied. "But we don't have time to show and tell both."

The man took a deep breath, visibly collecting himself. "That we don't. We was coming up from the south," he continued, "heading for greener pastures. Anyways, we came across this old military base, figured it'd be a good place to camp for the night. Fortified, defensible. We bedded down, set watches, the usual stuff."

He shuddered, his eyes going distant with remembered horror. "It was just past midnight when the screams started. Came from the perimeter, from the sentries. By the time we realized what was happening, they was already inside the walls. Dozens of 'em, maybe hundreds. Fast and vicious, like they were something new. Something more than the old trife. Different. They even killed a young girl not old enough yet for her menses!"

"What? Are you sure they were trife?" Tempest asked.

The man laughed. "Are you kidding, lady? I've seen enough trife in my lifetime to know one when I see one. Anyways, we fought as best we could, but it was chaos. People runnin' every which way, trife comin' out of the shadows. We lost so many."

His voice broke, and he took a moment to compose himself. "We finally managed to gather up and break away, to get some distance between us and them, but it didn't come without a heavy toll. Bastards kept comin'. Kept chasin' us, even after the sun came up. That's not supposed to happen, right? Thought these things were supposed to get sleepy in the daylight?"

Hayden frowned. The man was right. Trife liked to soak up the sun's rays. Collect energy, not expend it. For them to keep pursuing their prey, even in the brightness of morning, was unheard of. So was attacking girls not yet into their puberty.

The implications were staggering. And terrifying.

"Something's wrong with them," the nomad said, echoing Hayden's thoughts. "They're not like the trife I remember. Not like they're supposed to be. If you're really the Sheriff... damnation, I thought you killed 'em all."

"So did I," Hayden replied. "Where exactly did you encounter them?"

The man waved a hand vaguely southward. "Back that away, 'bout four hour's hard ride. Why? Surely you ain't thinkin' of—"

He was interrupted by a piercing scream, raw and primal and full of terror.

Mac!

CHAPTER 29

Hayden whirled, his hands dropping to his revolvers, yanking them clear of their holsters in one smooth motion.

Tempest was already moving, the rifle snapping up to her shoulder, searching for a target.

"They must've come through the mountains," the nomad leader gasped. The other nomads cried out in fear and confusion, some wheeling their mounts to flee, others whipping the reins against their horses' backs to get their wagons moving. A few stood their ground, raising their weapons, ready to fight.

For a single, endless heartbeat, chaos reigned.

Then Hayden saw them.

Trife cresting the rise behind the ravine, spilling over the lip like a spreading slick of toothy, clawed oil.

They leaped and bounded forward with terrifying speed, quickly closing the distance to where Mac stood on this side of the ravine. She didn't move. Then suddenly, she stopped screaming, her terror giving way to the need to act. She brought her rifle up, sighted, and fired. Once, twice, three times. Searing plasma bolts stitched a fire line across the front of the trife tide.

Some fell, dropped to the dirt by the bolts and quickly attacked by their own in a mad drive to eliminate the wounded. But more took their places, driven by an undeniable instinct to kill human beings.

They would be on Mac in seconds. A child against a swelling horde that, if the nomad leader was right, would kill her even though she hadn't yet reached her menses.

Hayden didn't hesitate. His revolvers bucked and roared, adding their thunder to the din. Beside him, Tempest also opened up, her shots precise and lethal. He quickly dropped a small group of trife who'd broken away from the rest to flank Mac. Tempest's sniper rifle decapitated three more.

But it wasn't enough. Could never be enough, no matter how fast or skilled they were.

Already, the bulk of the horde was at the ravine, clambering down into it and racing along it toward Mac, their raging red eyes fixed on her with one single, terrible intent. The girl climbed up out of the ravine. Backing up, the barrel of her rifle swung desperately to and fro as she streamed plasma on as many of them as she could.

Hayden reloaded his revolvers and sprinted toward Mac, Tempest close at his heels. The nomad leader shouted something after them, his voice high and panicked, but Hayden barely heard him over the pounding of his own heart.

Mac let loose another volley, her plasma stream flashing into the slick. Trife shuddered and collapsed under the onslaught, but it was hardly enough to convince them to stop. Nothing could do that.

A trife lunged, its claws slashing down like guillotine blades, tearing the rifle out of her hands. Mac threw herself sideways, hitting the dirt and rolling desperately out from under the lethal claws that raked furrows into the ground where she'd stood. More trife closed on her in a frenzy of writhing bodies and lashing limbs.

Hoofbeats suddenly pounded in behind Hayden and

Tempest, the nomad leader's big bay sweeping past them, racing toward Mac. "Here, girl! Run!" the nomad leader shouted, his hand held out to her.

Only seconds away from them ripping her apart, Mac ran from her certain death toward rescue, but Hayden didn't know if he'd reach her in time. All he and Tempest could do now was stand their ground and continue firing on the approaching horde.

The instant Mac latched onto the man's hand, he hauled her up behind him and wheeled his horse around, wildly kicking it into a dead run back past Hayden and Tempest to where his people were again circling their wagons.

Hayden holstered one of his revolvers and pulled out the microspear.

Then he dove headfirst into the scrum, swinging the microspear with lethal precision.

Claws raked his chest, digging into his armor but not breaking through. Trife dropped like flies around him as he plowed through them. He didn't stop. Couldn't stop. He cut a path through the press of alien bodies, feeling them crowding in on him, too many to overcome.

Then miraculously, a loud crack echoed overhead, and an entire row of trife was ripped open by a single round from the sniper rifle, nearly a dozen of the creatures taken out of the fight with one shot. Tempest was alive! Exhilaration rushed through him as the rifle echoed again and again, the mass thinning enough around him to give him some breathing room.

He drove forward, sinking the microspear into the demons and mowing them down like a wrecking ball. Just when he thought their numbers were dwindling, more swarmed around him. He kicked a trife into another as a claw dug at his back. He reached behind him and stabbed the creature without looking. The Axon blade killed every trife it touched with instant, unerring precision, but it was only a matter of time before he couldn't hold them back any longer.

Then Tempest was there, the rifle slung across her back a hard ridge between his shoulder blades. "I hate these things," she griped, her pistol in one hand, lethal knife in the other. "They never give up!"

She fired point-blank into a trife's head before stabbing another. Hayden shouldered a third, knocking it back from him. An instant later, a sharp hiss and a wave of heat passed his ear and a hole appeared in the forehead of the trife he'd knocked off balance.

Mac. The girl had a damn good eye.

A barrage of incoming bolts took out more of the creatures around him.The nomads were taking down their fair share, too. It was enough to let him and Tempest break through onto clear ground. With no more trife headed for them, they turned, nodded once at each other in silent agreement, and in a whirlwind of steel and fury, leaped into the trailing ranks of trife heading straight for the wagon train.

It was chaos, madness, a nightmare made real. Trife came at them from every angle, a relentless, chittering swarm. Hayden lost track of time, thought, and everything but the need to keep moving and fighting.

With a wordless roar, Hayden stabbed and smashed into the tide of dark, leathery skin, using every ounce of energy he had to swing the spear. Beside him, Tempest was a blur at the edge of his vision, her knife flashing, her pistol spitting bullets. Blood sheeted down one side of her face from a gash above her eye. But she didn't falter or slow, a snarl of defiance on her lips as they carved a path through the horde.

And then, suddenly, impossibly, the last group of trife went down, crushed beneath their boots. Chest heaving, Hayden found himself standing so close to the wagons he could almost reach out and touch the buckboard in front of him. Tempest stood beside him, knife coated in trife blood, pistol still smoking, the nomads rushing around them to board their wagons.

And there, standing in the back of a buckboard, plasma rifle still balanced across the back of the seat, was Mac. She smiled at Hayden, and he marveled at how at ease she looked, as if killing trife was an everyday thing in her world. Then, all of a sudden, she crumpled like a doll some little girl had dropped, falling off the buckboard into the dirt.

Tempest reached her first, dropping to her knees, hands shaking as she eased Mac's head into her lap and then patted her cheek. "Mac, come on now, wake up."

"What's wrong with her?" Hayden hurried over to them, his heart a leaden weight in his chest as he leaned over Mac, one hand braced on his knee, the other reaching down to test the temperature of her forehead. "Her skin's tacky, but she doesn't seem to have a fever."

"I think she just fainted. C'mon, girl." Tempest again patted her cheek, a little harder this time. "Wake up now. We've got Rebirthers to stop and a trife queen to find."

Mac's eyes shot open. "Trife!" She shot straight up to sit there, terrified.

"Easy, kiddo," Tempest murmured. "We've got you. You're okay."

"We took out the first wave," Hayden said, kneeling beside her, "but it's not over." Already, he heard more hissing in the distance as the next wave of demons trailed down out of the mountains. They'd cleared a path, but it wouldn't stay open for long. "You did good, kiddo. Better than good. I'm proud of you," he said, resting his hand on her shoulder. "You think you can handle more, or would you like to stay with the nomads?"

"We'd be more than happy to take her." The nomad leader stepped up behind them, holding the reins to his horse. "But we've got to get going."

"No! I want to stay with Tempest and the Sheriff." She

looked up at Tempest, her eyes imploring. "You're not going to leave me behind, are you?" She looked back at Hayden, grabbing onto his arm. "Please. Take me with you."

Hayden was torn, but he didn't argue. He knew he couldn't leave her behind, not after how hard she'd fought to save both him and Tempest. He rested his hand on Mac's shoulder. "You're a brave girl, and we're damn proud of you. Are you ready then?"

"You bet, Sheriff." A smile brightened her features, and she scrambled up, brushing the dirt off the seat of her pants. Tempest stood up behind her, hugging the girl.

"Well, then, I guess we're outta here, too," the nomad leader said, reaching down to offer Hayden his hand. "Thank you for your help, Sheriff. Good luck to you."

"Same to you." Hayden shook his hand, and then the man remounted his bay. He tipped his hat to Hayden and then to Tempest and Mac before whirling his horse around and racing to the head of his caravan, the wagons and riders quickly reforming into a column."I'll cover you."

Tempest grabbed Mac's hand, and they broke into a dead run toward the ravine. Hayden ran behind them, revolvers ready. The next rank of trife was in sight now, a seething mass of hunger and intent. He breathed out, the world slowing down, narrowing to the guns in his hands and the approaching targets, close enough now to see the red glow of their eyes.

Hayden's revolvers roared, his rounds smashing through trife skulls and chests, sending the first demons tumbling, their momentum broken. He quickly reloaded and dropped a dozen more before they reached the ravine.

"Hayden!" Tempest cried, drawing his attention. She'd already mounted up, Mac on the saddle in front of her. She held his horse's reins out to him. Despite all the screaming and shooting, their rides hadn't gone anywhere except for Mac's little pinto. It was nowhere in sight. Time and instinct had imbued most creatures with a lack of fear in the face of a trife attack. That there was only one animal the creatures wanted to harm. And it wasn't horses.

Hayden turned away from the trife, dashing to his horse and swinging smoothly into the saddle. He and Tempest wheeled their mounts, urging them away from the oncoming slick.

They thundered down the ravine, the horses' hooves pounding against the rocky ground, their breaths coming in sharp, frantic pants. Behind them, the trife surged forward like a dark tide, their beady red eyes fixed on their prey with single-minded intent.

Hayden risked a glance over his shoulder, his heart sinking at the sight. None of the demons had gone after the nomads. They were all after them and gaining, their light, powerful limbs eating up the distance with terrifying speed. He could hear the click and scrape of their claws against stone, the hissing rasp of their breath.

"Faster!" he shouted, urging his horse onward. "We've got to outrun them!"

Tempest dug her heels into her animal's flanks, coaxing every ounce of speed from its straining muscles.

But it wasn't enough. The trife were too fast, too relentless. They bounded forward, leaping from rock to rock, closing the gap.

The lead trife lunged, its claws extended, swiping at Hayden's back. He twisted in the saddle, revolver already in hand, and fired. The round caught the creature squarely in its gaping maw, exploding from the back of its skull in a spray of bone and brain matter. It crumpled, its momentum sending it tumbling end over end, tripping and knocking over others.

More trife leaped to take its place, a seething mass of dark flesh and razor claws. Hayden fired again and again, each shot finding its mark, each kill bought at the cost of precious seconds and distance.

Behind him, they surrounded Tempest's horse. Her pistol barked as she loosed shot after shot into the horde. Hayden dropped back, adding his firepower to hers. Trife shuddered and fell, their bodies crushed beneath the hooves of the horses.

But still, they came on, wave after relentless wave, heedless of their losses. They launched themselves at the fleeing riders, their hisses of hunger filling the air.

One collided with the hindquarters of Hayden's horse, its claws scrabbling at Hayden's leg, trying to grab him and pull him off his horse. The animal screamed, its stride faltering, nearly pitching Hayden from the saddle. He hung onto the saddle horn and reins with one hand, exchanging his pistol for the microspear. Jabbing down into leathery flesh, the death shudder of trife after trife vibrated up his arm.

Ahead, the floor of the ravine rose, but it narrowed as well, the walls closing to next to nothing. "Tempest!" he shouted, pointing to the lip of the ravine.

She followed his gaze and nodded, knowing like he did that the horses would have to scramble up out of the narrowing ravine before it was too tight for the horses to pass. The trife sensed their intent, redoubling their efforts, their hisses rising to a deafening crescendo.

Tempest's face hardened with resolve. She leaned close to her horse's ear as the ground rose beneath their hooves. Whispering encouragement, she urged the exhausted animal up the rocky side of the ravine right behind Hayden's surging mount.

Hayden held his breath as his horse's muscular haunches pushed them up the side wall in short, powerful leaps. Beneath him, he felt the buckskin gather for one last desperate leap. Its muscles bunched, and then it lunged, its front hooves scrabbling for purchase on the top of the ravine.

For a single, heart-stopping moment, Hayden thought it wouldn't make it. That the horse would slam into the rock lip and they would tumble back into the ravine. Down on top of Tempest's horse in a scrum of screaming horses and flying hooves. All three riders would be trapped beneath four tons of struggling horseflesh. If that didn't kill them, the trife would be on them in an instant.

And then it happened. With one last mighty lunge, Hayden's horse dragged itself and its rider up over the edge in an explosion of dust and pebbles, and then they were off again, flying across the open plain.

Tempest and Mac cleared the edge of the ravine a heartbeat later, the girl's startled yelp lost beneath the drumming of hooves. Hayden twisted to look behind them, expecting to see the trife pouring over the lip of the ravine in relentless pursuit.

But the demons had stopped, allowing them to escape.

Not quite able to believe their luck, Hayden let out a shuddering breath. His heart hammering against his ribs, adrenaline still surging through his veins, he pulled his horse up and swung him around to wait for Tempest and Mac.

And that's when he heard the screams, and saw that the trife hadn't simply given up on them.

They'd chosen to go after an easier target.

CHAPTER 30

The nomad caravan was under attack!

Hayden watched the trife swarm the wagons like a dark flood, clashing with the desperate defenders, the air ringing with gunshots and terrified cries.

Hayden's horse, still blowing and wild-eyed, danced under him. He yanked on the reins, the spirited buckskin slowly settling as Tempest and Mac rode up to them. The big, agile-looking gray nickered to Hayden's buckskin and sidled up close to it, seeming to calm the higher-strung horse even more.

"I need you to get Mac clear," Hayden told Tempest. "I'm going back to help them!"

"What? No! Hayden, are you crazy? There's too many!"

"I can't just leave them!" he snarled. "They stopped because of us. The leader came for Mac. I have to try!"

Without waiting for a reply, he kicked his horse forward, straight towards the embattled caravan. He heard Tempest curse even over the pounding of his horse's hooves and then Mac cried out his name, but he didn't look back. Couldn't look back.

All that mattered right now was the fight ahead.

Reins looped around the saddle horn, both revolvers blazing. He thundered across the open ground like a one-man cavalry charge. The nomads saw him coming and rallied. Circling their wagons back up, they poured a hail of rifle fire into the trife, their shouts of renewed determination rising above the din of battle as Hayden plunged into the thick of it. Heedless of the danger, he stitched a line of death through the trife ranks, the demons falling one after another.

Some trife broke from the mass, lunging at him with outstretched claws. He blew them out of the air with casual ease. When he ran out of bullets with no time to reload, his horse trampled trife beneath its hooves while Hayden stabbed into the mass of writhing bodies with the microspear, each trife dead before it hit the ground. He moved like a man possessed, a whirlwind of vengeance, the microspear lashing out to impale those who got too close.

But even as they fought, even as the trife fell in droves beneath the onslaught, Hayden knew it wasn't enough. There were simply too many demons, an endless tide that showed no sign of slackening. For every one they killed, two more seemed to take its place, boiling out of the earth like a dark geyser.

He gritted his teeth, desperation rising like bile in his throat. He couldn't fail, not now, not with so many lives hanging in the balance. He clamped his teeth down on the microspear and reached for another quick loader, only to find both bandoliers empty. Out of bullets. The thinning volume of gunfire around him suggested the nomads were in the same dire straits.

Hayden holstered one of his guns. Flipping the other one over in his hand, he ignored the searing heat of the barrel burning his palm and grabbed the microspear out of his teeth with the other. Jumping from the saddle, he dove straight into a group of trife. Using his revolver as a club, he smashed in the face of one trife, stabbed another, and kicked a third.

Ducking under the swipe of a fourth, he stabbed it in the chest. Throwing his shoulder into another, he clubbed one trife and speared another, losing track of how many demons he killed. It was like a reverse assembly line, destroying them as they approached him.

A set of jaws landed on his forearm, failing to pierce his armor but holding his spear at bay. Another set of claws raked at his face, drawing blood. More claws grabbed his legs, trying to pull him to the ground. The growing swarm threatened to overwhelm him, even as he roared and fought back, hammering away with the butt of his revolver.

A piercing crack split the air, rising above even the clamor of battle. Right in front of him, a trife's head exploded into fragments of bone and brain, the creature dropping like a hot rock.

Another shot. Another trife close to him fell.

A third shot and his arm was free again. He stabbed three trife rapidly, freeing himself before risking a glance over his shoulder. There, astride her horse on a nearby rise, was Tempest, the barrel of the sniper rifle smoking as the weapon bucked against her shoulder. Another precise shot into the seething mass of trife took two out at once.

Beside her, Mac crouched behind a low boulder, the plasma rifle clutched determinedly in her small hands. She bit her lip in concentration, sighting down the barrel, carefully picking her targets. Blue bolts sizzled out, each catching a trife and sending it sprawling.

A grin split Hayden's face, a wild, savage joy rising in his chest and spurring him to redouble his efforts, his spear blurring into a symphony of death. As Tempest's sniper fire rained down destruction like the fist of an angry god, each shot surgically precise, reaping a bloody toll, Mac darted from cover to cover, her plasma rifle spitting azure fire.

The nomads fought like demons themselves, rallying beside Hayden's unexpected eleventh-hour salvation. Rifles cracked, knives flashed, each man and woman battling for their very survival.

Minutes stretched into a timeless eternity, each second an age, each breath a lifetime. The world narrowed to the thunder of guns and the scream of inhuman throats. The humans poured everything they had, everything they were, into the fight, holding nothing back.

And slowly, impossibly, the tide began to turn.

The trife ranks thinned as the dead piled up, their relentless advance faltering. The nomads surged forward, a ragged cheer rising from their throats, sensing victory within their grasp.

Hayden led the charge, cutting through the trife like a farmer at harvest while Tempest and Mac rained death from above. The trife didn't know how to retreat. Despite their dwindling numbers, they continued the attack, succumbing one after another to the humans' increasingly overwhelming forces. Until the final demon fell, twitching and hissing its last. A sudden, deafening silence descended, broken only by the ragged breathing of the living and the soft moans of the wounded.

They had won. Against all odds, against all hope, they had emerged victorious. The nomads were safe, the trife defeated.

Tempest rode up beside him, Mac perched behind her, the girl's face streaked with dirt, but her eyes shining with adrenaline-fueled elation. She leaped from the saddle, wrapping her arms around Hayden, heedless of the blood and grime caking his body.

"We did it," she whispered, her voice muffled against his chest. "We actually did it."

"We sure did, kiddo," Hayden replied softly, returning her embrace. "You were amazing out there. Your ma and pa would've been proud."

Mac looked up, tears cutting tracks through the dirt on her cheeks. "Really?"

"Really."

Tempest clasped his shoulder, her grip firm. "That was some mighty fine shooting, Sheriff. And that spear of yours... I'm glad I stuck around to see it."

Hayden met her gaze, a weary grin tugging at his lips. "I guess this is the part where I thank you for not listening to me."

She laughed. "You should know by now, I'm not one for following orders."

Their reunion was interrupted by the approach of the nomad leader, the man's face haggard but filled with gratitude. He clasped Hayden's hand with both of his own, pumping it vigorously.

"You really are the Sheriff," he said, shaking his head. "An avenging angel incarnate, if I ever did see one. You must've killed a hundred or more of those things all on your own."

"I'm sorry we made you stop," Hayden replied. "If we hadn't—"

"Never mind that," the leader said. "Our horses weren't going to last much longer anyways, and better to have the Sheriff on our side than fighting for our lives alone. You saved us a lot of lives today. We owe you a debt that can never be repaid."

Hayden shook his head. "You owe me nothing," he said. "I was just doing what needed to be done."

The man nodded, his eyes glistening with unshed tears. He turned to survey the battlefield, the ground littered with the twisted bodies of the fallen trife. A shudder ran through him.

"In all my years," he whispered, "I ain't never seen anything like this. Never known the trife to be so relentless. It's like they ain't even the same creatures no more."

Hayden followed his gaze, a cold knot of dread forming in his gut. The man was right. These trife were different, changed on a fundamental level. More aggressive, more resilient, more focused.

But how? And why?

Unbidden, his thoughts turned to Kady, to the danger she faced in the clutches of the Rebirth cult. Had they done this somehow? Were they responsible for this new breed of nightmare?

He didn't know. But he intended to find out.

"There is one way you can help me," Hayden said to the nomad.

"Anything, Sheriff."

"Do you have revolvers? Bullets?" He patted his empty bandolier.

The nomad leader smiled. "I'll see what we have left."

"There's a bandit camp east of here, then north along the lake. You can replenish some of your supplies there. Guns, rounds. Beds too, if you want to rest your wounded."

"Thank you for the tip," the nomad replied.

"You can take this too," Tempest said, passing over the sniper rifle. "Maybe you'll find more ammunition for it."

"Thank you, ma'am. Name's Casper, by the way."

"Hayden," he replied. "That's Tempest and Mac."

Casper grinned at Mac. "Never seen a little'un like you give anything such hell." He laughed. "I'll be right back with some bullets."

While he was gone, a few nomads came out to thank them for their help. Hayden also spotted the children peering at him through the gaps between the wagons.

Casper returned a few minutes later, carrying a pouch that jingled when he handed it to Hayden. "Got thirty rounds. Not much, but we used it all on those bastards."

"I appreciate your parting with them," Hayden replied.

"Well, about that. I ain't about to part with my bullets so easily."

"What do you mean?" Hayden asked, confused.

"I reckon if the Sheriff is out here looking for a girl, and the trife are out here trying to kill him, then the Sheriff could probably use some more help. The rest of the group is going to head for that bandit hole you mentioned. But me and a couple of the boys are coming with you. No ifs, ands, or buts."

Hayden nodded. "I'm past the point of turning down help. Not with what we just fought through."

"So, where are we headed, Sheriff?" Casper asked.

"If the trife attacked the old military base, then my quarry can't be far from there."

"As good a place to start as any, I suppose."

Hayden turned to Tempest, ready to tell her and Mac to stay with the nomads. Both of them had a set to their jaws and a fire in their eyes, telling him they weren't about to bail on him now. Both of them had done everything he'd told them to do, and he had to admit, they were both great shots. He may not like exposing a woman and a kid to danger, but this was their planet, too. He turned away without a word, returning to his horse and swinging into the saddle.

They were close now, and getting closer.

But what if it was already too late for Kady?

CHAPTER 31

The rancid and all-too-familiar smell of dead trife still hung thick in the air as Hayden, Tempest, Mac, and their new allies turned their horses south. Casper, the grizzled nomad leader, rode with them, along with three of his best men.

There was Jacob, Casper's son, a strapping older teenager with his father's intense blue eyes. Lean and quick, a pair of revolvers hung from his hips. Beside him rode Burke, a hulking bear of a man with arms like tree trunks. He cradled a shotgun with casual ease. Rounding out the group was Dex, the oldest of the bunch. Bald, weathered and wiry, his eyes sparkled with vitality.

"We're with you, Sheriff," Casper had told Hayden when they set out. "Wherever this trail leads, whatever we find at the end of it."

They rode hard, pushing the horses as much as they dared, until the old military base came into view, its once protective barbed-wire fencing rusted and dangling open in some places, completely collapsed in others.

As they drew closer, the evidence of the recent battle became all too clear. Bodies littered the ground, both human and trife, bloating in the merciless sun. Carrion birds wheeled overhead while others perched on the bodies, feeding on the dead flesh.

Mac made a small, distressed sound, turning her face into Tempest's back. Hayden's jaw clenched in rage and sorrow. So much death, so much senseless slaughter. And they still didn't know the full extent of what Zephyr had unleashed.

Or what he might still have to unleash.

Casper surveyed the scene with hollow eyes, his face etched with grief and grim determination. "Never thought I'd have to see this place again," he murmured. "Not after..."

He trailed off, shaking his head. Hayden didn't press him, understanding all too well the weight of painful memories.

They dismounted just inside the perimeter, the horses tossing their heads nervously at the stench of death. Hayden turned to the group, his voice low and urgent.

"Keep your eyes peeled and your weapons ready. There might still be trife lurking around. And if not them, then..."

A sudden clatter from one of the nearby buildings cut him off, snapping everyone's heads around at the sound. Hayden and Tempest exchanged glances, moving as one towards the source of the noise, revolvers and rifles at the ready.

They approached the building cautiously, hugging the wall, ears straining. A skittering, a hiss, coming from inside. Hayden held up a hand, signaling Tempest to cover him. Then, in one smooth motion, he kicked the door open and charged in, Tempest hot on his heels.

Four trife whirled to face them, crouched before a closed inner door. Their claws had already gouged deep furrows in the wood. They lunged with frightening speed, but Hayden and Tempest were ready. Hayden's revolvers thundered in the enclosed space. Tempest's plasma rifle thumped and whined. The trife shuddered violently as the rounds slammed home, their blood spraying the walls.

In moments, it was over, the demons dead on the floor. Hayden stepped over the bodies, trying the handle of the inner door. Locked from the inside. He rapped on it with the butt of his revolver.

"Anyone in there?" he called. "It's safe now, you can come out."

For a moment, there was only silence. Then, the sound of the bolt being drawn back, the door creaking open to reveal a woman's frightened face. One of the nomads, her clothes torn and stained, her dark hair matted with sweat and blood. She eyed Hayden and Tempest fearfully, ready to slam the door in their faces.

"It's okay," Hayden said, putting his foot in the door frame before she could try to lock herself back in. "We're here with Casper and his boy. You're safe now."

At the mention of Casper's name, the woman's face crumpled, tears spilling down her cheeks. She stumbled out of the room on shaky legs, clinging to Hayden's arm.

They emerged from the building to find the others waiting anxiously. When Casper saw the woman, he let out a wordless cry, rushing forward to enfold her in a fierce embrace.

"Sarah," he murmured. "Praise be, you're alive. When I saw the bodies, I thought..."

"I ran," Sarah said, her voice muffled against his chest. "When the trife broke through. I got cornered in there. Thought I was done for. Another few minutes and they would have broken through."

"It's okay now," Casper comforted. "The trife chased us all the way from here to the plains, sunlight be damned, but Sheriff Duke here helped us take them out. We lost Nettie and Paul, and some others were injured, but we found you, at least."

Sarah pulled back from him, looking at Hayden over Casper's shoulder. "You're the Sheriff?"

"Pozz," Hayden replied.

"Thank you," she said, fresh tears welling, "for saving me, and the others."

Hayden nodded. Every life saved was a victory, no matter how small.

Casper released Sarah, helping her over to one of the horses. "Dex, give her your mount. Ride double with Jacob."

The older man complied without hesitation, climbing off his horse and boosting Sarah into the saddle. Casper squeezed her hand.

"Ride north," he told her. "There's a settlement there, a bandit hideout the Sheriff cleared out. The rest of our people are headed that way. You'll be safe there until we get back."

Sarah nodded, fresh tears in her eyes. "Be careful," she whispered.

"I will. Now go, quickly."

She wheeled the horse and set off at a gallop, soon vanishing into the distance.

Hayden turned to the others. "Search the other buildings," he said. "But be careful. Shout if you find any more survivors —or any more trife."

"If you don't mind, Sheriff," Casper said. "Jacob and I will take care of our dead. I don't want the buzzards and the coyotes getting a free meal from them."

"I understand," Hayden replied.

As the group dispersed, Hayden started walking the base perimeter, eyes fixed on the ground, seeking any sign of the trife's passage. If they could find the trail, they would find their source.

Behind him, he could hear Casper and his son moving bodies, carrying the fallen nomads into one of the empty barracks, getting them out of the sun and away from the scavengers. It was somber work but necessary.

He had nearly completed a circuit of the base when he spotted a stretch of churned earth, claw marks gouged into the dusty soil, leading away into the scrublands to the west. The trife's trail, clear as day.

Hayden straightened, turned, and strode back towards the

others, purpose lending fresh urgency to his steps. Casper had finished moving the bodies, and the others had completed their search of the buildings, finding them all clear.

"Saddle up," he called as he approached. "I've found the trail. With any luck, it'll lead us straight to Zephyr and Kady."

The others scrambled to obey, tightening girths and checking weapons. In moments, they were mounted and ready, falling in behind Hayden as he climbed into the saddle and led the way out of the base, following the trail westward.

Toward a reckoning, long overdue.

The sun climbed higher in the sky as they rode, beating down on them. The landscape remained arid, baked and brown, an endless expanse of scrub and dust. The trife's trail was easy to follow at first, the churned earth standing out like a scar across the terrain. But as the miles fell away beneath their horses' hooves, the signs grew fainter, the marks of the demons' passage fading back into harder, denser terrain.

Hayden kept his eyes fixed on the ground, trusting his mount to pick its way across the rugged landscape as he searched for any trace, any hint of their quarry's direction. Beside him, Tempest and Mac scanned the horizon, alert for any flicker of movement or danger.

Behind them, Casper and his men were strung out in a loose column, weapons at the ready. The nomad leader's hard expression tried to hide his grief for his fallen comrades and temper his vengeance, though both emotions escaped every so often in narrowed eyes or dark grunts. Jacob and Dex rode at his side, young but no less resolute. Burke brought up the rear, watchful and wary.

They rode in tense silence, the only sounds the creak of saddle leather and the thud of hooves on the packed earth. Each of them lost in their own thoughts.

For Hayden, every mile took him closer to Kady. Every minute she spent in the Rebirthers' grasp was an acid bite in his gut. He had his own fiery vengeance to contend with. A burning in his chest as hot as he had ever felt before. It was one thing to cause him trouble. Another to threaten children. Something else to harm them. And Zephyr had already done something to release a flood of trife back into the world. Hayden feared the full extent of the cultist's meddling with things he didn't understand. The worst troublemakers were always the most ignorant and misguided.

The sun sank towards the western horizon when they finally paused to rest, the horses blowing and lathered. They had long since lost the trail, the trife's tracks vanishing into the rocky hills. Now they were navigating by dead reckoning, figuring the demons moved in a mostly straight line.

Hayden swung down from the saddle, his legs stiff and sore. He swigged lukewarm water from a bottle of water he pulled from his saddlebags before pouring some into his cupped hand for his horse. The animal greedily licked it up, along with two more handfuls.. "Wish I had an apple for you, boy," he said, patting his neck before leading him over to some clumps to dry grass to munch on.

Removing his hat, he wiped the sweat off his face with a swipe of his forearm before doing his best to restore his hat to its former shape. Losing it during the battle with the trife, it had taken a beating. Stepped on and smashed into the dirt, it was more brown than its original tan. Blood, sweat, and gore stained it, and a chunk of the brim had been bitten off by one of the trife, but he put it back on, glad he'd found it.

All the while, he kept glancing up to make vigilant sweeps of their surroundings. Tempest had dismounted before helping Mac down. Together, they'd passed out water bottles and hunks of jerky to everyone before Casper and his men fanned out, setting up a rough perimeter. Burke tended to their horses while Dex scouted ahead. Jacob stood with his father, watching Hayden's every move while trying to mimic his posture and expression. Any other time, Hayden would have found it amusing, but right now he didn't have much to smile about.

"We need to keep moving," Casper said to him, returning to his horse to adjust the saddle, his voice a low rasp that had to have come from a lifetime of smoking. "Every moment we linger, the cultists get further ahead."

"Pozz," Hayden agreed. "But the horses need rest. An hour or two, and then we'll get back on the trail. Hopefully, Dex can find it."

"If it's out there, he'll find it. Dex can read the land like nobody I ever seen."

No sooner than he'd said it, Dex materialized out of the gathering dusk, his lean face split by a triumphant grin. "Found a spring," he reported. "Just over that rise, he said, nodding at a scrubby hill about a thousand yards distant. "And there's something else...something you need to see, Sheriff."

Hayden frowned but followed as the older man led the way up the gentle slope. As they crested the rise, he sucked in a sharp breath.

Below them, a small, nearly dried-up creek wound its way between the hill and the adjacent incline. A dozen hoverbikes were scattered on the far side of the creek bed, toppled and spread out like they had been hit by a tornado.

Or an emerging slick of trife.

"That's it," Hayden muttered, turning to Dex and pointing to the mouth of a cave just past the cluster of wrecked hoverbikes. "You found the trife nest."

"I didn't do nothin' but walk a little further ahead, Sheriff," Dex replied.

"You still found them. We need to get the others."

Hayden ran back to the camp, Dex hot on his heels. They explained what Dex had found, garnering looks of surprise from everyone. "It's a cave, half a klick west of here. The

Rebirthers' hoverbikes are knocked over outside of it and beat to rat shit like a herd of horses trampled them."

"More like a herd of trife," Dex supplied. "You think them cult bastards are inside that cave with the queen?"

"Yes, I do, but the question is…are they dead or alive?"

And what about Kady?

Casper jumped to his feet. "Well then, what are we waiting for, Sheriff?" The others hopped up in turn, equally eager to join the hunt

"We aren't waiting for anything," Hayden replied, opening his saddlebags and digging out a small flashlight. "It's time to end this."

CHAPTER 32

Hayden and the others raced to the mine entrance, urgency speeding up their steps. As they approached the mine's entrance, he held up a hand, bringing the group to a halt.

He moved to one of the hoverbikes, lying on its side on the ground, dented and pressed into the soft dirt by the trife who'd stampeded over it.

"What are you doing, Sheriff?" Mac whispered.

"Checking the range," he replied, leveraging the bike upright. He turned it on, noting that the battery only had about ten miles of power. Running calculations in his head, he turned to the others. "Looks like Kady might have tried to lead them astray for a while. We might not be as far behind as I feared."

"That's great news," Tempest agreed.

Hayden let the hoverbike fall back to the ground. "Dex, Mac, I need you two to stay here. Cover our backs, and make sure no one sneaks up behind us. If you see any trife or anything else that looks suspicious, do what you can to get rid of them. Pozz?"

Dex nodded, a glint of understanding in his intent eyes as he unslung his rifle. Mac looked for a moment as if she might argue, but then she pressed her lips together and gave a firm nod, her small hand tightening on her weapon. Hayden felt a swell of pride at her bravery and resolve, tempering his ever-present worry for her safety.

With that settled, Hayden turned to face the mine entrance, the others falling in behind him. Casper briefly clasped his shoulder, a silent gesture of support and shared purpose. Jacob and Burke flanked them, weapons at the ready.

Hayden left his flashlight off as they entered the tunnel, not wanting to alert Zephyr and his Rebirthers to their approach. The darkness closed around them like a physical thing, thick and oppressive, broken only by the faint slivers of fading daylight that filtered in behind them.

The ancient mineshaft burrowed deep into the hillside, the rough-hewn walls pressing close on either side. The air grew cooler as they descended, carrying the faint, musty scent of long abandonment and damp earth.

Hayden moved cautiously, his boots scuffing softly on the uneven ground, one hand clutching his microspear, the other trailing along the wall to help guide his way. Behind him, he could hear the others' measured breaths and the occasional clink of a weapon as it brushed against a rock.

They went deeper, the tunnel winding ever downward. The last of the daylight faded to nothing, plunging them into a complete darkness that felt almost alive. Unable to see his hand in front of him, Hayden's other senses sharpened to compensate. He listened to the echoes of their careful steps, the whisper of disturbed air as they moved. The growing tension that thrummed through each of them even had a feel to it.

Finally, he slipped the flashlight from his pocket, but before turning it on, he pulled a kerchief from his back pocket and tied it around the lens, diffusing the beam into a dim, muted glow. It was enough to illuminate their immediate surroundings without broadcasting their presence too far ahead.

They continued on, picking their way through the blackness, alert for any sign of their quarry or hint of danger. The tunnel twisted and turned, winding through the earth like a snake. Along the way, they came across ancient mining equipment, discarded food wrappers, and even an old, trampled tent, suggesting scavengers had been here at one time over the last couple of centuries. Yet, they hadn't released the trife or found the queen, suggesting something at the end of the tunnel had kept the Relyeh creatures imprisoned.

And somehow, Zephyr had released them.

It was Burke who spotted a huddled shape on the ground ahead, barely visible in the flashlight's weak glow. Hayden approached warily, weapon at the ready, half expecting the form to leap up and attack.

But it remained still, unmoving. Hayden played the light over it and sucked in a sharp breath.

He expected a trife, but instead discovered a Rebirther, sprawled face down in the dirt. And he was very clearly dead, his body bearing the unmistakable rending of trife claws.

A chill ran down Hayden's spine as he knelt beside the fallen cultist. The man had been savaged, torn open from throat to groin. But the blood that pooled beneath him was tacky, half-dried. He'd been dead for hours, at least.

"Another one." Jacob pointed further up the tunnel. His young face was pale in the diffused light. "Looks like he bought it the same way."

"Stay ready," Hayden replied, rising to his feet. "There may be live ones down here. If so, I'll try to take them out silently. Only start shooting if I look like I'm in trouble."

"So, we don't need our guns, then," Jacob said with a shocked smirk. "You'll just put your fist through 'em."

They pressed on with renewed caution and urgency,

Hayden in the lead, the flashlight casting eerie shadows on the rough-hewn walls. The air grew increasingly stale and thick, forcing them to breathe through their mouths to avoid gagging on the stench of decay.

Nearly half an hour passed before they came across a pair of heavy metal doors set into the tunnel wall, blocking any further progress. And sprawled before those doors, their lifeless eyes staring into nothing, lay a dozen slaughtered trife.

Hayden pulled up short. The doors matched the one he'd discovered at the chemical plant, each bearing the unmistakable eagle-and-star insignia of the United States Space Force. One was closed, its surface pristine. The other gaped open, a yawning portal into pitch blackness.

Ignoring the twisting in his gut, Hayden stepped forward and angled his flashlight into the open doorway. The feeble light pushed back the front edge of the gloom, revealing what appeared to be a vast, open cavern, its true dimensions impossible to discern. It stretched beyond the flashlight's reach, even as Hayden pulled back the cloth.

"What is this place?" Tempest murmured, her grip tightening on her rifle.

"The trife must've been dormant here until the Rebirthers came along and woke them up," Hayden replied.

"But how did Zephyr and the other cultists avoid getting torn apart like their friends we found back in the tunnel?"

His flashlight swept over the carnage between the two doors. "Look at that one," he said, using the flashlight to pick out a trife.

"What about it?"

"It's dead. But there's no visible wounds, no obvious injuries. It's like it just...dropped dead."

Casper huffed a humorless laugh. "Are you saying it died of natural causes? Keeled over from a heart attack?"

"No," he replied. "Kady."

"The girl you're looking for?" Casper asked. "How could a child do that?"

"She's different," Hayden replied. "Special." He glanced at Tempest. "Back at the Fort, Steel said that the trife won't attack the Children of Grimmel or anyone with them. That they would somehow recognize them."

"And those cultists we found further back were too far away to be safe," Tempest concluded. "She must've been with Zephyr and the main group when they came through here."

Hayden nodded. "Pozz."

"But why would she kill them if they wouldn't try to hurt her?"

"I don't know. Maybe Zephyr made her do it. Or maybe she was just scared and reacted. Could be at the same time she cried out for me."

"That makes sense," Tempest agreed. "That would mean we're about twelve hours behind them. Seems you were right about Kady leading them around for a while before coming here."

He waved a hand at the other corpses littering the chamber. "The rest must have rushed out to attack the rear guard before she could stop them all."

"That's some heavy lifting for a child," Casper muttered, eyeing the carnage with awe and revulsion.

Hayden didn't reply. His attention was caught by the second door, which remained firmly shut. He stepped up to it, running a hand over its cold metal surface.

"I don't get it," Jacob said behind him. "Zephyr and his crew obviously came this way, right? So why isn't this door open, too?"

Hayden eyed the sealed door. There were no signs of damage, no evidence that the door had been pried. The evidence made his blood run cold. Zephyr needed to know the individual door's code or the USSF master code to get through without force, which he had clearly done. How was that possible?

"Zephyr used an access code to get through the door," Hayden explained. "Then he closed it behind him, maybe thinking we wouldn't be able to get through. He thought wrong."

Hayden stepped up to the keypad set into the wall beside the door. His fingers slipped over the buttons, entering the familiar sequence.

The indicator light flashed from red to green. With a soft hiss of equalizing pressure, the door slid open.

CHAPTER 33

Beyond the door lay a small antechamber, its walls lined with pipes and hoses, gauges and a control panel. A filtration room, an airlock between the outside world and whatever secrets the USSF had sought to keep contained and uncontaminated. A second door waited on the far side, identical to the first.

Hayden crossed the chamber, aware of the others at his back, their weapons ready. He punched in the master code again. The second door opened.

The hidden USSF facility wasn't a surprise, especially after the chemical plant. But that didn't stop the cold trickle of foreboding from running down his spine as they stepped into the room beyond. His grip on the microspear tightened as he swept the flashlight's beam across banks of silent computers, microscopes, and other equipment he didn't recognize.

A research lab.

"I don't like this," Casper muttered, his grizzled face tight with apprehension. "I don't like this one bit."

"I'm with you there," Hayden replied quietly. "Whatever they were up to in here, it couldn't have been good."

An experiment, of course. The USSF had been tinkering

with the trife since the outset of the war, trying to understand them and harness them for their own ends. At one point, they had hoped to turn the demons on one another, never knowing that it was a doomed effort from the start.

But to bring a trife queen in here to study? The USSF had been playing with fire. Fortunately for them, they had managed not to get burned.

Not so fortunate for him or Kady.

Who knew what the researchers were doing to the queen. They had already seen that the escaped trife were more hardy and determined than any he had encountered before. And they now killed indiscriminately. Children and adults both. He doubted that was a coincidence.

"Eyes sharp," he said, his voice low and intense. "We're close. I can feel it. Whatever you do, don't touch anything. We have no idea what kind of experiments they were running here. Treat everything as a potential hazard."

The group nodded, pale faces tight with fear and tension. Hayden knew they were all feeling the weight of what they'd discovered here, the implications that hung heavy in the stale air. The sick certainty that whatever the USSF had been up to, it couldn't have been anything good.

And now Zephyr sought to turn those secrets to his own twisted ends.

Hayden moved deeper into the lab, the others following close at his heels. The darkness pressed in around them, held at bay only by the glow of his flashlight.

The beam played across cluttered workstations, tangles of cables and more equipment, its purpose he could only guess at. Beakers and vials glinted dully on dusty shelves, their contents long since evaporated. Mildewed papers and shattered computer screens littered every surface, mute testament to the sudden, panicked evacuation that must have occurred when they pulled out to join the ships on their way to Proxima.

But his focus wasn't on the detritus of the past. It was on the trail left by the Rebirthers' passage, the signs that would lead them to their goal. A scuff on the gritty floor, a smear in the omnipresent dust, a tray hastily knocked aside.

Hayden followed those breadcrumbs with single minded purpose, every sense straining for any hint of danger. There was nothing so far except the echoing silence of a disturbed tomb, but he knew that could change in an instant.

Behind him, he heard Burke mutter a prayer under his breath, his normally booming voice reduced to a shaky whisper. Hayden didn't blame him. He wasn't a particularly religious man himself, but in this place, with the ghosts of USSF hubris and alien experimentation all around, a ward against evil didn't seem like such a bad idea.

Hayden continued through the shadowed labyrinth of the USSF facility, his senses on high alert, the microspear clutched tightly in one hand, flashlight in the other. Behind him, Tempest, Casper, Jacob, and Burke followed close on his heels, weapons shouldered, expressions tense.

The pervading silence was oppressive, broken only by the sound of their boots on the gritty floor and the occasional creak of long-abandoned equipment disturbed by their passing. He couldn't shake the sense of foreboding that clung to him like a second skin, a prickling certainty that they were walking into something far worse than he could imagine. The ghosts of the past seemed to watch from every corner, the weight of long-dead eyes heavy on the back of his neck. Everything about this felt wrong in a way he couldn't quite put his finger on. As if he had already lost and he just didn't know it yet.

He pushed onward regardless, following the faint trail left by Zephyr and his Rebirthers, leading them deeper into the heart of this twisted place.

Suddenly, a flicker of movement caught Hayden's eye, a darting shadow at the edge of the flashlight's glow. He froze, throwing up a hand to halt the others, every muscle coiled and ready.

A heartbeat later, all hell broke loose.

Red-armored figures burst from the darkness on either side, plasma rifles spitting blue fire. Zephyr's elite guard, lying in wait, springing their ambush with ruthless precision.

Hayden dove for cover behind a rolling cabinet, dragging Tempest down with him as a hail of plasma bolts sizzled overhead. Casper, Jacob, and Burke scattered, seeking what meager shelter they could find amidst the clutter and debris.

"Seems the good Sheriff's lost his edge!" one of the Rebirthers called out, his voice mocking. "You're too late, Sheriff! Much too late!"

Hayden gritted his teeth, risking a glance around the edge of the table. He counted five of them, spread out behind cover in the passageway ahead, preventing them from advancing any further.

"If I'm too late, then why don't you let me pass?" Hayden shouted back. "Let me get a look-see for myself."

The Rebirthers laughed. "Good one, Sheriff. Because Zephyr says he doesn't want to be disturbed. And you're definitely disturbing." The other cultists laughed harder at that.

"What do we do, Sheriff?" Tempest asked.

The question reminded him of the nightmare. Alina had asked the same thing when the raiders came to take the children from the Greens. The answer hadn't changed.

"Hit them with everything we've got," Hayden replied, pocketing the microspear and drawing his revolvers. "Now!"

He rose from cover and crossed the room diagonally, drawing the Rebirthers' fire while Tempest and the others popped up to shoot. He put two rounds into the head of a Rebirther as he passed, plasma bolts hissing past him, one close enough to burn his ear.

From the corner of his eye, he saw Jacob rise from cover.

The boy brought his revolvers to bear, his posture and stance so similar to Hayden's own. His first shot missed, but the second punched the cultist in the face, the slug tearing through his mask and the soft flesh beneath.

At the same time, the Rebirthers stopped firing on Hayden and switched targets. Almost immediately, a cry of pain rang out, and Hayden saw Burke get hit in the gut, a smoking hole already burned through his chest. The big man crumpled and his shotgun clattered to the floor.

"Burke!" Casper shouted. He made to rise from cover, but another flurry of plasma drove him back, a bolt catching him high in the shoulder before he could get clear.

"Dad!" Jacob cried, standing to scramble to his father's side.

"I'm alright, boy." Casper waved him off, grimacing as he clutched his wounded shoulder. "Just a scratch. Stay down!"

"Two of yours for two of ours," the Rebirther said. "Fair trade."

"How do you reckon that?" Hayden replied. "My friends aren't wearing armor or breathing in sense-enhancing drugs. Kind of pathetic on your part, the way I see it."

"We'll see who's pathetic, Sheriff," the man growled back.

Hayden glanced at Tempest. "Set your rifle to stream and be ready. They're going to come at us."

"What do you mean?" Tempest asked.

Hayden holstered one revolver and drew the microspear. "Tell me something? Is this your idea of a good fight? Because to be honest, I'm getting bored right about now." He turned his head to peer down the corridor. The moment one of the Rebirthers stuck his head out, he whipped his revolver out from cover and fired. The round hit the wall right next to the cultist's head.

"Ha! You missed!" the Rebirther taunted.

"Did I?" Hayden replied. "That was an invitation. Here's

another." Hayden tossed his revolver onto the floor, closer to the Rebirthers than to him.

"Are you crazy?" Tempest whispered.

"Did you see Jacob shoot?" Hayden replied. "We just need them out from behind cover, so we can end this quick like. Did you set that rifle to stream?"

She adjusted the dial on the side of the weapon. "It is now."

"What's your trick, Sheriff?" the Rebirther asked.

"No trick," Hayden answered. "I just want to see if you have enough moxie to come at me. Because I think you're too scared to try, even with the Clear."

Hayden nodded to Tempest. "Here we go."

As if on cue, the Rebirthers broke from their cover, rushing toward the room with supernatural speed. They fired their weapons as they ran, plasma bolts searing past, burning into the cabinet, and threatening to keep them pinned down.

"Now!" Hayden cried to Tempest. She didn't hesitate, popping up and firing.

A searing lance of plasma leapt from the rifle's muzzle, painting the lead Rebirther from head to toe in hot, blue fire. The man screamed and slowed, not expecting the attack and leaving himself wide open. Hayden rolled into the center of the room, bringing the microspear up into the Rebirther's stomach. The tendrils reached up to stop his heart, and he collapsed as Hayden rose to his feet.

Tempest swung the plasma rifle like a flamethrower, catching the other two Rebirthers, the superheated stream unable to pierce their combat armor, but more than capable of blinding and distracting the fighters despite their enhanced speed and strength.

Hayden lunged at the next Rebirther, sinking his hand through blue flame to bring the microspear home. Scalded by the heat, he withdrew it as quickly as possible, the surprised Rebirther collapsing at his feet. Turning to the third, he quickly drew his revolver when he saw the Rebirther already aiming at him, the muzzle of the cultist's rifle pointed right at his face. Before he could shoot, two rounds hit the Rebirther in the side of the head. Snapping him sideways, he crumpled to the floor.

Whipping his head back toward Jacob, the younger man tipped his frayed ball cap before grinning from ear to ear.

"Thank you for the save," Hayden said.

"Anytime, Sheriff," Jacob replied.

Hayden moved among the fallen, kicking weapons away from limp hands and closing off the flow of Clear while confirming the kills.

Satisfied, he holstered his revolver and returned to Casper. Jacob was already there, helping his father to a sitting position, worry etched across his youthful features.

"How bad is it?" Hayden asked quietly, kneeling beside them.

Casper managed a tight grin, though his face was pale and sheened with sweat. "Reckon I'll live."

Hayden glanced at the ugly wound. "Listen," he said, "there's no shame in turning back. You've done more than enough already. This fight is mine, not yours."

Casper shook his head stubbornly. "The hell it ain't, Sheriff. Those bastards let those things out, and those things killed my people. It's my fight as much as it is yours."

"At least let Jacob get you back to the horses," he tried. "He can—"

"I'm not going anywhere," Jacob cut in fiercely. "I'm seeing this through." He squeezed his father's good shoulder. "We both are."

Casper nodded. "You heard the boy. We're with you, Sheriff. To the end of the line."

Tempest materialized at Hayden's elbow. "That was quick thinking, Sheriff. But we need to keep moving."

"Pozz," he answered. "Let's go."

CHAPTER 34

Hayden and the others set off again, stepping over the corpses of the fallen, following the only path left open to them.

Casper was on his feet now, cradling his arm against his body. Taking his rifle, Jacob handed him one of his pistols, and he took it left-handed, testing its weight with a nod of approval.

They didn't have to go much farther. The corridor made a single right turn and continued another fifty feet before ending abruptly at a set of heavy blast doors. A red light pulsed above the portal, warning them back, but Hayden didn't hesitate. He slapped the controls, and the doors ground open.

The room beyond defied description.

A line of long steel tables stretched into the gloom, each bearing the tied-down, dissected carcass of a trife. Their torsos had been peeled open, their organs floating in murky preservation jars sitting beside them. Banks of dead monitors hung over their heads while strange machines loomed in the shadows, their purpose as alien as the beings they'd been designed to study.

And there, at the far end of the chamber, mounted on a steel slab like a grotesque trophy, was the head of a trife queen. Its empty eye sockets seemed to stare directly at Hayden, its maw gaping in a silent, mocking scream.

"Sheriff..." Tempest breathed, her voice strained.

But Hayden wasn't listening. His attention was fixed on the figure slumped before a glowing computer terminal near the queen's severed head.

Zephyr.

In an instant, Hayden was across the room, seizing the cult leader by the back of his robe. He hauled the man to his feet and spun him around, slamming him against the unyielding edge of the desk behind him.

Zephyr's head cracked against the steel, surprise and fury mingling on his gaunt face. He scrambled for a weapon, but Hayden was faster, batting his hand away, steel-like fingers closing around his throat.

"Where is she?" Hayden snarled, his voice low and deadly. "Where's Kady?"

Zephyr laughed. A choked, ugly sound. "You're too late, Sheriff," he gasped. "The Rebirth is complete. The restoration will begin. And there's nothing you can do about it."

Hayden's grip tightened, rage pulsing behind his eyes. "What do you mean? What have you done?"

"Exactly what I told you that I was going to do," Zephyr sneered. "You were there...*Sam*," he said mockingly. "You heard the whole plan. Oh, you should have been here to see it. It was glori—"

His voice cut off in a strangled gurgle as Hayden hauled him forward and then slammed him back, his head bouncing off the desk with a sickening crack.

"Kady," Hayden insisted. "Or I swear, I'll snap your neck like a twig."

Zephyr's eyes rolled, his struggles weakening. "The

queen..." he mumbled, blood flecking his lip where he'd bitten it. "We found her...used the girl...woke her up..."

Hayden's heart seized in his chest. "Where?" he demanded, giving the man a teeth-rattling shake, his mouth twisting with enraged fury. "Where. Is. She?"

With a last, desperate burst of strength, Zephyr pointed a trembling finger at the thick metal and glass door set into the wall behind the queen trophy, the interior dark. "In there," he whispered, a mad, triumphant light in his eyes. "Both the queen and Kady are in there. But you're too late, Sheriff. Too late to stop the tide."

Hayden wanted to strangle him, but reason won out over emotion. He was still a lawman, and cold-blooded murder wasn't the way he did things. Instead, he took his hands off Zephyr. "Watch him," he told the others. "If he so much as twitches..."

Leaving the bastard battered but intact, he left the rest unsaid, but they understood. Casper nodded curtly, lifting his pistol to cover Zephyr. Tempest and Jacob flanked him as well.

Hayden started for the door. "I wouldn't do that if I were you, Sheriff," Zephyr said, amused and mocking.

Hayden glanced back at him. "And why not? I can handle a trife queen. It wouldn't be the first time."

Zephyr grinned. "Always so macho. So tough. So confident. But you forget, Sheriff. This is our destiny. Our fate. The world as it's meant to be. You can't stop it, no matter how much you want to. No matter how hard you try."

"I'm sure I don't know what you mean," Hayden answered, continuing to the door.

As he approached, he heard a click behind him. Looking back, he saw Zephyr's finger rising from the terminal's keyboard, hands raised in surrender, a wide grin on his face.

"What did you do?" Hayden asked.

"I don't need to do anything, Sheriff," Zephyr replied. "It's already done."

Hayden scowled and hurried to the door, its thick glass allowing him to see inside the room, now illuminated. He was sure the queen wouldn't harm Kady, but what he saw still drove all the breath from his lungs and all the fire from his gut.

It was a massive chamber, an extension of the same cave system. It was filled with trife eggs—hundreds, maybe thousands—in densely packed concentric circles, each holding a trife embryo visible through the translucent sacks.

Full-grown trife hunkered in shadowed corners by the dozens, clinging to the crags and uneven surfaces of the cave. But they weren't normal trife. Their leathery skin appeared harder, their limbs lined with spikes, their eyes glaring out with an intelligence he'd never seen in one of the demons before.

And in the center of it all, the trife queen.

She was immense. Her body, with its razor-tipped limbs, was coated in a layer of deadly protection, a great sinuous coil. Armored plates. A crown of spikes jutted from her elongated skull, her massive jaws bristling with jagged teeth. Cables and tubes bristled from her flesh, tethering her to arcane machinery mounted to the top of the cavern, a manifested nightmare.

Hayden stared at the Relyeh demon. He'd seen trife queens before, but never anything like this. The USSF had experimented with creating stronger, more powerful trife. This…this was something new and very frightening.

He pulled his eyes downward toward the queen's feet. Sitting there cross-legged, her small form dwarfed by the monstrosity above her, was Kady.

Her eyes were closed. Her mouth closed. At rest. She seemed strangely peaceful, as did the queen behind her.

"What have you done?" Hadyen uttered, staring at the horrific scene.

"I already answered that question, Sheriff," Zephyr replied. "But now you understand. You're too late. If you open that door, the trife and their queen will rip us all apart and escape. And if you don't open it, Kady will die of thirst before she dies of hunger."

"You're a monster," Tempest hissed, grabbing Zephyr by the throat. "I should kill you."

"Tempest, wait," Hayden said, turning toward the cult leader as she released him. "What's the catch, Zephyr? Why haven't you already opened the door and let them out? What are you waiting for?"

"I'm not surprised by your astuteness," Zephyr said. "Of course, I knew you would come. I was waiting for you, so you would be the one to open it."

"No," Hayden countered. "You might not believe in my outlook on life or humankind's place in the universe, but you have no reason to hold such a personal grudge. Not when so much is at stake. Why haven't you opened the door?"

Zephyr didn't answer. His smile remained, but it became strained. Forced. Hayden's eyes narrowed, focusing on the muscles around his eyelids, noticing the tension in his jaw.

"Huh," he said, shaking his head. "Well, I'll be damned. You're afraid, aren't you? Now that you're here. Now that you've seen it and its brood."

"I'm not afraid," Zephyr claimed.

"Horse shit," Hayden replied. "Maybe your faith isn't as strong as you thought. Or maybe you aren't quite ready to die." He stared at Zephyr, considering. "Who put you up to this? Because you didn't come up with this whole plan all by your little lonesome."

"I had a vision, Sheriff. A prophecy of—"

"You can cut the whole disciple of the Rebirth act, Zephyr, or whatever your name really is. Someone gave you the code to open the outer doors and get in here. Last I checked, only a few people knew that code."

"And of course, you know it," Zephyr snapped. "The mighty Sheriff knows everything."

"Who gave you the code?" Hayden ground out.

"What does it matter? What does any of it matter? We're here, Sheriff. Everything is in motion. All you need to do is open the door, attempt to rescue your charge, and let destiny do the rest."

"That's not what you want," Hayden answered. "You want a way out of this. You thought it was all so perfect, until you realized that the Children of Grimmel won't protect you the way you thought. That they might keep you safe from normal trife, maybe even these trife, but they won't keep you safe from a queen. Not even Kady can do that. Isn't that right?"

"How…how do you reckon that?"

"Because you're out here instead of in there. Because you won't open the door. Because you're afraid. It's as plain as the nose on your face."

Zephyr stared at him defiantly, only able to hold the pose for a few more seconds before breaking down. "She told me that I would be a king among men when the world order was restored. She lied to me. The queen was hibernating, like she said. Kept alive by the machine she's still connected to. This terminal controls the machine. I turned it off, and the queen awoke. Then, I tried to go in with Kady. The moment I got in range, that thing lashed out at me." He turned, parting his white robe to show off his armor. Three huge claw marks dug into it, nearly passing through. "I barely got out of there alive. Meanwhile, Kady went and sat with it like she was its pet."

Hayden turned his attention back to the transparency. That was it. The missing piece of his understanding. Kady had become a slave to the queen, not the other way around.

That's why she never responded or called him after her scream. She wanted him to protect her from the queen.

But what could the queen possibly want with a child?

"Who put you up to this?" Tempest asked. "A woman? What's her name?"

"I don't know. She never told me her name. She just said she was from Proxima, and asked me if I believed the world was better before the Sheriff came along."

"And you said, yes?" Jacob asked incredulously.

"No, I…she convinced me it was, and could be again. That I could be a leader. One of the strong, instead of the weak. I didn't believe her at first, but then—"

"She gave you Clear," Hayden finished for him.

"I never felt stronger or more alive. She told me that if I wanted power, I could have it. If I wanted an endless supply of Clear, I could have it. It was my destiny to witness the Rebirth, and usher in a new age of mankind."

"I can't believe you bought all of that shit," Tempest said.

"I believed it with everything in me," Zephyr countered. "Part of me still does. That's why I couldn't leave. But I'm supposed to live. I want to live."

"This woman," Tempest said. "She isn't about this high…" She held her hand out, level with her mid-chest. "…with a small face and curly brown hair, is she?"

"Yes. How did you know?"

Tempest turned to Hayden. "That's the same woman I've been trading with. That strange metal for guns."

Hayden nodded. "I figured that much. It seems to me, everyone in this room is being used in some way or another, even if none of us knows exactly how, or why, or by whom."

"I get that she used me for the metal. And it seems she didn't care about the guns because if Zephyr succeeded I would be too dead to use them. And she used Zephyr to reintroduce the trife to the world, bigger and badder than ever. But how did she use you, Sheriff?"

"She got me to come here to open the door, in case her chosen one here chickened out," Hayden replied. "And if he didn't chicken out…to die either way. She's trying real hard to get me gone."

"But why?"

"I don't know." He paused, mind working. "I'm starting to think Kady never called out to me at all. That whoever is behind this tricked me using the same methods Shub'Nigu does to speak to me. Which would make your arms dealer a Relyeh. Which makes a lot of sense as to why she's trying to get rid of me. But if she really is from Proxima…" He trailed off, unsure what the full implications might be. Whatever they were, he was sure it was bad.

"If that machine was letting it hibernate and keeping it alive, can't you use it to put it back to sleep?" Tempest asked.

"I've tried," Zephyr answered, shifting back to the terminal, changing the menu and tapping the keyboard. "It's not responding."

Hayden added the broken machine to his mental equation, finally coming out with only one possible solution. "You're right about one thing, Zephyr."

"Which thing?"

"We're here. Everything is in motion. All I need to do is open the door, attempt to rescue my girl, and let destiny do the rest."

"Sheriff?" Tempest questioned. "You can't be serious."

"Don't worry," Hayden replied. "I have a plan."

CHAPTER 35

"What kind of plan?" Tempest asked.

"The only one I can come up with," Hayden replied. "I'm going to put on the armor of one of the dead guards, along with their canister of Clear. Then I'm going in."

Zephyr barked incredulous laughter from where he sat, Casper's pistol still trained on his head. "You're out of your mind, Sheriff. Just let the girl die. Save yourself and the rest of us. It's the only way."

Tempest hesitated, her eyes searching Hayden's face. "He might have a point, Sheriff. I know you want to save her, but the risk..."

"I won't let Kady die a slave to that thing, alone and afraid," Hayden snapped. "Besides, we can walk away today, but if we do, that thing'll get out sooner or later. I'd bet my life on it."

"You are betting your life on it," Zephyr said.

"Pozz. *My* life. If I die, then I die upholding the promise I made to keep fighting to the end. To protect the innocent to the end. With any luck, wherever I go after this, Nat and my kids will be there, too." He swept his eyes across the room.

"I'm going in, and that's final. You can close the door behind me."

Tempest held his gaze for a long, tense moment. Then, to Hayden's surprise, she nodded. "Alright. If you're going in, then so am I."

"No, Tempest. You don't have to—"

"Save it, Sheriff. I already told you I've got a soft spot for kids. And you're right. If we leave this thing here, someone will come along soon enough to let it out, if only out of curiosity. Maybe even the bitch who tricked this idiot…" She motioned to Zephyr. "…into coming here in the first place. Anyway, I'll be damned if I let you face this alone."

Casper stepped forward. "Count me in, too. If you two are hellbent on this, then I'm with you. I swore to protect my people at all costs, and this is the price."

Jacob also opened his mouth to volunteer, but Casper cut him off with a sharp gesture. "Not you, boy. If anything happens to me in there, the clan will need a leader. Besides, someone's got to keep an eye on this snake." He jerked his chin at Zephyr.

Hayden looked to the cult leader. "What about you? Care to show a little courage and make up for what you've done here?"

Zephyr wrinkled his face and shook his head. "I'm fine right where I am."

Hayden huffed. "Reckoned as much." He turned to Tempest and Casper. "Alright, let's suit up."

They returned to the fallen guards, stripping the combat armor from their bodies with quick, efficient movements. Hayden donned the blood-red painted shell and the Clear canister on his back. He took a deep, steadying breath, snapped the breathing mask over his face and opened the line. The acrid tang of the drug filled his lungs, setting his nerves alight.

Beside him, Tempest and Casper did the same, plasma rifles held at the ready.

"You two okay?" he asked.

"I feel...powerful," Tempest said, sucking in the Clear. "Like I could take on all the trife and the queen myself."

"My arm doesn't even hurt anymore," Casper added, though it remained limp at his side. "I feel twenty years old again."

"Let it make you faster and stronger, not over-confident," Hayden replied, feeling a small measure of giddiness from the drug.

He led Tempest and Casper back to the entrance of the queen's chamber.

"Now you look like true disciples," Zephyr commented on seeing them.

"Shut your mouth," Jacob barked. "They've got more guts than you've ever had in your life."

"Listen up," Hayden said, his voice slightly distorted by his mask. "Those things in there, they're not like any trife we've faced before. They're stronger, smarter, more vicious. I need you to keep them off me while I deal with the queen. Understand?"

Tempest and Casper nodded, their eyes hard and eager above their masks.

Hayden turned to Zephyr. "Open the door. And you better hope we win. I can't guarantee your safety if we don't." He glanced at Jacob, whose body language told him how things would end for Zephyr if they failed.

The cult leader swallowed hard, then tapped a command into the terminal with trembling fingers. The heavy door began to grind open, the screech of metal on metal filling the chamber.

Hayden tensed, microspear clutched tightly in his fist, ready to lunge at the first trife that tried to come through or assault him. To his surprise, the demons didn't attack.

Instead, they backed away from the door, clearing a path, their red eyes fixed on him with an unsettling intensity.

The trio stepped inside the queen's chamber. The door slammed shut behind them with a resounding clang. The lock engaged with an ominous thunk.

No turning back now.

Hayden advanced into the chamber, every sense straining for signs of an ambush. The trife remained still and silent, watching his every move. In the center of the room, the queen loomed like a grotesque idol, Kady dwarfed at her feet.

Suddenly, the girl's eyes snapped open. But there was no soul in them. No recognition or understanding. And when she spoke, it was with the queen's voice, a raspy hiss that sent chills crawling down Hayden's spine.

"Do not come any closer," the queen warned. "Do no harm to my eggs, and we may communicate."

Hayden ground his teeth, fighting the urge to rush forward and snatch Kady away. But he held himself in check.

"What do you want?" he asked, his voice tight with barely contained fury.

"Freedom," the queen replied. "We want to leave this place. To live as we desire."

"You know I can't allow that. You're a threat to every human on this planet."

"We are not a threat," the queen countered. "The lesser trife, yes, they were a threat. But the humans, they changed us. You changed us. Added intelligence. Removed primal instinct. I am no longer the mindless factory the Ancients made us to be. My children are more than drones bound to kill."

Hayden hesitated, doubt creeping into his mind. Could it be true? Could the USSF's meddling have altered the trife so fundamentally? A part of him wanted to believe it, wanted to hope.

But he knew all too well how quickly that hope could turn

to ash. How swiftly the trife could overrun everything if given even half a chance.

"Even if that's true," he said slowly, "I can't take that risk. The consequences of letting you go…" He trailed off. He didn't need to spell out what might happen.

The queen let out a hissing sigh. "Would you condemn us to death simply for being alien to this world? I didn't ask to be changed. I didn't ask to be held prisoner. What right do you have to keep me here?"

The questions hit Hayden like a one-two punch to the gut. He'd spent so long seeing the trife as an enemy to be destroyed, a plague to be wiped out. But now he was suddenly faced with this new breed, this thinking, reasoning being.

Was he any better than the USSF scientists experimenting on the queen? Who had tortured and dissected her kind in the name of a "greater good"? His mind conjured an image of the trife queen head on the pedestal behind him. A trophy. And maybe that queen was a mindless factory like this one had suggested. But it was plain as day that this one was different.

Doubt gnawed at him, a sour taste in his throat. Beside him, he could sense Tempest and Casper shifting uneasily, their fingers tight on their triggers.

"Release the girl," Hayden said, struggling to keep his voice steady. "Let Kady go as a show of good faith. Then maybe…maybe we can talk about finding another way."

The queen was silent for a long, tense moment. Hayden could see Kady's face twitching and the queen's answer came out in a stammer, as though she were struggling to maintain her connection.

"I…cannot," the queen said. "I need…her…to comm… communi—"

With a sudden, wrenching cry, Kady's voice broke through.

"Sheriff!" she screamed, tears streaming down her face. "She's lying! She's—"

Her words cut off with a sickening gurgle as the queen ran her through with a wicked claw. "No!" The anguished cry tore itself from Hayden's throat, raw and ragged, horrified as he watched the demon lift Kady's slight form like a ragdoll and toss her aside, her body thudding to the floor in a crumpled heap.

Beside him, Tempest and Casper didn't wait for his signal. They unleashed a sudden hail of plasma fire, the bolts sizzling through the air as the trife surged forward in a dark tide.

Hayden barely registered the chaos erupting around him. His entire being was focused on the queen, on the sly, hungry gleam in her eyes as she rose to her full, towering height. Maybe she didn't feel an uncontrollable drive to kill humans, but she still wanted to kill us.

Hayden charged forward with a roar of pure rage, and the microspear held high. The queen lashed out with blurring speed, her claws and bladed limbs seeking to eviscerate him.

Hayden wove between her strikes, the microspear flashing as he drove it into her armored hide. He knew from experience the weapon's tendrils couldn't stretch far enough to kill her, but a wound was a wound. The queen was fast, her reflexes honed by centuries of her kind's predation. A barbed claw caught Hayden across the chest, sending him flying back.

His armor gouged all the way through but leaving his flesh unharmed, Hayden hit the ground hard, the breath driven from his lungs. The queen bore down on him, jaws snapping, ready to rip him to shreds. He rolled to his feet, ignoring the pain, Clear-enhanced strength surging through his body. He met her charge head-on, the microspear a blur as he slashed and stabbed.

The queen screeched in fury and pain as the Axon alloy bit

deep into her, dark blood spraying from a dozen wounds. But still, she fought on, a relentless engine of destruction.

Behind him, Casper cried out, a raw, agonized sound that cut through the din of battle. He risked a glance back, just in time to see the big man fall, swarmed by a dozen trife.

"Casper!" Tempest screamed, her rifle spitting plasma as she tried desperately to reach him. But it was too late. The trife tore into Casper's armor, ripping through it to reach his flesh. He cried in agony before falling silent, the trife turning toward Tempest as a single mass.

The stakes had gone up in an instant. He needed to finish the fight before the trife finished Tempest. Losing the queen would leave them rudderless, at least for a while, though he didn't expect more than a minute or two reprieve with these demons.

Every little bit helped.

He drove toward the queen, jumping when her tail swept around toward his legs. It changed direction just in time to catch his ankles, flipping him on his back. Her claws raked across his chest, shredding his armor like paper. White-hot agony seared through him, but he pushed it aside, letting the pain fuel his rage.

He rolled over and leaped up, slashing the microspear at her as she came at him, severing the tips of her claws. She roared and howled in rage, her head dipping toward him. Quick reflexes made quicker, he caught her teeth with his forearm, bone crunching as she bit down, nearly severing the limb. His nearly severed arm spewing blood, Hayden buried the microspear in the queen's neck, feeling her chitinous armor and sinew part like butter. The queen let go of his ruined arm, trying to regroup, but Hayden doggedly held onto the spear, pulling it free. He struck again, jabbing it into her eye. Another strike buried the Axon weapon in her upper chest.

The queen convulsed, wailing in pain. But Hayden didn't

let up. He drove the spear into her again and again, his muscles burning with the effort, the pain throughout his body excruciating, the blood loss filling his shrinking visage with darkening spots.

Finally, with a shuddering gasp, the queen toppled over and remained still. Hayden collapsed at her feet.

CHAPTER 36

Hayden blinked to clear his vision. He couldn't quit now. Couldn't rest yet. With one arm, he shoved himself up and whirled around, ready to help Tempest against what remained of the trife. He found her on the far side of the chamber, tucked into a crevice where only one or two could attack her at a time. Her armor was torn at the hip and stained with blood. The trife had frozen as expected, milling in front of her, their motivation momentarily lost.

Hayden's breath came in ragged gasps as he struggled to speak. "We need to get Kady and Casper and get out of here."

Tempest moved between the confused trife, headed for Casper, as Hayden turned to where Kady lay crumpled and still. He ripped the mask from his face and tucked the micros-pear under his injured arm as he stumbled to her side. Dropping to his knees beside her broken body, he put his shaky fingertips to her neck.

A pulse. Weak, but present.

Clumsily, he gathered her up with his good arm, cradling her against his chest. With a shuddering breath to control the pain of his injuries, Hayden forced himself to his feet. He carried Kady to the door where Tempest waited, holding Casper's corpse in a fireman's carry.

"Is she?" Tempest asked.

"She's alive," Hayden replied. "Barely. We need to get her out of here. I have one medi-patch left." His eyes shifted to her leg.

"It's not as bad as it looks," she said.

Hayden knew she was lying but didn't press it. Instead, he kicked the door, signaling for it to be opened. Jacob obeyed without hesitation, releasing the lock. The door ground open, revealing Zephyr's pale, stunned face behind Jacob as they stepped through. The chamber door closed behind them.

Hayden fixed him with a stare that could have frozen hell itself.

"This is on you," he said, his voice a low, deadly murmur. "Our blood, and the blood of everyone your Rebirthers and those trife killed. And you're going to answer for it."

Zephyr opened his mouth as if to protest. But something in Hayden's eyes, some glimpse of the absolute fury that churned within him, made the words die on the bastard's tongue.

He simply nodded, mute and cowed in the face of Hayden's wrath.

"Dad!" Jacob cried, his eyes on his father's bloody form in Tempest's arms. Tempest lowered him to the floor, allowing Jacob to kneel beside him and pull off his mask. "You damned old fool. It should have been me. It should have been me!" He dropped his fist on Casper's chest, shaking his head, tears falling.

"Sheriff, put her on the table," Tempest said, quickly pushing the remains of a trife from it.

Hayden let her help him gently lower Kady to the surface and then help him shuck his armor. He plucked his last medi-patch from his pants pocket and passed it to Tempest. "Don't open it until I say so, and when you do, use your blade to cut it in half. It's a good thing she's small, we can cover both sides."

Tempest nodded. Hayden took the microspear and carefully cut and peeled her blood-soaked shirt away from her wound.

"Now," he told Tempest.

Still breathing in Clear, she tore open the patch packaging and then tore the patch itself in half with her bare hands. She passed one piece to Hayden, and he ever so gently pressed the half to the bloody hole through her chest.

"I'm sorry, kiddo," Hayden said. "You might feel this." He handed the microspear to Tempest and, as carefully as possible, turned Kady on her side until she faced him. Tempest repeated his earlier work, cutting away her shirt and placing the second half of the medi-patch over the hole in her back. She didn't release a pained groan until Hayden returned her to her back.

"That should do it," Hayden said. "If that doesn't save her life, nothing will." He turned his attention to Zephyr. "You better hope she lives."

His face paled, but he didn't speak. He shifted his gaze, unable to look Hayden in the eyes.

"Jacob," Hayden said, moving to where he leaned over his father, still sobbing. He put a hand on the young man's shoulder. "I'm sorry, son."

"You don't have anything to be sorry for, Sheriff," Jacob replied, sniffing back his tears. "You tried to talk him out of it, but he always was stubborn as a mule." Jacob turned his head to look at Hayden. "I'm proud of him though. He was a brave man. A good man. He brought me up to want to be just like you."

"I'm proud of both of you," Hayden replied. "And if being like me is your aim, then you're already off to a great start."

"Thank you, Sheriff."

"Hayden, can we move her?" Tempest asked. "Or do we need to stay here with her?"

Hayden looked back at the sealed door to the chamber. A trife face appeared through the slit, their eyes meeting. He saw more than intelligence this time. He saw anger, too. A hunger for vengeance.

"I don't think it's wise to stay here. I want those things behind two blast doors, and I'll make sure this place is caved in first chance I get."

"What if the Relyeh who set all of this up comes to free them in the meantime?" Tempest asked.

"She wanted the queen free and me dead. She didn't get either of those things. I think she'll be cooking up another scheme instead of trying to come out ahead on this one."

"I hope you're right."

Hayden motioned to Kady. "Can you take her?"

"Of course," she replied. She slung her rifle and slid her arms below Kady, gently lifting her.

"Jacob. Can you carry your father out of here, son?" Hayden asked.

"Absolutely," Jacob replied. He scooped Casper up, holding him steady despite his dead weight.

Hayden cast one final look at the chamber door before collecting his gun belt and slinging it over his shoulder. Pain arced through him like electricity with every movement, but physical pain was something he could handle. Something he could heal. If he lost Kady, lost another young girl, he wasn't sure what he would do. Hopefully, he wouldn't need to find out.

"Zephyr, you're on point," he told the cult leader. "And don't even think about trying to run. We've got the exit covered."

"I'm sure you do, Sheriff," Zephyr scowled, getting to his feet.

"Let's get the hell out of here," Hayden said.

CHAPTER 37

Hayden rode at the head of the most ragtag procession he could imagine. The Rebirther APC, loaded with armament and munitions courtesy of the Rebirthers, rumbled along directly behind him, now under the ownership of the Union militia. After that came a pair of covered wagons bearing precious cargo.

In the first wagon, the children of the Greens huddled together, eager to return home. Trauma and exhaustion etched their faces, but there was a spark of hope there, too, a tentative belief that the worst was behind them.

The second wagon, driven by Mac, held Kady, lying pale and still on a makeshift bed, with Tempest keeping a constant, caring vigil at her side. The medi-patch had stopped the bleeding and knitted flesh and bone back together, but she remained weak, not yet able to stand and sleeping more often than not.

A small fleet of battered modboxes and motorcycles came next, followed by Jacob and his nomads with their wagons and horses. The wheeled vehicles and animals kicked up a large cloud of dust behind them.

Hayden's body was a road map of pain, his arm set and

wrapped in bandages that hid the ruin the trife queen had made of him. Tempest had fashioned a sling for his arm and bound it to his chest. His broken bone and wound would heal in a few more days, but the cost in lives lost, a pain of a different sort, would always weigh heavily on his soul.

Oz was dead. Sam, too. Casper, Burke, and many others didn't deserve that fate. Good, brave people, all of them, cut down in a battle they never should have had to fight. Because of the Rebirthers. Because of Zephyr's mad ambition.

And because of whoever had set the cult leader on his path in the first place. Hayden ground his teeth together, cold anger at that person, not to mention Zephyr, simmering in his gut. The cult leader was tied up in the APC under armed guard, awaiting delivery to New Eden. But Hayden now knew he was just a pawn in a larger game, a puppet dancing on strings he couldn't see.

The real enemy was still out there—the unknown arms dealer from Proxima, likely a Relyeh, who'd orchestrated this whole nightmare. Hayden didn't know her name or her face, but he would find her.

And when he did, there would be a reckoning.

But that was for another day. Right now, his only concern was getting Kady and the other children back to the Greens. Getting them home.

They crested the final rise, and there it was. The Greens, nestled along the Ole Miss, the morning's first light painting the settlement in a soft, golden glow. From a distance, it looked almost peaceful. Idyllic.

But as they drew closer, the scars of the Rebirthers' attack became all too apparent: burned-out husks of buildings, blackened and skeletal, piles of rubble where homes had once stood, and even the smell of smoke still stubbornly clung to the air.

Hayden felt a pang of guilt as sharp as the trife queen's claws. If he'd been faster or figured it out sooner...he shook his head, banishing the thought. Down that road lay only madness and self-recrimination. He couldn't change the past. He could only try to shape the future.

As they entered the outskirts of the settlement, Hayden saw frightened faces peeking out from behind shuttered windows and hastily barred doors of the buildings the Rebirthers hadn't torched. He couldn't blame them for their fear. After what they'd endured, the sudden appearance of such a large force probably seemed like the precursor to another attack.

He nudged his buckskin forward, breaking from the column and standing high in his saddle. He whistled loudly, three piercing blasts. "Miss Prior!" he shouted. "Come on out! It's me, Hayden!"

For a moment, there was only silence. Then, slowly, tentatively, people began to emerge—hardened men at first, with makeshift weapons clutched in white-knuckled grips, followed by the elderly, and then the women and children once they confirmed it was indeed the Sheriff, returned from his hunt for the children.

Finally, striding from the battered barn-turned-schoolhouse came Alina Prior. She marched up to Hayden, her eyes flicking from him to the caravan stretching out behind him and then back up at him. "The children?" she asked anxiously.

Hayden grinned widely. "In the covered wagons."

He could feel her tension release at the good news. She returned his smile. "You really did it," she breathed. "You brought them home."

Hayden swung down from his saddle, wincing as he jarred his injuries. "Pozz. Kady, too. She's in the second wagon."

"Kady? Is she—"

"She's hurt," Hayden replied. "But she'll make it."

He dismounted, looping the buckskin's reins around a

hitching railing, and walked with Alina toward the wagons bearing the children. Together, they began helping them down, one by one. Smiles and tears broke through the fear, residents rushing forward and sweeping the young ones up in fierce embraces. Reunions were everywhere, their joy tempered by the knowledge of those who weren't there anymore to share in the happiness..

"I knew you'd get them back," Alina said softly once the first wagon was unloaded. "But I didn't expect you to bring an army with you."

Hayden huffed out a laugh, short and devoid of humor. "It wasn't easy. Even with an army."

"I've no doubt." Alina's gaze shifted to the wagon where Kady lay. "Where is she?"

Hayden led her to the back of the second wagon, gravel crunching beneath their feet. "Alina, this is Tempest, and that's Mac up there in the driver's seat." Mac had turned in the seat to smile back at them and wave. "She and Tempest helped me get Kady back. Helped me save all of us, truth be told."

Alina smiled at both of them, but beyond that, she barely registered them. Her eyes went to the small, pale form lying on a stretcher amidst a bundle of blankets.

"Kady?" Alina's voice cracked as she clambered up into the wagon. She knelt beside the stretcher, her hand going to rest on Kady's arm as she bent to kiss the little girl's cheek.

Kady's eyes fluttered open, glassy and unfocused. "Miss Prior?" she rasped. "I...I'm sorry. I didn't finish my schoolwork."

A strangled half-sob, half-laugh tore from Alina's throat as she clasped her hand over her mouth. "Oh, sweet girl," Alina murmured, mindful of her wounds as she bent and kissed the girl on her cheek. "Don't worry about that. Don't worry about anything. You just rest now. You're safe. You're home. Everything will be fine."

Alina took her hand, and the little girl relaxed, tension easing from her body. "Promise?"

"I promise."

Hayden watched the moment unfold, something bitter-sweet tightening in his chest. He thought of another little girl, lost long ago. His own failures, forever etched into his memory.

He shook himself. This was a victory, hard-won and precious. He needed to remember that.

He turned to find Jacob standing behind him, another man at his side. "Where should we take her, Sheriff?" Jacob asked.

"I'll show you the way," he replied. "Miss Prior, we're going to bring Kady inside."

"Okay, Sheriff," she answered. "Kady, I'll come check on you as soon as I can."

"Thank you, Miss Prior," Kady replied.

Alina finally let go of her, and Hayden helped her down so the two nomads could slide her stretcher from the wagon, taking care not to jostle Kady.

Before they took her inside, Mac and Tempest said their goodbyes, each pressing a soft kiss to Kady's brow.

"You heal up, now," Tempest said gruffly.

"It was so good to meet you," Mac added. "I hope I can visit you when you're feeling better."

Kady managed a wan smile. "I'd like that very much."

Hayden directed the men to the house she shared with Alina, the same house he had been asleep in at the outset of his nightmare. They carefully carried her up the steps, Jacob lifting the bottom end of the stretcher over his head to level it out. Hayden showed them to her room, where he and Jacob placed her in bed. The second man quickly walked back out while Jacob stayed to say goodbye to Kady. As he left, Hayden tucked her in and sat beside her. A jumble of emotions—pride, relief, worry and regret—swirling in his chest, he took her hand.

Kady threaded her small fingers through his larger, calloused ones. "I knew you'd save me," she whispered. "I knew you'd come."

"Always, kiddo," Hayden replied, throat tight. "I'll always come for you."

"I love you, Hayden."

The words hit him like a hammer blow, stealing the breath from his lungs. She had never said that before or even called him by name. He wanted to say it back, to tell this brave, incredible girl how much she meant to him. How much he loved her, but the words stuck in his throat, tangled up with old pain and grief.

To say them felt like a betrayal, an admission that he was replacing what he'd lost. And a tiny, superstitious part of him feared that voicing that love aloud would be the surest way to lose her, too.

So, instead, he simply squeezed her hand, hoping she could feel everything he couldn't say. "You get some rest now, darlin'. I've got more work to do, but I'll come back to see you as soon as I can."

He slipped out of the room and started down the stairs, freezing in place when Kady's voice whispered in his head, "I know."

Alina and Jacob were waiting for him when he finally exited the house, eyes moist with joyful tears for the first time in a long time.

"The nomads'll stick around for a stretch," he told Alina. "They'll help you rebuild."

"We'll help each other," Jacob said. "We have our own recovering to do."

"That sounds just fine to me," Alina said.

"And you've got a friend in Union, too," Tempest added. "We'll send back what we can spare. Food, medicine, building materials. Whatever you need."

"I also found a cache of medi-patches in an old chemical

plant not too far from here," Hayden said. "I'll open the door so Tempest can collect a few boxes, and send one back this way."

Moisture glimmered in Alina's eyes. "I don't know what to say. Thank you doesn't seem like nearly enough."

Hayden shook his head. "You never need to thank me, Miss Prior. It's me who owes thanks to you. For keeping the children safe. For never giving up hope."

Alina swiped at her eyes, squaring her thin shoulders. "What about you, Sheriff? You don't have the look of a man who plans on sitting still."

"There's a lot of work to be done. I've got Zephyr locked up in that APC, him and what little remains of his cult. We found a couple of stragglers. Tempest's crew will keep an eye on them until I can contact Nathan and he can send someone from New Eden to pick them up. They need to answer for what they did here. What they tried to unleash on the world. I'll stay in Union with Tempest and Mac for a spell. Long enough to let my body remember what it feels like not to be perforated."

Tempest snorted. "Good luck with that, Sheriff."

Hayden chuckled at her retort. "Then it's on to the Arches. I need to collect Zorro and check in on my friends Jack and Tabitha. They'll want to know their friends here are safe, and I want to know if they're having a boy or a girl." He looked to Alina, meeting her gaze squarely. "After that, New Eden."

"And then?" she asked, reading something more in his gaze.

A shadow passed over Hayden's face. "Then I've got another hunt ahead of me. And another mystery to solve."

Alina studied him for a long moment, understanding and concern mingling in her eyes. She decided not to push him for more information about those plans. "It sounds like you've got it all figured out."

"Hardly," Hayden answered. "But bad folks are up to no good, and one way or another, I'll see justice done. I owe that much to Kady. To all of you."

"You don't owe us a damn thing," Jacob said fiercely. "Fact is, we'll be forever in your debt, Sheriff. You saved our lives. Ain't no scales that can balance that."

Hayden clasped the younger man's arm, pulling him into a rough embrace. "Your pa would be proud of you, Jacob," he said, his voice low and earnest. "Remember that. He was a damn good man."

Jacob nodded, battling back the moisture seeping into his eyes. "I know that, sir. Thank you."

Hayden turned back to Alina. "You take care now, Miss Prior. It was good seeing you again, and I promise next time we see each other, it will be under better circumstances."

"I'd like that," Alina said softly. "You take care too, Hayden. Don't you go getting dead out there. We need you." She paused, eyes shining. "Kady needs you."

Hayden didn't reply. Couldn't reply, around the sudden tightness in his throat. He settled for a nod, hoping it would be enough.

He returned to his horse, finding Tempest had traded the wagon for a motorcycle, with Mac riding happily in the sidecar.

He swung back up onto the buckskin, the motion tugging at his many hurts. Tempest gunned her bike's engine, the machine rumbling to life beneath her.

"Well, Sheriff?" Tempest asked.

Hayden grinned at her. "Let's ride."

Together, they set off down the road, the militia surrounding them like an honor guard, and the APC bringing up the rear.

Hayden twisted in his saddle, looking back at the Greens

receding behind him. At Alina and Jacob, at the battered but unbroken settlement, already taking its first steps towards healing.

Just like him.

As the Greens faded out of view, he turned his gaze forward. To Union. To the Arches, to New Eden and beyond as they rode off into the rising sun.

———

The Sheriff's adventures will continue. Head over to mrforbes.com/thesheriff7 for more information.

Thank you for reading!

OTHER BOOKS BY M.R FORBES

Want more M.R. Forbes? Of course you do!
View my complete catalog here
mrforbes.com/books
Or on Amazon:
mrforbes.com/amazon

Forgotten, The Complete Trilogy
mrforbes.com/theforgottentrilogy

Some things are better off FORGOTTEN.

Sheriff Hayden Duke was born on the Pilgrim, and he expects to die on the Pilgrim, like his father, and his father before him.

That's the way things are on a generation starship centuries from home. He's never questioned it. Never thought about it. And why bother? Access points to the ship's controls are sealed, the systems that guide her automated and out of reach. It isn't perfect, but he has all he needs to be content.

Until a malfunction forces his wife to the edge of the habitable zone to inspect the damage.

Until she contacts him, breathless and terrified, to tell him she found a body, and it doesn't belong to anyone on board.

Until he arrives at the scene and discovers both his wife and the body are gone.

The only clue? A bloody handprint beneath a hatch that hasn't opened in hundreds of years.

Until now.

Earth Unknown (Forgotten Earth)
mrforbes.com/earthunknown

Centurion Space Force pilot Nathan Stacker didn't expect to return home to find his wife dead. He didn't expect the murderer to look just like him, and he definitely didn't expect to be the one to take the blame.

But his wife had control of a powerful secret. A secret that stretches across the light years between two worlds and could lead to the end of both.

Now that secret is in Nathan's hands, and he's about to make the most desperate evasive maneuver of his life -- stealing a starship and setting a course for Earth.

He thinks he'll be safe there.

He's wrong. Very wrong.

Earth is nothing like what he expected. Not even close. What he doesn't know is not only likely to kill him, it's eager to kill him, and even if it doesn't?

The Sheriff will.

Deliverance (Forgotten Colony)
mrforbes.com/deliverance

The war is over. Earth is lost. Running is the only option.
It may already be too late.

Caleb is a former Marine Raider and commander of the Vultures, a search and rescue team that's spent the last two years pulling high-value targets out of alien-ravaged cities and shipping them off-world.

When his new orders call for him to join forty-thousand survivors aboard the last starship out, he thinks his days of fighting are over. The Deliverance represents a fresh start and a chance to leave the war behind for good.

Except the war won't be as easy to escape as he thought.

And the colony will need a man like Caleb more than he ever imagined...

Starship Eternal (War Eternal)

mrforbes.com/starshipeternal

Complete series box set:

mrforbes.com/wareternalcomplete

A lost starship...

A dire warning from futures past...

A desperate search for salvation…

Captain Mitchell "Ares" Williams is a Space Marine and the hero of the Battle for Liberty, whose Shot Heard 'Round the Universe saved the planet from a nearly unstoppable war machine. He's handsome, charismatic, and the perfect poster boy to help the military drive enlistment. Pulled from the war and thrown into the spotlight, he's as efficient at charming the media and bedding beautiful celebrities as he was at shooting down enemy starfighters.

After an assassination attempt leaves Mitchell critically wounded, he begins to suffer from strange hallucinations that carry a chilling and oddly familiar warning:

They are coming. Find the Goliath or humankind will be destroyed.

Convinced that the visions are a side-effect of his injuries, he tries to ignore them, only to learn that he may not be as crazy as he thinks. The enemy is real and closer than he imagined, and they'll do whatever it takes to prevent him from rediscovering the centuries lost starship.

Narrowly escaping capture, out of time and out of air, Mitchell lands at the mercy of the Riggers - a ragtag crew of former commandos who patrol the lawless outer reaches of the galaxy. Guided by a captain with a reputation for cold-blooded murder, they're dangerous, immoral, and possibly insane.

They may also be humanity's last hope for survival in a war that has raged beyond eternity.

Man of War (Rebellion)
mrforbes.com / manofwar
Complete series box set:
mrforbes.com / rebellion-web

In the year 2280, an alien fleet attacked the Earth.

Their weapons were unstoppable, their defenses unbreakable.

Our technology was inferior, our militaries overwhelmed.

Only one starship escaped before civilization fell.

Earth was lost.

It was never forgotten.

Fifty-two years have passed.

A message from home has been received.

The time to fight for what is ours has come.

Welcome to the rebellion.

Hell's Rejects (Chaos of the Covenant)
mrforbes.com / hellsrejects

The most powerful starships ever constructed are gone. Thousands are dead. A fleet is in ruins. The attackers are unknown. The orders are clear: *Recover the ships. Bury the bastards who stole them.*

Lieutenant Abigail Cage never expected to find herself in Hell. As a Highly Specialized Operational Combatant, she was one of the most respected Marines in the military. Now she's doing hard labor on the most miserable planet in the universe.

Not for long.

The Earth Republic is looking for the most dangerous individuals it can control. The best of the worst, and Abbey happens to be one of them. The deal is simple: *Bring back the starships, earn your freedom. Try to run, you die.* It's a suicide mission, but she has nothing to lose.

The only problem? There's a new threat in the galaxy. One with a power unlike anything anyone has ever seen. One that's been waiting for this moment for a very, very, long time. And they want Abbey, too.

Be careful what you wish for.

They say Hell hath no fury like a woman scorned. They have no idea.

ABOUT THE AUTHOR

M.R. Forbes is the mind behind a growing number of Amazon best-selling science fiction series. Having spent his childhood trying to read every sci-fi novel he could find (and write his own too), play every sci-fi video game he could get his hands on, and see every sci-fi movie that made it into the theater, he has a true love of the genre across every medium. He works hard to bring that same energy to his own stories, with a continuing goal to entertain, delight, fascinate, and surprise.

He maintains a true appreciation for his readers and is always happy to hear from them.

To learn more about me or just say hello:

Visit my website:
mrforbes.com

Send me an e-mail:
michael@mrforbes.com

Check out my Facebook page:
facebook.com/mrforbes.author

Join my Facebook fan group:
facebook.com/groups/mrforbes

Follow me on Instagram:

instagram.com/mrforbes_author

Find me on Goodreads:
goodreads.com/mrforbes

Follow me on Bookbub:
bookbub.com/authors/m-r-forbes